FOURTH DAY

NORTHWEST COUNTER-TERRORISM TASKFORCE - BOOK 4

LISA PHILLIPS

TWO DOGS PUBLISHING, LLC.

Copyright 2019 Lisa Phillips

All rights reserved. This book or any portion thereof may not be reproduced or used in any manner whatsoever without the express written permission of the publisher except for the use of brief quotations in a book review.

Trade Paperback ISBN: 979-8-88552-091-1

Cover design Ryan Schwarz

Edited by Jen Weiber

Published by Two Dogs Publishing, LLC.

1

"I need help!" Allyson huffed out a breath, then yelled again. "Medic!" The muscles in her back screamed as she hauled her teammate through the warehouse door and out into the chaos.

Sirens. Lights. Emergency vehicles.

With Max pressed up against her side, she could feel the warm blood seep into all three layers: her T-shirt, uniform shirt, and vest, all pulled down over her hip. "Medic!"

Her boot caught on the uneven concrete. Several people reached out to catch both her and Max. As she righted herself, she felt her phone buzz in her pocket. All her teammates were here, so who was calling her?

She dismissed the thought, shoved back a few strands that had escaped her ponytail and followed behind Max, now being carried by two of her teammates. ATF. Her friends and family, all rolled into one. They just didn't know she felt that way about them. And they *never* would. It wasn't that kind of team. Yeah, they bet their lives on each other, but that didn't mean they needed to be more than work colleagues.

"Hey." Someone snagged her elbow. Someone with a low voice and a southern twang.

She stopped and looked up at Carl. The motion made her rifle bump up against her, and she righted it.

"Did you get hit?"

She shook her head, glancing at the red stain. "All this is Max's."

Carl opened his mouth to say something else, but she walked away. Allyson climbed into the ambulance and rounded the EMT to speak to the injured man.

She crouched by his head. "You good?"

The skin around his eyes was pinched with pain, his face flushed. "If I am, it's thanks to you."

"Is she coming with?"

She ignored the EMT's question. Max said, "Call Lynnie."

"I'll see you later." She squeezed his shoulder and forced her body to climb back out of the ambulance. She stumbled and nearly fell to the ground, but managed to stay upright. Her phone started up, buzzing again.

Before she could reach for it and see who it was, she got a slap on the shoulder. "Let's go."

Two of the guys on her team stood around her. Carl and Finn.

"In a minute." She needed a minute. Couldn't they see that? Allyson wanted nothing more than to lean forward, plant her hands on her knees. Take a second and just breathe.

They would laugh about that for a week.

But who could blame her? It had been a crazy last few days— ever since they got word through the wires that a high-level target had escaped federal custody. An explosion where he'd been held. Then there had been a terrorist attack at the rally.

Multiple crime scenes, even before they'd been assigned to this breach.

She squeezed the bridge of her nose. Her ATF team had worked the house explosion all day, then wound up here helping with the takedown. They'd gotten the suspect back—he was in custody, and she'd heard word the Northwest Counter-Terrorism

Task Force had cleared the whole thing up. Including a Secret Service assistant director who had been in on it. A dirty cop.

Allyson's stomach rumbled. She hadn't eaten. Hadn't slept in probably three days. Maybe she should take a week off. Even she needed a break sometimes.

"Are you sweating?"

She lowered her hand and ignored their glances. "Probably just rain."

Finn nudged her shoulder. "That's what they all say."

She grinned. They were twin idiots, frequently referring to each other as their *brother from another mother*. Whatever that meant.

She looked around. Firefighters were here. Cops, local and state. There were a million FBI agents all over the place like ants. Her team was all filthy. Sweaty. She shoved at the rifle slung across her back. Time to get rid of it, clock out. Take a shower. Tomorrow she'd probably be back at the stadium, continuing the scene investigation there.

Allyson's group supervisor, her boss, wandered over. Special Agent Daulton handed them each a water bottle. In her pocket, her phone rang again. She twisted the cap on the bottle and downed half of it, turning to continue surveying the area.

Across the parking lot, the Northwest Counter-Terrorism Task Force team all headed to their cars. Arms slung around each other. Laughing. Bantering, like her team did. Just not sticking around to do the cleanup here. Their man was caught, job done.

They all looked like nothing big had happened, and now it was time for them to celebrate.

The lone man at the back of the group turned. Slender. Tall. That weathered face and those deep-set, dark eyes. Jeans and a western-style shirt.

Finn nudged her shoulder again. "Your boyfriend probably wants to invite you to the team dinner."

She glanced at him. "I will get out my stun gun."

Out the corner of her eye, she saw movement. Sal was actually walking over. Right now? She looked awful. She probably smelled like smoke from the stadium bomb. Or the house that exploded, the one where Yewell had been kept prisoner by the Secret Service—a whole investigation in itself. Especially considering the fact the assistant director had been working with him, betraying everything he'd sworn to uphold.

Now Yewell was in custody. The threat had been eliminated, and she was covered in dirt from rolling around on the floor with a gunman. Not to mention the blood.

Just because it was another day on the job didn't mean she had to like it.

His brows drew together. "You okay?"

Her team milled around, pretending they weren't listening. Allyson was pretty sure she heard one of them snort.

Motioned to the blood. "Not mine."

"Is Max okay?"

She pointed at the ambulance, driving out of the parking lot. "He asked me to call his wife."

His mouth shifted. That was all he gave her.

She shrugged. "You were the one undercover in a terrorist organization."

Daulton took a couple of steps closer. "Alvarez, we'll need your statement, given your involvement in this." He looked at his tablet. "Plus a statement from a 'Drew North'."

Allyson turned to her boss. "Why are we point on this?" There were a million FBI agents here, and her team was better dealing with the aftermath of the explosion. As the ATF, it was kind of their thing, actually.

Alvarez said, "Drew left already."

Her supervisor sighed.

"I'll hit your office first thing in the morning and lay it all out for you."

"Copy that."

"Thanks for your help on this."

Allyson glanced between them. "Help?"

"We got our result," Daulton said with a shrug.

"Result?"

Sal nodded. "Tell your undercover I appreciate his help getting into Yewell's operation."

Daulton nodded, then walked away.

She looked at her teammates who'd taken a couple more steps but were obviously still listening to everything. Nosy, or trying to protect her?

"So…" she started. "I'm gonna get back to work now." She folded her arms. "Plenty of stuff still to do."

Sal's teammates hadn't left yet, but they seemed to be getting impatient. He didn't make a move to leave. Just frowned some more and continued to stare at her like they weren't all waiting for him.

"What?"

He sighed.

Someone called out, "Let's go, Sanchez."

She glanced over her shoulder. "Be there in a second."

They were trying to protect her. It seemed they didn't think much of Sal, even after what happened at the Seattle federal courthouse. The scar on her arm itched, but she didn't touch it. Did his itch sometimes? It had been two years. Maybe it shouldn't still be bothering her.

"Deputy Alvarez!" Victoria strode over on her heels. She looked like she'd just stepped out of a board meeting.

Allyson said, "Don't get in trouble on account of me." Her phone rang again, so she pulled it out. She didn't recognize the number.

Sal lifted one finger to Victoria, then turned back to Allyson. "I'll see you tomorrow?"

"I may have to go to the house you guys blew up and take another look. Or the stadium." She wasn't about to tell him she liked to double check and make sure she hadn't missed anything. "I don't know where I'll be."

He frowned. "What house we blew up?"

"The house where Yewell was being protected by the Secret

Service."

"At the behest of the current administration."

She shrugged. "Doesn't matter who's sitting in the chair, we all still follow whatever orders we're given."

"Well, yeah."

Allyson was a little more "boots on the ground" than that, which was why she was ATF and hadn't applied to the Secret Service. And she had thought Sal was as well. After all, instead of investigating with his team, he'd gone undercover.

"Copy that." It was her boss.

She turned to see what was going on.

"Load up." He motioned for all of them to get rolling. "Someone just drove a truck into the side of a gun store. We've gotta roll."

———

She looked completely exhausted. Sal couldn't bring himself to watch her respond to another call out, especially while he headed to a restaurant with the rest of his team. Not when the reason she was so wrung out was because they'd been dealing with his task force's fallout for days.

He said, "I'll go with you." Even though he was exhausted, his head still full of everything that had happened with Yewell.

"Aren't you guys going somewhere to celebrate?"

He shook his head. "I'm not hungry and you're a man down, so I'll tag along." Sounded good out loud, not just in his head. Thankfully.

The ATF didn't need a complete team just to respond to a robbery, but he still waved off his own team to leave.

Victoria frowned. He turned back to Allyson and took a few steps with her.

As he walked, he decided it might be worth being part of this call out as a marshal. Victoria had handed him back his badge and gun as soon as the operation had been over. No way was he going to stay out of a gun store robber case when it could've been done by someone he'd met before. It might be a case the marshals would eventually find themselves working on.

Keep trying to convince yourself.

The fact was, he'd nearly died today. One of her teammates had been shot. He pretty much just needed to face the fact he was only going because he wanted to spend more time with Allyson.

His teammates all knew what he was doing. When he glanced over, this was confirmed. Dakota wasn't happy. Haley was confused. Their significant others would reassure them it was all good. Right now Talia and Mason were only concerned with each other, which was fine considering the past few days. Their lives had been turned upside down.

Another of his teammates in a relationship.

Even Victoria had someone to worry about. Welvern had been shot and was in the hospital. His recovery from being hit by a rifle round would be long.

The team's vehicles pulled away from the curb. It almost felt easier to watch them go than it would've been to even out the numbers at dinner. Especially knowing he was about to leave them anyway.

Could he get on a task force with the ATF? That might be fun. But hearing more about small town life from Drew had made him wonder about being a sheriff.

Going home.

Back to those open skies. Snowcapped peaks. If he returned to Wyoming, he could find a town where they would take a US Marshal as a sheriff. Or vote him in the normal way. Somewhere without the memory of his father's final breath as a weight against his chest.

Despite that thought, the yearning for *his* mountain was there.

Allyson climbed into the back of an SUV and left the door open. He got in, and they were driven to the gun store. He closed his eyes because neither of them had the mental energy for small talk right now. Not when everything they said to each other had a level of emotional impact he still hadn't figured out. The why, or the what—as in, what to do with these pent-up feelings.

He needed to decide what he was going to do next, given this life was making him seriously antsy. It happened every few years. Usually he just asked for a transfer. This had been the longest stretch working with one team.

Was it time to move on?

When they pulled up at the gun store, he opened his eyes. And immediately gaped. A huge rental truck had smashed into the side of the wall.

Doors were opened. Slammed. As a group they walked to the uniformed officers on scene.

Allyson's boss, her group supervisor, was a former NYPD detective who'd come over to the federal side years ago. He spoke with the officer. Sal moved closer to hear and felt Allyson squeeze in beside him.

"...called the rental company."

She glanced over and met his gaze.

Sal mouthed, *You okay?*

She nodded. *You?*

He scrunched up his nose, unsure how to answer that. Their relationship—if he could even call it that—had always been complicated. It had developed into maybe becoming something a couple of years ago. Right before the situation they were both working at the courthouse erupted. Now he had nothing to show for it but a bunch of scars.

"The truck was supposed to be returned tonight at midnight, according to the company's computer."

Sal glanced at the cop. "So they decided to do one last job before they returned it?"

Allyson leaned around her boss and told the officer, "They usually steal the keys out of the return box and drive the truck off the rental lot. Use it in one job, grab as many guns as they can, and race away in a secondary vehicle."

He figured she also said it for his benefit.

The officer took in the blood all down Allyson's side.

Sal moved the conversation forward. "Have there been any other similar robberies in the area recently?"

One of the ATF agents—he was pretty sure the guy's name was Carl—chuckled. "You almost sound like a real cop, Deputy."

Sal shot him a look that made him laugh. All of them knew what marshals did. They'd worked together before, but the friendly rivalry was part of it. Gone were the days of agency secrets and backbiting. 9/11 had changed more than just TSA policy and federal policing, it had changed the whole culture of law enforcement. Refusing to be part of the team these days got innocent people killed, and no one wanted that.

The cop walked them through the scene.

"You think they left something behind?"

Allyson shrugged. "We'll look at the surveillance video."

They headed for the office, and the employee there showed them a grainy image of three guys with hooded sweatshirts hauling out armfuls of guns and boxes of ammo. It could have been someone he knew. There was also literally no way to tell.

One of Allyson's teammates wandered in and peered at the screen. "Military trained."

Sal said, "Yep."

The employee shifted in his seat. "You can tell that?"

Allyson said, "Look at the way he holds them."

Sal said, "Can we have this enhanced and get more from it?"

Both Allyson and her teammate reacted like that was a dumb question.

"Sure," the employee said. "If it was high-quality digital footage. It's a surveillance video. Blurry's all you're gonna get."

Sal was pretty sure Talia could work with that, and that she'd done so in the past. Was he going to call her right now, though? She'd been grazed by a bullet today. He decided to let her have her evening.

She was happy, like the rest of the team. While they moved on, Sal would be right here, unsure of what to do. Nothing in his life had progressed, not for years. Probably not since his father died. It was like the breath of his life had ceased at the same time, laying in that damp grass on the side of a mountain watching the sunrise.

Allyson and her teammate headed out, so he followed back to the main part of the store. The whole place was disheveled. Half empty shelves, and destruction. The cab of the rental truck was inside the store, drywall dust and debris everywhere.

Allyson stood to the side, holding her cell phone to her ear. The rest of the agents stood in a huddle in conversation with Daulton, their supervisor, who broke off when he saw Sal approach.

Allyson said, "Slow down."

He looked over. She'd gone pale and was almost crying. Sal started toward her before he even thought about it.

"Tell me where you are. I'll come and get you."

2

Allyson gripped the phone. She listened to the short breaths on the other end of the line, hearing the fear in her friend's voice. Was it really Vanessa? After all these years, how could she be on the other end of the line?

Allyson shivered as the sweat from earlier chilled against her skin. "Can you hear me?"

Nothing but crackles answered across the connection. She hadn't seen Vanessa in years—since college, in fact. Because she'd disappeared from their college dorm one night. No sign of her. No explanation. No answers as to what had happened. The frustration, and the mystery were what made Allyson become a federal agent in the first place. She'd wanted to find lost people, protect innocents and take down bad guys.

She gripped the phone. "Vanessa, are you okay?"

Sal shifted into view. He touched her elbow and frowned.

She could hardly explain right now. Vanessa needed to answer. Her long lost friend had asked for help, frightened and upset. It had been years. Was she still being held against her will?

How had she gotten Allyson's work number?

Where was she?

There were so many questions swirling in Ally's brain that she could hardly even think through what to say. What to do.

She wanted to reach for Sal. She was exhausted, and now she was handed this on top of everything else? She had to force her brain to function. She only had enough energy to say, "Vanessa, can you hear me? Can you answer me?"

Sal gave her elbow a squeeze. She shifted closer, but that was all. She wanted to lean into him, only her team was probably watching. She sort of cared. Not totally. What they thought wasn't the point right now. She knew they'd probably rib her for whatever this was between her and Sal. It had been brewing for so long they should be used to it by now, but every time it was like they were realizing it anew all over again. When they weren't making cracks about him already being her boyfriend.

But whatever their reaction, it wasn't her priority. Right now she needed to figure out what was going on with Vanessa.

She needed to know Vanessa was safe.

At least her boss was here. She might need his help in a minute and would definitely need his authorization to break from what she was doing to go to Vanessa if needed.

"Vanessa."

She wasn't going to stop trying to get her to respond. Not until the line went dead.

"Vaness—"

"Ally." Her voice was breathy. Different than it had been years ago, and yet achingly similar. She could even picture her friend's face. "I need your help."

"Are you hurt?" The only image she had of Vanessa in her mind was from age nineteen. They'd been roommates at the University of Seattle.

Allyson was the daughter of a Presbyterian minister. Vanessa's father had been in construction, working long days all year round. Their mothers hadn't been there, but for entirely different reasons. An immediate bond, but then Vanessa had disappeared.

Most of the other students—including the boyfriend Allyson

hadn't even known Vanessa had—figured she just took off on a whim. Like she'd gone to California or something. A few of them had even thought Allyson killed her and covered it up.

Allyson had talked it over for hours on end with Vanessa's father, never able to figure out what had happened to her. In the end, the police labeled it a cold case. There had even been a documentary on the local news about it in the years since.

"I think…someone is after me."

Allyson's whole gut clenched. This was her chance to get answers about what had really happened. She'd be able to help her friend, finally. "Can you tell me where you are? I'll meet you."

"I'm coming to Seattle."

So she wasn't here already but on her way? "You're coming right now? Where are you?"

"I think I'm being followed, and I don't want them to catch up to me." Allyson heard her suck in a breath. "You're the only one who can help. The only one I trust."

Her chest tightened. "Who are you running from?"

Had her friend been a captive all this time? That was a horrifying thought. It meant Allyson was the worst friend ever, never finding Vanessa. Allowing her to stay in that situation forever.

"I don't want them to catch—" The line crackled. "…help."

"I'll help you, of course I will." Allyson paused so she could try to get a hold of herself. "Can you still hear me?"

"…help."

"Vanessa?" Allyson thought she might be able to hear her friend crying. "It's going to be okay, I'm going to help you."

"I knew I could trust you. I knew you'd help me." Her voice cracked. "But I'm not Van anymore, and I haven't been for a long time. I'm Bridget McNamara."

"I'm a cop." She had to know that. "Tell me where to meet you, and I'll do everything I can."

The line crackled again. "…where I am."

"Vanessa, can you hear me?" Allyson turned to Sal. "I need a trace on this line. So I can get her location." Why hadn't she thought of that before? The call could end any second, and then she would have nothing.

"I can call Talia." He reached to pull out his phone.

She turned back around and tried to figure out how to get the location faster than that before Van was gone. There was no way to do it, considering she was out in the field and not at the office. No one else was available without calling the FBI. And it would take too long to explain everything to them.

"Vanessa?" There was nothing on the line but dead air. She looked at her phone screen. "She's gone."

Sal lowered his phone before he'd even dialed. "What's going on?"

Allyson blew out a breath. "A friend of mine needs help." Her pointer finger traced across the keys, and a second later he got a text.

"What's this?"

"Seattle PD case number." Allyson barely managed to get the words out before she had to bend forward and suck in a few breaths.

It was like her body had just now caught up with what was happening. She stared at the phone in her hand, then straightened. "She said her name is Bridget McNamara now."

Would she call again? Allyson half expected it to ring. For her considered-dead, old friend to call again, and continue hauling the past right back to center stage. After all these years. Once could have been a trick. A mind flip, like the premise of some awful practical joke, or a horror movie.

Maybe this wasn't even real. Maybe she was at home having a nightmare, a phone call from a woman she'd assumed for years to be dead.

"Tell me." There was so much compassion in his gaze, she just wanted to fall into it. Get lost. Maybe drown. All those lame romance novel expressions. But they were all true. She was at the end of her strength, and he was everything she needed.

She opened her mouth to ask for help.

"Sanchez!"

———

DAULTON STRODE OVER. "You're done for the day. Go get some sleep, look for your friend tomorrow. Let us know if you need anything." He glanced at Sal. "You'll make sure she gets home?"

Trusting Sal with that responsibility was new. Sal didn't seem to think it unusual, though. "And I'll help find your friend."

Allyson pressed her lips together. "I wish I knew where she was right now."

"She'll call back. As soon as she does, you can go to her. Right?" He squeezed her shoulder. "And we'll run the name she gave you."

She glanced between her boss and Sal. "I'd like to head to the hospital and check on Max."

Daulton nodded. "Do that. Fill me in, and then go home."

"Yes, sir."

As soon as the boss walked away, Sal drew her to the side so they could talk. "Tell me about that call."

He hadn't gotten ahold of Talia yet. His teammate, a computer genius, was at dinner. Probably with no electronics in the restaurant but her phone. Still, he hadn't had the chance to dial.

Allyson faced off with him, their gazes almost level because of her height. "You find people, right?"

He could tell she was barely holding herself together. "You need a ride to the hospital?" They could talk about all this in the car.

"I'm good." She stepped back. Always walking away from him.

"Your boss just asked me to drive you."

"I'll call for an Uber." Still walking away from him. "Let me know if you come up with anything."

That was a heck of an assumption. Probably a whole bunch of them.

He'd help her.

He'd find her friend.

He'd call her when he did.

She'd handed him a case number and a name. Her history with this person caused that phone call to shake her. Did he want to get involved?

Sal had to face the fact that the same part of him who saw his team all paired off with their significant others, knowing they didn't need him the way they used to…also saw Allyson and her need.

This wasn't something she wanted her own team to help her with? No, she'd asked him. She'd leaned on him.

He'd been feeling superfluous. Now, not so much. He had something to sink his teeth into.

Sal stood outside the gun store and watched her walk away. The ship had probably sailed. He'd waited too long, not sure about pursuing a relationship with her. Then he'd just gotten busy with work. Distracted. He'd seen her once in a while.

Sal had to wonder—again—how he was going to work her out from under his skin.

Was it really just a case of quitting and finding a small town in need of a sheriff? Or he could be a PI. Maybe a bounty hunter, even. Could be he just needed to take that open marshal position in Cheyenne. Though, probably if he was going to do that then he should have emailed back the senior US Marshal there weeks ago when he'd seen the position post.

Or he could go home. Clean out his dad's cabin. Sell it, and figure out what to do next.

Maybe that position in Cheyenne was just like what could have been with Allyson. Another "too little, too late" situation. A missed opportunity. He didn't want to consider that he might be sabotaging his own intention to move on with his life by thinking about her instead of moving on.

That infernal war raged in him constantly. The opposing armies fought a battle between the part of him that wanted to have something good in his life and the part that wanted to stay right here.

Inertia.

Allyson.

The team.

A life in the mountains.

Didn't matter what the reason was, he hadn't gone yet. Maybe it was straight fear. Could be he hadn't made the decision simply because he didn't want to fail.

At least he knew he could help her friend. That was what he did. And if he wasn't going to make headway doing anything else, then he could at least do that. Find an innocent. Put something to rights.

Sal got one of the uniformed police officers to drop him at the office. He rode the elevator up to the floor where the task force offices were. He used his key code to get in the door and flipped on enough lights to see where he was going.

Even while her mouth challenged him to find her friend, she was pleading with him with those eyes. All this while she'd been visibly exhausted. He couldn't say she was the only reason he was helping, though she was a big reason. Sal sighed and jabbed the button to fire up his computer. He waited while his computer finished some update or another, and then looked up the case number Allyson had given him.

Missing persons cold case. A young woman, Vanessa Freethey, had gone missing one night, a student at the University of Seattle. Her roommate? Allyson Sanchez.

That was the connection.

A friend gone. Did Allyson blame herself? He could only imagine how it must've felt to never know what happened to someone she cared about.

Sal looked up the name she'd mentioned to him. Bridget McNamara. A few hits showed up, so he dug into each. Only one was a woman whose history didn't go back past five years. A created identity? The woman lived and worked in San Francisco, for what looked like a pharmaceutical company, an executive assistant.

The same woman who had called Allyson? Maybe. There was no picture of Bridget on the company website.

The search took him to a police department report. A coworker of Bridget McNamara hadn't shown up for work yesterday. Was something going on at the pharmaceutical company, something that meant Bridget needed to flee to Seattle and seek out the help of a friend? A friend who'd thought she was dead.

Talia would know better than him where to look for more information. For connections. He slid the phone closer, then figured it was a better idea to send both her and Haley an email. One of them should be able to help him. Halfway through typing out the email, the front door clicked.

Victoria strode in on her signature heels, wearing her normal skirt suit and blouse. Her hair was straight and blonde. Mostly he'd refer to her age as "undetermined." She could pass for anything from late thirties to early fifties, more with the use of makeup.

He leaned back in his chair. "I thought you were at dinner."

"I ate fast. Now I'm headed to the hospital to check on Mark."

No time for a cup of coffee, then. So why had she stopped by?

"He's out of surgery?" The FBI assistant director, Mark Welvern, had been shot a few days ago.

"They expect him to wake up at any time."

He nodded. "That's good."

She didn't seem convinced. Instead, she leaned over and looked at his screen. "That ATF agent has got you doing her research?"

Victoria knew exactly what her name was. "What's your problem with Allyson?"

"Did I say I had a problem?"

Sal shot her a look. Innocent wasn't a state she could convince him of. "She's a friend of mine. A colleague. I'm going to help find this missing person if I can."

"A female federal agent like that?" Victoria shook her head. "She's not one of us, and she never will be." She folded her arms. "It's probably a trap."

3

Allyson held a paper cup of coffee loosely. Her favorite coffee shop had run out of sleeves, but she wasn't going to let that stop her from getting her caffeine jolt. She headed into the Seattle office of the ATF, seriously dragging.

She'd gotten a couple of hours of broken sleep. Tossing and turning, waiting for the phone to ring and praying that Vanessa would be on the line. Her friend hadn't made contact again, but the prayer time had helped.

She said, "Hi," to the guys, and nodded to a couple of others. "How's Max?"

"Lynnie is there." She got an eye roll at that, and nodded as she said, "He'll pull through." She wasn't sure the same could be said of his marriage.

Allyson sat at her desk and logged on to her computer. Four scenes, not including the call from her friend. There was so much paperwork to do, it would probably take a week. Not that she had much time to get it done. The safe house, the stadium, the warehouse, and the robbery. She had to write up her take on all of it when she'd rather be out knocking on doors. Maybe checking airports, train and bus stations for Vanessa on their surveillance.

There was a difference between agents who went out and solved cases, and the ones who sat in an office, wanting to solve cases from their desks. She'd never been that type of cop. Probably never would be.

Half an hour of focused typing later, Allyson stretched and looked around. Across the office, in the conference room, she spotted Sal through the windows. He had to be giving his statement.

There was a recording device on the table between Sal and the undercover agent her team had brought on long-term to Yewell's operation. Not a job they'd thought would lead to an opening for someone like Sal to get in with the group.

Also present in the room were Daulton and two FBI agents. He had to be debriefing them all on the undercover operation. He'd managed to get into Yewell's crew—thanks to their guy—and had been there when the man was finally taken down. When the Secret Service's assistant director had been revealed as a traitor.

Two men in custody, along with the rest of Yewell's crew—those who weren't dead.

Allyson made her way to the door that had been left slightly ajar and hung there, close enough to hear what they were saying. The longer he talked, the more incredulous she became.

It was incredibly reckless what he'd done. Hearing all about it didn't make her feel better. Yes, Deputy Marshal Salvador Alvarez was good at his job. But that didn't mean he hadn't put his life in serious danger. And only a short time after he'd been previously injured.

He'd been right there in the middle of it all, along with Drew North.

She felt the reaction well up in her. Hot anger unfiltered due to her exhaustion. Her emotions were always closer to the surface when she was overtired.

Ally didn't want to know how it would feel if he was killed.

He'd been hurt plenty of times, that was nothing new. Dead would be a whole different story.

She blew out a breath and pushed aside those morose thoughts. Instead, she wondered if he'd found out anything about her friend.

She realized he'd glanced at her. Along with a couple of the FBI agents. The undercover ATF agent had a slight grin on his face. Ally lifted her chin. Sal returned it with a nod. He had something.

She wandered back to her computer and decided to run the number from which Vanessa had called her. It came up as unregistered, so a burner phone. What kind of person was Vanessa that she'd gotten her hands on a burner?

Allyson sent an email to the agents who helped them find information—their variation of CSI, though most of it was electronic. Their version of Talia was actually a team of two agents. She asked them if they could try and track the closest cell towers. See where it pinged off previously, and whether it was still on. Find out if Vanessa was really in Seattle now, running for her life.

Allyson leaned back in her chair and ran her hands down her face.

"That doesn't look good." Sal dragged a chair over and sat by her desk. He hissed out a breath.

"You okay?"

"Old injuries."

Before she could ask more about it, her phone beeped. She leaned down and read the subject. "My boss wants an update on the FFL robbery from last night."

Sal was quiet for a second. "We didn't stay that late."

"Doesn't mean I'm not on the case." She shrugged. "Among others."

"I'm still looking at your friend's info. So far on Bridget McNamara I've got nothing except an executive assistant working for a pharmaceutical company."

He told her the name of the company, and she typed it into

her computer. Found the website. Pulled up the page of employee bios.

"She's not on—"

She scrolled down. A picture of her redheaded college roommate stared back at her.

"It's her." Ally chewed her lip. Could Vanessa really be on the run and in trouble? "I can't believe someone missing all this time can suddenly be here—and also nowhere to be found. It makes no sense that she was fine and still she didn't contact me all these years."

"No social media friend requests?"

"I'm not on social media, so I'll have to use one of our dummy accounts to look." Most ATF agents weren't present much online. As a small agency they did undercover work, and it just wasn't worth the risk of being targeted. "I'll call and find out if she turned up to work this morning."

"Is it worth having the FBI pay the office in San Francisco a visit? Get them to ask about both her and the missing coworker."

She nodded. "Someone local should go, at least."

"The fact that she reached out is good. You can help her."

"I'm going to try. But if I can't find her, then how can I make sure she's safe? I don't even know where to start looking. And I doubt I'll be able to track her down after all this time unless she contacts me again." What if she had waited all these years to finally find Vanessa, only to have her turn up out of the blue right before something even more terrible happened?

"I sent everything to Talia and Haley. I'll let you know what they come up with."

Allyson nodded, even though she didn't like the idea that his coworkers were part of this. She was going to accept the help, regardless of her opinion of them.

Her phone buzzed with an email.

"Is it her?"

"It's the list of guns that were stolen from the store." Which would help when they tracked them down. Or *after* they were used in the commission of a crime. She sighed.

"What is it?"

"I'm tired, that's all." Or she needed a change. Too bad she'd never thought of what she might want outside of the ATF. "Maybe I'm getting too old for this."

"No, that's not it."

How did he know? Whatever his tactic for getting a result, it seemed like he always knew what she was really thinking.

"Need help on this case?"

"Which one?"

He actually smiled, something he didn't often do.

"You have a nice smile." She realized what she'd said. "Doesn't your team need you?" They were his priority. Always had been, always would be.

She saw something in his eyes then. Like maybe no, his team didn't need him right now. And he didn't seem like he thought that was a good thing.

Allyson glanced at her monitor. She stared again at the photo of her friend and swallowed her pride. "I'd appreciate whatever help the task force can give me."

———

"This isn't about the team." She did know that, didn't she? Sal leaned closer to her, over the corner of her desk so she'd hear his low voice. "I'm going to do what I can to help you."

"Thanks."

After he'd satisfied that promise, he would be free to leave. Free to spend time alone, in the mountains, working her out from under his skin. He was good at being a marshal. He had enjoyed working on the task force, for Victoria, the past few years. But he had to admit, at least to himself, that he was ready for the next stage of his life. This need for change wasn't going to be satisfied with two weeks doing nothing, going crazy. He needed to make a move somewhere else. Do something else.

"What's that on your face?"

He frowned and shrugged one shoulder.

She understood enough to say, "It looked nice. Maybe wistful, even."

"You ever just want to go do something else?"

She frowned.

"Change your life. Quit. Move away. Go a totally different direction?"

"You want to leave?"

"Sometimes." He needed to be honest, despite how she might react. What they had was truthful, and they had upheld that unspoken arrangement for years. "Not just that the grass is greener on the other side. More like, I just need something…different."

"Is it like wanderlust?"

"Maybe." He still leaned in, close enough to whisper. "Where do you go on vacation?"

She frowned. "My dad's cabin."

"Have you ever been outside the state of Washington?"

She shrugged. "For work, sure." But there was something in her gaze.

"There's a wide world out there."

"And I should be going to visit all those places?"

"Maybe it's just that I don't let myself settle. I refuse to be satisfied with the same thing for decades. Probably because my father never aspired to anything other than exactly what he was."

"The sheriff of Arapoe County."

Sal blinked. "Did you do a background check on me?"

"Uh, no…Google."

He laughed. All the while he did so, Victoria's caution from last night rang in his ears. She thought Allyson didn't fit in with the team? That was fine. They weren't looking for anyone else to join.

Given the conversation they'd just been having, he wondered if the fact Allyson *wasn't* part of the team might make her all the more attractive to him. She could be some of the "different" he'd been eyeing for a while now.

Sal sat back in his chair, realizing he often felt more at home in the ATF office than he did in the task force office. He could say the same for a few of the police stations throughout Seattle. He enjoyed the camaraderie, but not when the people around him were at odds.

Like Victoria and Allyson.

There was enough of a battle going on inside him that he didn't need to be in the middle of those two women and their conflict as well. And yet, here he was.

"So you're ready to leave Seattle?"

Sal shrugged. Honest, but not necessarily something he wanted to say out loud to her. Not when words had power.

Allyson turned back to her computer, biting her lip. It was almost like she was hurt. Great. He'd made her mad. Or upset. Or this was about her being so tired and having no filter.

He poured her a cup of coffee, then one for him too, and delivered it to her.

"Peace offering?"

She gave him a small smile. "Thanks, Sal."

He couldn't help being drawn to her. Especially considering she needed support.

He was between cases, and his team had resources. Her people weren't who she'd gone to for assistance on this. He was. Victoria's opinion of her said more about Victoria than it did about Allyson.

The fact Allyson was so by-the-book probably rubbed up against his boss's former career as a spy. Victoria had been trained to be independent, to color outside the lines. Spies had to make the situation work in their favor, using whatever resources they had.

Sal wasn't so sure he'd have been able to do that. He had skills he employed undercover, but there was always procedure. He had plenty of lines he wouldn't cross.

Living with no boundaries would be a nightmare. Allyson was all cop. Victoria and Allyson, a spy and a cop, and not likely able to find a middle ground considering the places they were coming from. He was a hunter. Where did he fit? Definitely not between them.

Sal didn't think he'd ever be able to figure out a common ground. Not the least because they were two women.

"Are you going to sit by my desk all day?"

Sal sipped his coffee. "Are you going to be here all day when you're supposed to have taken the day off?"

"No one else is taking the day off." She held her hands over the keyboard, fingers poised and ready to continue typing. "Besides, I have work to do."

"And I should leave?"

"I was just curious why you're still here when we both have stuff—"

She was interrupted by his cell phone ringing.

Sal dug it out of his pocket and flipped it open. "Alvarez." He grinned at Allyson, who grinned back and then went back to her work.

"It's me."

Dakota. "Hey. What's up?"

"When will you be in the office? I need to talk to you about something."

It was on the tip of his tongue to ask if it was about Allyson, but he bit the words back. That wasn't something he needed to say out loud in the ATF office. "About what?"

"About *something*. That's what I said, right?" Dakota sighed. "Plus the coffee pot is broken. Will you be much longer?"

"I'll be there in twenty. Is something wrong?"

"It's not a case," Dakota said. "It's personal."

Sal's stomach clenched. What could have gone bad since he'd seen her last night? "Is something up with Josh?"

"No, of course not. Nothing's wrong. But it is related."

But she wasn't going to just spit it out? "Just—"

"I'm not talking to you about this over the phone, okay? I just need to know when you'll be in the office."

A dog barked in the background, a familiar sound considering Josh had a former marine canine, and she'd pretty much been taken on as the task force dog.

"UPS is here."

He smiled. "I'll be there as soon as I get there."

She ignored the comment and just said, "Good."

Urgent, but not life threatening. Not work, personal. What was it? Had to be something significant considering she'd just let go of a serious chance to pick on him about that comment. *I'll be there when I'm there.* Something was up if she'd let that go.

A part of him didn't want to be drawn into whatever problem she had. That was for Josh to solve, right? And her fiancé was more than capable of handling her. That was the job he'd signed on for.

"Hang on." Dakota went quiet for a second, then said, "Talia needs to tell you something."

"She's in—"

"Hey." Dakota had to have handed her the phone.

He said, "You're in the office?"

Talia answered, "Uh, yeah."

Sal took a breath. Apparently showing up to work today wasn't as surprising as he'd thought, considering she and Allyson had both done it. "Everything okay?" Maybe she knew what was up with Dakota.

"Question."

"Fire away."

"I need Allyson to confirm. Is the woman she knew in college, the one who went missing, the same woman that works at the pharmaceutical company?"

She knew he was here? What was he thinking—of course she knew. "Allyson said it was."

The woman herself glanced over at him. Sal said, "One sec. I'm putting you on speaker." He hit the button, then said, "Go ahead, Talia."

"Bridget McNamara's coworker, the chief of operations, never showed up to work yesterday."

Allyson leaned closer to the phone. "I saw the police report."

"The cops found his body. He's dead."

4

———————

"**Y**our office has a security code?"

"Yours has swipe cards." Sal tugged down the handle and pushed the door open.

"Yeah." Great. Now she sounded dumb. She swallowed down the embarrassment and took in the Northwest Counter-Terrorism Task Force office.

And gaped.

The wall to the right was all windows, beyond which was the Seattle skyline. Inside was all red brick and electronics. There were a few key things that indicated it really was the office of a federal law enforcement agency. However, they clearly managed to get the best of most everything they needed.

No wonder they kept it so secret.

The whole gang was here even after the major operation yesterday. Niall, the NCIS Special Agent. Haley, his girlfriend, who was the office manager—and former Navy Intelligence. Talia, the NSA analyst and computer whiz. Dakota, with her Native American coloring, was Homeland Security Investigations, and Josh—who Allyson had never actually officially met—was the DEA agent.

A dog barked.

The animal was a German Shepherd, tall and slender. It stopped a few feet from her and barked, its whole body leaned toward her.

"Good girl." Dakota smirked but didn't look over from her computer.

Was Allyson supposed to be impressed? "You teach her to do that?"

Josh strode around his desk to the waiting area. "She's had what amounts to guard dog training."

The dog had stopped barking but still leaned toward her. She expected to see a flash of teeth at any moment.

"Neema, place."

The dog gave her one last death glare and then moved to the wall, where a dog bed had been placed in the morning sunshine. The dog sat. Not restful, but completely alert.

"Platz."

She lay down with a groan.

"Josh Weber." He stuck out his hand.

"Allyson Sanchez."

"Nice to meet you."

Huh. Maybe they weren't all so bad—

Allyson caught the death glare Dakota shot her before she glanced at her fiancé, lips pressed into a thin line.

"I'm Haley." The woman stood shorter than Allyson, her gaze assessing. Brows drawn together like she was trying to figure Allyson out. She had gorgeous dark features, and eyes that sparkled.

"Nice to meet you." Maybe she should just stick with this line until kingdom come. It seemed to be working for her.

Talia looked over from her computer and eyed her. "Victoria should be here soon."

"Thanks." Sal touched her back, between her shoulder blades. He pretty much shoved her forward, but she covered it well—she thought.

She didn't care much if they all gave her dirty looks. This

wasn't her team, and she already knew they were close. Probably it wasn't just about outsiders though. Probably it was just her.

Had she really taken half an hour convincing her boss this missing persons was an ATF case, not just a personal matter, only to come here and be party to this?

Talia's smile was proof enough. She hadn't managed to hide her reluctance at all.

Allyson said, "How are you doing? I heard you caught a bullet yesterday."

Several people in the room shifted. Tense movements. They didn't want to be reminded of what had happened?

"Graze." Talia shifted, and Allyson caught the edges of pain in the skin around her eyes.

"I'm glad it wasn't too bad."

Dakota's head whipped around. "She got *shot*. There's nothing *not too bad* about that."

Allyson stared her down. She wasn't going to cave.

Sal stepped in the laser beam of their locked gazes, breaking the tension. "Dakota, why don't we have that conversation now?"

Allyson didn't get a chance to hear her answer. Talia motioned to a chair and told Allyson to "take a load off."

Allyson sat to the sound of Dakota scraping her chair back. The two of them walked to the kitchen area at the far end of the open office, beside a hallway where the bathrooms were and a closed office door with a strip of masking tape on the door that read VICTORIA in permanent marker.

"You have information about Vanessa's coworker?"

Talia leaned back in her chair and nodded.

"Sure you're okay?"

"Mason told me to take two weeks off." Talia glanced at her. "I told him that if he wasn't going to, then neither was I."

"Didn't he just get promoted to acting assistant director?"

She smiled, the softening of someone thinking about the person they loved. "He's a shoo-in for the permanent position. I'm sure he'll get it."

Talia seemed happy. Content. Healed. Allyson didn't know her well enough to say something and share in that fact. Her opinion, or pleasure, didn't mean anything to the NSA analyst. She hadn't even thought the woman liked her—personally or professionally.

Maybe Talia was only being nice because Victoria wasn't here, and that was why Talia had told them the boss would be there soon. Allyson couldn't deny that might be the reason the atmosphere in the office wasn't full-on hostile.

She glanced at Sal and Dakota, who appeared to be having a heated and hushed conversation over by the coffee pot.

Talia said, "Are you okay?"

Out of the corner of her eye she saw Sal turn and look at her. She figured ignoring it was best. "Long night." Not to mention the fact that one of their agents had been shot in the warehouse. These people were all back at work, while others were trying to pick up the pieces.

Allyson stood. "Maybe you could just…email me everything."

She started to walk away. These people were going to do whatever they were going to do, and she didn't have the emotional energy to shore up her defenses. She didn't want to wind up bitter at them. They didn't need that. Not when they actively worked to turn the tide of crime and terrorism. They saved innocent people's lives, just like she did, and actively sought justice for wrongs that had been done.

Talia called after her. "Sit back down, Special Agent Sanchez."

A thought occurred to her as she turned around. "Because you're not done cloning my phone?"

Talia actually laughed. "I need you to have all the information, so you're properly equipped when your friend calls back. Yes, I'm accessing your phone so that I can deliver it." She paused, then explained, "Also so I can try to figure out where she is now."

Allyson sat back down.

"The missing pharmaceutical employee was found on the side of the highway. Cause of death is blunt force trauma."

"Car?"

Talia shook her head. "Smaller than that. Investigating detectives found a series of emails between the chief operations officer and Bridget McNamara. Threats and hostility on both sides. They got a warrant for her condo and found signs that she fought with someone. DNA was run, it's the dead guy's blood."

Was Bridget being framed, or was Vanessa a killer? "On the phone she sounded distressed. She reached out for help, and I'm going to help her."

"Even if she's a murderer?"

"Everyone is entitled to tell their side of the story."

Allyson didn't like bullies, and she had a compulsion to help victims. The deep things that drove her had everything to do with being alone after Van had gone missing.

Being questioned.

Those side glances from teachers and students. She'd been at dinner with her father, a minister, at the time of the abduction… kidnapping. The night Vanessa had run away. She still didn't know which it was, but she was closer to finding out the truth about what had happened. No one had been able to accuse Allyson of involvement because of her alibi. Still, that didn't mean people hadn't talked behind her back.

"This is our case now."

Allyson blinked. "Excuse me?"

"Bridget McNamara's boss is Malcom Kennowich."

Everyone in the room braced. Allyson glanced around. "That means something to you guys?"

"Malcom Kennowich is the man behind Cerium. The man who had me sold. We've been chasing him for months, trying to figure out who he is."

And Allyson had just tossed him into their laps.

———

THAT WAS why they'd had her come to the office?

"…talk to you."

He turned back to Dakota. She should have just spat it out.

"It's more important than a thirty second question/answer by the sink."

Sal gritted his teeth. "I'll make time. But I have to deal with this right now." He pointed toward Allyson, who had stood up again. Didn't look like Talia would be able to get her to sit back down this time.

Dakota started, "I know how to deal—"

"Don't." He didn't need her attitude when he knew—or at least was mostly sure—it was because she saw everything changing around her and was getting freaked out at the speed of it. Even though Dakota was the one who'd fallen in love first. Before any of the other team members.

He said, "Not right now."

Allyson's whole demeanor was stiff. "You guys aren't taking my case." She shot him a look. Hurt. Disappointment.

He didn't know which was worse. Together they caused a sharp pain in his chest. "Ally…"

She looked like she wanted to be halfway out the door.

It was Haley who said, "We've been tracking this guy for months, trying to figure out who he is and who has been selling modified CX gas, stirring up all kinds of mayhem. He almost destroyed us. We've barely survived up until this point. But we think this Kennowich is Cerium, and your missing friend could be the key to busting the case wide open."

Talia said, "If we can find her, then maybe we'll be able to prove it. Prove she didn't kill that guy."

"Which means you don't know for sure if the two things are linked," Allyson countered. "My friend's call for help might have nothing at all to do with your case against Kennowich."

"But it could—"

"You aren't taking my case."

He strode after her, shooting a side glance at Talia. "You didn't think to warn me about the connection?"

"There wasn't time." Talia didn't get up. Clearly she didn't think there was anything wrong with springing this information on all of them.

He picked up his pace, even though it made a low thrum of pain slice through his leg.

None of the others had seemed surprised. Maybe it was just him and Allyson that Talia had sprung this information on. An attempt to get her honest reaction to this news about her friend's involvement with a criminal.

Sal pushed through the door into the hallway where Allyson waited for the elevator, jabbing the button. The set of her shoulders said more than any words needed to. She was hurt, but she hid it well under a layer of irritation.

"I can smell what you guys are doing from a mile away."

"You think we're trying to steal your case?"

"I know you didn't know." She turned around. "And I know you've been looking into this Cerium thing for months now. But whatever's going on with Vanessa, it's *mine* to deal with."

"You're right to be the one to help your friend. She called you."

How was he going to convince her that his team wouldn't hijack it, though? She was never going to believe he didn't bring her here just so they could absorb her into their investigation, or hijack the search for her friend.

"I didn't share it with you so you could take over."

"That's not what I'm doing. I want to help you."

"Because you have nothing better to do?"

He couldn't tell her why. She would get the wrong idea if she thought he was there because he had feelings for her, and that wasn't going to help him be able to walk away later. Too much had happened between them. Too much water under the bridge, or so the saying went. It wasn't like it would ever work, and the fact was he'd waited too long. They were past the point he could have transitioned them from friends to something more.

He'd missed his shot with her.

She would never be happy thousands of miles from here in a small town, and he couldn't live in the city forever.

After all, when he'd brought up his urge to get away, she'd barely known what he was talking about, the idea was so foreign to her.

Sal moved closer to her. "I had no idea your friend's disappearance was connected to our case. I thought we were just coming here to hear about the murdered guy." But they should pool their resources, right? That would be a quicker win for everyone.

The idea they could get the Cerium guy energized him.

"Great. Job done, you know all about the murder and so do I." She turned and jabbed at the button again. "Now it's time to go find Vanessa."

Before the cops did?

He was just about to say, "Fine," when the elevator doors opened.

Allyson flinched and took a half step back.

Victoria, several inches shorter than Allyson, but somehow more imposing, stepped out. "She knows about Kennowich and the Cerium connection?"

Allyson braced. "You're not taking my case from me." Then she stepped onto the elevator. "I don't care who this guy is y'all are chasing."

Victoria's eyes narrowed.

Sal stepped between the open doors. He reached around to press the button that would hold the doors open and looked back at his boss. "How is Welvern doing?"

"He's out of surgery, and he woke up." Her face went carefully blank. "The prognosis is good, though he's going to have to work his way back to being fighting fit."

Sal nodded. Maybe Victoria was venting her frustration on Allyson, considering she wasn't a personal friend. It was possible she was more willing to get mad when she had no connection. No camaraderie or friendship to burn. Which just made Allyson a handy punching bag.

Was that what was happening? And were the rest of them taking their cue from her?

It was possible there was another reason Victoria was stressed, but he didn't know what it would be.

Regardless, this was hardly the way a State Department Director should be acting. Not the first indication he'd had that Victoria wasn't a professional politician or diplomat. She definitely had her own ways of doing things. And it was often not the wisest, most people-friendly course of action. He'd actually respected that about her.

Was it possible to bring some harmony between the two of them?

"We're pooling our resources." The last thing he wanted was to be in the middle of two strong women at odds with each other. "We need to find Allyson's friend, and that's not going to happen by standing around talking."

Victoria lifted her chin. "Keep me apprised."

He didn't miss the look the two women shared before the elevator doors slid shut.

Here he was trying to make peace, and they were just going to continue with this animosity? Honestly, that irritated him. Not that he thought his work environment had to be harmonious all the time. That wasn't realistic. People butted heads and miscommunicated.

But why couldn't they figure out how to be professionals about it, rather than falling back on all that passive-aggressive stuff? They didn't need to be friends. They just needed to get over their hang-ups enough to show each other a little more respect.

The elevator opened in the lobby, and he stepped off the elevator.

"Guess I'm not the only one who's mad."
He turned to Allyson. "Let's just find your friend."
Hopefully fast.
Then things could go back to normal.

5

"Copy that." Sal hung up and tossed his phone into the cup holder.

"Was that about Kennowich?"

He shook his head. "It was the Marshal's office in Portland, about a case from last year."

She'd been searching online via her phone, looking into the pharmaceutical company Bridget McNamara worked for and reading everything she could find on the man who employed her friend. Was he involved in her disappearance years ago? It wasn't impossible, but still very unlikely.

And until she found Vanessa to ask her, Allyson would continue to not have an answer.

Sal gripped the wheel as he drove, the muscles of his forearms flexing. He insisted they get coffee and something to eat while they figure out a plan to find Vanessa. Allyson would've been fine on her own, but he made the decision. She had too much respect for him to argue with that. It was his steadiness that helped her stay calm. Despite being angry at his team, Allyson could admit—at least to herself—that maybe she was better with him here.

It was like he was completely at peace, both with who he was and where he was. Probably also with what he was capable of.

Had she ever been that sure of herself? He just had that…calm about him. In a way no one did these days. Everyone seemed to live their lives on their phones. She used hers for work but, at home, barely looked at it.

Would it ring now? She took a second and prayed, as she did often when she needed movement on a case. However Vanessa had managed to get a call out to her, Allyson felt that window may have closed. Otherwise her friend would have tried to contact her again, right?

So had the phone broken somehow? Or had she been captured? Maybe something else happened. Thinking of the terrible possibilities made her shudder.

If she made contact just once more, Talia could track the call. Given what she had done to Allyson's phone at the office, she figured the NSA analyst would know the second it started to ring. She would happily give up a little privacy for that protection.

Besides, it wasn't like there was anything personal on her phone.

Every awful conclusion to a case went through her mind, a trailer of all the times she had failed. All the hurt and pain she had seen.

That day everything erupted at the federal courthouse. The day she'd had to watch Sal get overpowered, and then fight to get the suspects back in cuffs. And then, there it was, right at the end —the grand finale of her mistakes. That split second before she'd pulled her stun gun to take down the bad guys had felt like an absolute eternity. Sal had been hit and kicked several times before she and the other ATF agents managed to get everyone off him.

That feeling of helplessness wasn't something she liked. The fact they both still had scars wasn't something she liked to think about…the experiences that unfortunately connected them.

Ugh. She'd been trying to occupy her thoughts to keep from thinking about him. But here she was, falling into that spiral of distraction because of her attraction to him. She had to stop allowing her mind to wander. After all, look at what had happened at the federal courthouse? Not that she'd been swooning over him at the time, but the fact was, she'd lost focus, and if there was ever a time she needed to focus, it was now.

Her phone buzzed about the same time his did. When she looked down at the screen, she saw it was a group thread including her, Sal, and Talia.

"Talia's facial recognition program got a hit. She has Vanessa on a surveillance camera at a shopping center early this morning. She's tracking her, trying to figure out where she went after that."

"Good. Let's pray she comes up with a solid lead."

Allyson nodded. She knew he was a believer as well. Probably a huge part of that peace he had, and why she felt so calm around him. But it wasn't like they shared that stuff with each other. Her own faith was pretty low key.

"Is Talia bringing in the FBI, or is it just your team going after my friend?"

He glanced at her, but she didn't see what the look was. "They'll keep her safe."

So maybe she'd had a *tone.* But that hadn't been what she was asking for assurance on. She wanted to know that he would do what he could, not that he had faith in his team. Their friends' opinions would tear them apart, even if they tried not to allow that to happen. She'd figured out that much, and also figured it was why he'd never asked her out.

There would be no way to stop the wedge that would form between them. It was already there, even now. Before either of them had even voiced anything about their feelings for each other.

She knew they had a connection. They'd been through an intense experience and shared something that involved the darkest of fears—death.

His team didn't get that.

She decided then that she didn't care if they were going to swoop in. She would get her friend to safety before they showed up. Allyson was going to keep Vanessa from winding up in their custody. If she was innocent, there was no way she'd allow Van to end up in *anyone's* custody. At least as much as she could help it.

Sal was the wild card. She didn't know which way he would go. In the heat of the moment he was going to make what he thought was the best decision. She admired that about him, even as much as it frustrated her. He had a core of nobility that was missing in a lot of men she met—good guys and bad guys.

He would do what he thought was right, even if she didn't agree with it. There also wouldn't be much she could do, considering it was just her. She'd have to combat what she could, but that would be the end of it. She wanted to work with his team about as much as they were interested in having her join them. Talk about mutual respect.

Ally glanced out at the mountains in the distance. Maybe she should just jump on her motorcycle and take off. Get lost.

He'd mentioned wanting to get away from it all. What had rolled through her then was...fear. Did he want to leave her?

Allyson had to face it. "Sometimes…when I get restless…I take my motorcycle up to my dad's cabin. It's where he got away from everything and took time to just pray in the quiet. Seek the Lord."

Maybe she should do that again. Or offer the option to Sal. Maybe he could use her cabin for a weekend.

There was something wild in him. Formidable, like the mountains. Craggy and harsh, but beautiful. Uncharted, yet solid and steady. *Ugh. You're doing it again.*

"Wilderness and the road is in my blood. It's what I do whenever I have time off." He smiled at the street ahead. "I have a spot where I camp, up in the mountains. Total silence except for the breeze, and the sounds of nature. No people. No Wi-Fi." He shot her a grin.

She mostly figured trying to "find yourself" was a total cliché. But maybe a cliché by its very nature was based on someone's true experience. Otherwise it wouldn't be so universally understood, right?

"You think that's what people need? Like we should all take the chance to unplug?" It was a legitimate question. She didn't feel that burning desire in her.

"I think it's about what your soul needs." He spoke more softly than she'd heard him speak before. "We all have a cry in us for something. Most people either don't know what it's asking for, or they think they have to pack it into a two-week vacation every year. Then the rest of their lives are soul sucking. People get divorced, or they fall into addiction, all because they refuse to admit what they really need. Some people just don't want to get off their backsides and go claim it. They settle, instead of taking the hard steps to grow."

Was that what she'd done? Settled. Refused to take the next hard step? "Maybe they just…don't know how to ask. Or what to ask for."

Their phones both buzzed again.

"Vanessa got into a vehicle." Allyson read aloud. "Talia has it parked outside a house."

***

SAL DROVE past the residence twice, then parked. No movement. All the blinds were drawn, which meant it could be empty or full of people, and they wouldn't know until an army poured out with guns drawn.

They walked together down the sidewalk. A simple holding of the hands would be the only difference between two people strolling beside each other and an official couple. If they wanted to not look like cops, they should probably grab each other's hand. And it was on the tip of his tongue to suggest it when they reached the car.

He'd memorized the model, color, and plates from a photo Talia sent over. So he didn't need to check back on their text string to make sure it was the right vehicle. Not many other red nineties cars on this street. A stack of what looked like mail sat on the front seat.

Allyson leaned in the window to look at the backseat. "Nothing."

Sal wasn't sure what to say, considering it was neither good nor bad for her friend.

"At least, no signs a kidnap victim was tossed back there."

He shot her a conciliatory smile. Unless they got the keys, there was little chance they'd get a look in the trunk.

Sal led the way up to the front door. He knocked once, and it swung slowly open. "Left ajar?"

"Or the worst kidnappers ever." She stepped around him and knocked again on the now-open door before calling out, "Federal Agents! Is anyone home?"

After a handful of quiet seconds, she announced her intention to enter. One hand unsnapping her weapon, she stepped inside.

The hallway branched off to several rooms and had a staircase to the left. He didn't hear anyone, and no one responded to her announcement. So, not an army then. "You take downstairs?"

She nodded.

Sal headed up, gun in front. The search was fast and simple. Furniture was minimal, and most of the closet space in the two bedrooms were empty. He checked under beds and behind hanging curtains.

As he searched, the conversation he'd had with Allyson crept back into his mind. When had he figured out that he wasn't getting nearly enough out of his job anymore? The idea must have been working around in his subconscious. It seemed like it took voicing it to Allyson to realize that what *he* really needed was to breathe that mountain air again. Maybe all the time.

He was nearing the end of his twenty years as a federal agent. It was past time to take her father's stance and get away to pray. When was the last time he'd done that?

"No one down here."

"Same up here." He trotted back down the stairs. "Basement?"

"Not that I could see." She took a second, and he could see her mind working on the problem. "We could surveil the house. Sit outside and wait for someone to show up."

"Let's check the garage before we do that," he said. "We also need to look for a shed, or somewhere else a person could be kept. Did you see any car keys?"

She shook her head and led the way to a door off the kitchen. Washer dryer. Dry dog bowl. Beyond that was another door. She waited for him to be ready; they nodded to each other, and he pulled the door open.

Allyson stepped through, gun first.

"She was in here."

He followed her into the garage. It was like stepping into a sauna. Stifling, hot air. A single chair in the middle of the empty space. Not even a box or plastic tote against the walls. On the seat of the folding chair was a smear of blood. Like a hand, or fingers, had wiped across the plastic.

Someone was held here. Whether that would turn out to be her friend was another question entirely.

"She could have escaped."

Sal crouched and looked at a strand of plastic on the concrete beside one chair leg. "Whoever was here, they broke free."

"Let go, or moved? Or she got herself loose somehow."

He nodded. Each of those things was possible.

The reality was that Allyson hadn't seen this woman for years. She had no idea what kind of person this lady was now, only the person she remembered knowing years ago. For only a matter of a few months, considering they had been first year roommates and Vanessa had gone missing weeks into the spring semester.

This woman who was also known as Bridget McNamara could —these days—be someone quite different. Capable of all manner of things. Who knew?

Sal walked back through the house, trying to figure out where she had gone next given this new information.

He stopped at the back door.

"Did you find anything?"

"Another smear of blood." He pointed at the door. "Right here." Someone had touched it. On their way out, or in the process of closing the door.

"I didn't see that."

He shrugged and pulled open the back door.

"Didn't your father teach you that stuff? I thought I remembered you telling me that."

"Yep." He stepped out. No shed, no gate that he could see. Was there one on the side of the house? Had Vanessa run out that way?

Allyson said, "Looking for clues, and finding things most people overlook."

He figured it was mostly instinctual at this point. He didn't have to think much about what he was looking for before he found a sign of someone. Man affecting the world around him. Or her.

Did he have that much of a grasp on human nature? That fight-or-flight nature, and how it played into the sequence of decisions a person made without even realizing it.

"Do you even know how you do it?"

He shrugged as she came to stand beside him. Was she asking about his tracking ability to hide the fact she was now seriously scared for her friend? "Call the local PD. They should get CSU down here to go over all the evidence. I'm sure there's stuff I missed."

"I don't know about that." She tipped her head to the side. "It would probably take you years to teach that stuff to me, right?"

Did she want him to? He glanced up at her, then crouched and looked at the blood on the door.

"I started learning as soon as I could walk. My father took me with him when he went hiking, hunting, and fishing. Taught me everything he knew. When he was young, he worked as a ranch hand on a huge spread in Wyoming. A true mongrel. Hispanic and Native American with a swatch of Caucasian."

"I thought he was a sheriff?"

"That came later." His gaze traced the patio, then in a straight line to the back fence. He stood up, hissing out a breath against the aches and pains he tried to ignore.

"Are you okay?"

"I've been doing physical therapy, but I'm still wondering if I'm too old for this. Too many back-to-back injuries."

He glanced at her and saw the nod. She said, "You need a month-long vacation."

"Ain't that the truth?"

They walked together across the lawn. He'd been able to keep it from the team so far, but he wasn't able to keep it from Allyson. There was something visceral between them, and he couldn't push it off. Couldn't ignore it.

"So you're *not* okay."

She needed to know if her partner was capable of having her back.

"It's nice of you to care, but I'm perfectly capable of doing my job."

Ahead of her now, he glanced back and saw her exasperated expression—that roll of her eyes. He smiled to himself while he tracked footprints to the back fence.

Whoever Vanessa was, and whatever part she played in Cerium, it was clear this woman needed to be found. Regardless of the "off" feeling he was getting from all this. He was a hunter, but that didn't mean the prey always made that hunt worthwhile. Satisfaction demanded the process feed something in him. Not a cheap imitation most people seemed to settle for so easily these days.

Sal peered over the back fence and saw what he was looking for.

Then he turned to Ally and mouthed, *She's right there.*

6

———————

She landed on the grass as quietly as she could. No way to avoid the surprise, though. She'd just jumped over the fence.

Allyson planted one knee on the gravel in front of a woman. A familiar face and yet, in a way, the person huddled before her was a total stranger. Older. Dressed in black skinny pants and a shredded and stained blousy shirt. Smudges of dirt marred her skin, and she had a deep purple bruise around her eye.

"Vanessa."

The woman flinched, eventually looking up. Blinked. "Allyson."

She nodded. "Yeah."

"You found me."

"I did." She reached out. "Can you stand?"

Vanessa's eyes shifted over Allyson's shoulder, looking at something beyond her. Behind her.

Again she flinched, and Allyson caught a quick intake of breath.

"That's my friend, Sal." She touched Vanessa's elbow and braced to help her stand. "He's a US Marshal."

Vanessa shifted, and Allyson helped her up. "Can you walk?"

She swayed. "I'm okay."

Allyson held onto her with two hands now. Vanessa moved, and then Allyson was swallowed up in a hug. She stiffened, her instincts catching on to how much closer her old friend was to her gun than she was. Then everything rushed back.

The loneliness. The loss of her friend, the first person after her father's death who really understood her. She had truly felt a part of Allyson's life. Other people who knew them both had said they thought Vanessa was a *faker*, like she was only pulling the wool over Allyson's eyes.

No one could fake that level of friendship. Not the way they'd been during that first semester of college. Vanessa had become her family in that short time.

Then there was Vanessa's father, who had drawn her into his family as well. As though she and Vanessa were sisters or something.

The tragedy was that Bill hadn't lived long enough to see his daughter found.

"You're here." Allyson let out a breath that sounded like it'd been held for ten years.

"I'm calling an ambulance." That was Sal.

Vanessa pulled back, retreating from Allyson's hug. Eyes wide, her gaze darted around. "No, no, no…no ambulances." She took two additional steps in retreat.

She reached out, but Vanessa got too far away. Allyson stopped. What was she going to do, grab her? Allyson tensed. What if her friend ran again? What would she do if Vanessa disappeared *again*?

Vanessa glanced between her and Sal, as though at any moment the marshal would attack her.

"Sal is a friend of mine and a good guy." The fact she wouldn't mind being more wasn't exactly the point right now. "He helped me find you. That's what he does." Both the helping part and the finding people part. "You're safe now, Van. We've got you, and we're going to make sure you continue to be safe and that you get whatever help you need, okay?" Allyson didn't wait too long, not especially needing an answer to that.

Sal took a step closer. "Are you hurt, honey?"

The soft tone of his voice made Allyson want to shut her eyes and just soak in it. Until it clicked that he'd never called *her* any kind of endearment. Now he was using one on a victim, her friend?

Allyson shrugged aside her jealousy. "Can you walk? We'll drive you to the hospital, but we really need to get you checked out." She gave her friend a small smile she hoped made Van feel better. "Make sure you're all right."

They headed for her car, Vanessa taking shaky steps as Allyson helped her along. Her friend's clothes were disheveled and dirty. There were smudges on the front of her shirt, blood from her split lip. Still, her clothing was clearly the expensive kind. Well made, maybe even tailored. A blouse. Slacks. She'd lost her shoes. Vanessa's bloody, cut-up feet left smudges on the concrete as they walked.

"Almost there."

As Bridget McNamara, she had been working for a top pharmaceutical company in San Francisco. She was an executive assistant to one of those c-suite, corner-office types. Not a world Allyson was all that familiar with, but she at least knew enough to know Van clearly hadn't been a kidnap victim for every one of those years. She'd managed to make something of her life, emerging from that pit to rise high.

And yet, she hadn't reached out to anyone throughout that time. She had never called to say she was okay. Not in all the years since.

They rounded the corner and headed for the car. Vanessa looked over her shoulder at Sal, bringing up the rear and Allyson felt her shudder. Because she was scared of men? She might have been abused. Allyson's stomach rolled over at the thought of it. She didn't work sex crimes, but sometimes it was part of what she did. She never liked those cases even if they were a reality of life.

"Who was at the house with you?" She waited for a second, and when Vanessa said nothing, she asked another question. "Where did they go?"

Someone had held her. Bound her. Hurt her. Where were they now?

"I think they left." Vanessa took a breath. "I got out of the garage. I heard them looking for me, but I think I was pretty well hidden."

Sal had managed to find her. The man who had picked up his pace to a run and now approached them, driving the car. Allyson helped her into the backseat and got in beside her. He then drove to the hospital while they sat in silence in the backseat.

Allyson didn't know what to say. She prayed the whole way there, lips moving quietly. Once Vanessa was seen by a doctor, and they knew the extent of the damage, then they could figure out how to move forward.

Would the task force show up then, swoop in, claim her as their witness? Probably Sal had gone to get the car not just because Vanessa shouldn't walk all that way, but also because it gave him time to call into his office and update them about her rescue.

Allyson tried not to be mad considering it hadn't happened yet. But it was a better distraction for her brain than being scared about what Van had been through.

When Vanessa climbed out of the car at the hospital, Allyson stalled her for a second with a hand on her arm. "I know you're hurt but…it really is good to see you."

Her friend sort of smiled, but it was wobbly and directed at the front doors of the hospital. Allyson spotted the sheen of tears in her eyes. It would be a long process, but time really would bring her friend back to herself. How long would she need Allyson's help to do that? She intended to stick with Vanessa for as long as it took. She was in this for the long haul, friends forever. Just as they'd sworn to each other years ago.

Did she know her father had died?

Sal held the door, and Allyson took her inside. Vanessa refused a wheelchair. She wanted to walk in under her own steam.

"I'll give you a hand." Allyson didn't really know what to do with herself but thought of something. "With the paperwork and stuff. You don't need to worry about that."

She glanced back and shared a look with Sal before he let go of the door to go park the car.

For a second there, it almost looked like he was proud of her.

———

SAL LEANED against the wall in the hall, outside the room where Vanessa was being checked out. The woman was clearly in shock, her rich-businesswoman clothes rumpled and stained. Chipped nails, like she'd fought someone. Gashes and scratches that would need to be cleaned. Who knew what internal injuries she had that the doctors hadn't found. Things that went deeper than the physical.

Allyson had been in the room since the doctor allowed her back there. Before that, she'd paced the hallway in front of him, back and forth at a clip. Still, in her restlessness, her boots made almost no noise on the floor.

He'd half expected the rest of his team to show up already. Despite the fact Bridget McNamara was Allyson's friend Vanessa, they were all anxious to find out what she knew about her boss Kennowich's activities. The things the team believed he'd been doing for months now. He'd told them to wait. That there was little chance Vanessa would open up to anyone except the woman she knew. The one person in the world right now that she trusted.

The door swung open before he could figure out how to delay them until a better time. But given Vanessa had just been admitted to the hospital, a better time could be days away. Would Allyson be okay with his team coming in to interview her friend in the meantime?

Allyson strode out, shut the door behind her. She sucked in a choppy breath, and her expression changed. As though she'd been holding all the emotion back. In one rush it came over her.

Sal crossed the distance between them and pulled her to him for a hug while she let out a sob. Was she going to lose it? He didn't think she was the kind of woman who did that readily, but what did he know? She sucked in a few choppy breaths but didn't break down into actual tears.

Had Vanessa told her about her experience?

He started, "Did she…"

Allyson stood back, shaking her head. "I had to tell her that her father was dead."

Ah. "Soon enough all the hard parts of this will be over. She'll find joy again, and you'll be able to help her move past this."

She nodded, pulled out her hairband and flipped her head forward. She ran her fingers through her hair, which he figured she did to compose herself. When she straightened to retie her hair, he saw that the wet in her eyes was gone.

Sal had never been on this end of things. He'd protected witnesses before, but nothing like this. Generally he worked on tracking down fugitives and keeping his team safe. The part where he just kept the rest of the task force alive was in itself a full-time job. Certainly it had been lately. During their most recent investigation, he'd infiltrated a terrorist organization to take them down from inside. He didn't usually work like this, on the back end, where it was about moving on from the terror of it all.

"Soon will be nice." Too bad she didn't sound super happy about that. "But that's not the whole reason I came out here, other than just needing a minute's break. She wants to talk to both of us."

"Is she okay?" Did she know who he was, or was she interested in the marshal badge and what he could do for her?

"She's been beaten, but the doctor said it was superficial. No broken bones. She wasn't raped."

Thank You, God.

Allyson nodded, evidently seeing the relief on his face.

He followed her into the room. Given his impression of the woman and how wary she had been of him, Sal hung back and stayed close to the wall. He didn't want to freak her out. The fancy clothes had been replaced by a hospital gown. Long blond hair fell past her shoulders, disheveled, making her look younger than Allyson. She picked at the blanket threads, manicured nails ripped and chipped, blood and dirt in the corners.

The woman had been through enough, and now appeared to have pulled herself together enough to speak with them.

Allyson wandered to the bedside and sat close to her friend, reaching out to run her fingers down strands of hair on the side of her face. Vanessa shifted into the touch. Seeming to preen under the attention. Kind of like a cat asking to be petted just so it had an excuse to purr.

Why Sal thought that, he wasn't sure.

Allyson shifted closer. "Vanessa?" Her friend said nothing, seemingly lost in a peaceful moment. "You wanted to speak with both of us?"

Finally, Vanessa nodded. She still didn't look at Sal.

It was clear they were awkward with each other, unsure how to be since it had been so long, and this was a delicate situation. He didn't know how to read where they were at, but he knew Allyson pretty well and she seemed unsure. One of the few times since he'd met her that he saw her like this.

Vanessa shifted. She worked her mouth like she was gearing herself up to say something that was maybe painful. He wanted to hear what it was, and not just because it was possible she knew who he was. Maybe she knew what his team did, and who they were, because of her boss. Their existence wasn't publicized.

He had to wonder if this was Kennowich's doing.

"I need your help." Vanessa looked at Allyson then. "That's why I called you. Because you're the only ones who can help me."

She did know who they were. Who *he* was. Why were they the only ones who could help her?

Sal said, "What do you need our help with?" And how did her kidnapping, and escape, play into all this?

Vanessa continued, "He's…" She didn't finish before a sob escaped her. She turned to Allyson. "Don't let him take me again. I can't go back to him."

"Who?"

"Malcom Kennowich. I finally got away, and I have a flash drive of information that can bring him down. That's why I need your help. Both of you." She looked at Sal then. "I saw that research lab in Portland on the news. I looked into what happened. I know it was you and your team who brought down that whole conspiracy."

They'd had help, but yes, his team did that. Still, her connection to Kennowich was entirely too coincidental considering they'd been looking into the man. Yes, she'd clearly been the victim of a kidnapping and attack, but there was something about this that didn't sit right with him.

He asked her, "Allyson was your intended route to the Northwest Counter-Terrorism Task Force?"

"You're the ones who can finally stop him." Her face had reddened, her voice breathy.

"I get that you need our help, but that means you have to be one hundred percent honest with me."

Displays of emotion from a victim weren't going to persuade him to believe her. This was their case, and that was why he would work with Vanessa. Listen to her, and take what she said into account as part of their investigation.

Allyson could help, but she was far too close to this. Too emotional—which was the reason she glared at him now.

He watched as tears rolled down Vanessa's cheeks. "He's planning something terrible. He's going to hurt a lot of people."

7

———

Allyson could almost see the fear move through her friend. She touched Vanessa's hand. "You're safe now."

She was doing the right thing, coming to them so they could prevent whatever Kennowich had planned. It was right to involve Sal. He was a marshal, and dealing with a witness in a situation exactly like this was what he did. Allyson was fully prepared to pick his brain to find out the best course of action to help her friend—and ultimately stop Kennowich.

What she *wasn't* going to do, was hand the case over to his team like a gift secured with a nicely-tied bow. Just because she was ATF didn't mean they could shut her out. Or relegate her to the position of "victim's friend" and "advisor" even though she had every intention of being both those things.

"I need to make a call."

She watched him leave, closing the door with a slight click on his way out to fill his team in. Or to call the local witness security people…or whatever he was doing.

Allyson turned back to her friend and smiled as if everything was fine—or would be. "Vanessa, is Malcom Kennowich the one who kidnapped you?"

"It's not like that." Her friend looked ready to cry. "It was an internship."

That was right, she'd had an internship first semester. Allyson hadn't really known what it was. Surely the police looked into it when they'd investigated Vanessa's disappearance?

Allyson had to tread carefully or Vanessa would shut down. She gently said, "And then one night…you just didn't come home?"

"He said it was time. That I needed to cut ties. Commit to him and the business."

"Like come to work full time, or live with him?" Had it been both romantic and business? Allyson had seen pictures of Kennowich. He was much older now, but still handsome. Did he have that charismatic, magnetic personality some people had that drew people in?

The way she'd worded it, Kennowich sounded like a cult leader. Had he brainwashed her into working for him all these years, instead of coming home? She watched Vanessa take a sip of water and wondered if this was a case of Stockholm syndrome. Maybe she should mention that to the doctor and get a psychological evaluation.

But why would Vanessa turn on him now? It could have something to do with the men who'd captured her. The fact she'd been running. Maybe she was on the outs with Kennowich for some reason, and so she'd run. Or had the fact she'd decided to run cause him to send people after her?

Only Vanessa could answer which side of this chicken-or-egg scenario she was on.

"Were you in San Francisco," Allyson asked, "all this time?"

Vanessa studied the clenched fingers in her lap. "I was in Miami for a few years learning the business. Then Chicago. I was even in Vancouver for a while."

He'd kept her on the move, hindering anyone's attempts to find her. Like the couple of private investigators Allyson had hired over the past ten years. And yet *no one* had realized the internship was the cause of it.

Allyson didn't like that. It smacked of payoffs, bribes, or just straight coercion. Everyone who had looked into Vanessa's disappearance had claimed to find nothing but dead ends. "And now you live in San Francisco?"

She nodded, looking a little startled. "That's right."

"Sal's team did their homework. That's how we managed to find you."

Vanessa flashed her a brittle smile. "I'm glad you did."

Allyson needed to tease the "threat" out of her friend. Find out what Kennowich was planning, preferably before Sal came back in. To do that, she had to get Vanessa to rely on her. Could they rebuild their friendship, even after all these years, or would their relationship always be tainted by the fact Allyson was a cop, and Van needed her help?

Vanessa grabbed her hand then. "Thank you for helping me."

"Nowhere else I'd rather be." Tears threatened at the edges of Allyson's vision. "I'm so glad you're here and safe now. I'm so sorry I never found you."

"He wouldn't have let that happen. There's no way you could have known."

She had to ask. "Did he ever..?"

Van looked away. "It wasn't like that. Not all the time. He saw something in me, and I'm good at my job now. Really good."

Yet she'd left. To do the right thing, or because she'd had no other choice? "I'm proud of you for taking a stand." Allyson touched her hand.

Vanessa turned her hand over and held on tight. "I had to. He's going to…hurt people."

"Tell me. So I can stop it."

Vanessa bit her lip. "I don't know if you can."

"But I'll try, right? That's why you came to me."

"I came because you cared about me. Because we were friends."

And yet she said that in the past tense. "It's still true." Allyson just needed to convince her. "But I'm also a cop, and that means it's my job to take the intel and try to stop the crime *before* it happens."

Usually they were about cleaning up the mess afterward. Getting justice for victims. They made sure the bad guy didn't do something worse next time because they'd gathered enough evidence there would be no way they wouldn't get a conviction.

Always a gamble, but the justice system was what it was and they just did their best to prevent more crime. Like putting the pin back in a grenade before it is released to destroy. Whenever they could get ahead of something, it was a serious win for the ATF. For all of them, really.

"You're a good person. Always were," Vanessa said. "I haven't been a good person for a long time, and maybe I never was one."

"That's not true. What you've done doesn't matter. It's the choices you make now that count."

"You really believe that?"

Allyson nodded. "Of course."

"You're my only family now."

She blinked. Vanessa really thought that? Allyson patted her hand while she processed the idea that this woman wanted to be that with her, even now. Of course *she* wanted it. She cared about her friend. But could she be her support system? Allyson had to wonder if she would be enough.

Back in the day, Vanessa and her father had an interesting relationship. They hadn't exactly seen eye to eye. Now with him gone, they didn't have anything and never would.

Vanessa needed Allyson's support all the more. She was right, they were the only family each other had. But whatever strain had been between them back in college wasn't because Vanessa had been a bad person.

"Whatever Kennowich made you do wasn't your fault." She paused. "Was it your idea?"

Vanessa looked away.

Life was never cut and dry, but it was like she'd convinced herself it was. Because she was somehow…poisoned? Tainted maybe, but not poisoned. "You might not be able to fix the past, but you can make the future whatever you want it to be."

Vanessa looked up at her then, hope shining in her eyes.

Sal chose that point to come back in, breaking the moment. He didn't look exactly happy. "I need to know what Kennowich is planning, and I need the physical evidence you have. Which means you need to hand me that flash drive."

Allyson stood so fast she almost stumbled. "Now hang on a second."

———

SAL LIFTED A HAND. "If it's as bad as she claims, then time is of the essence."

Not to mention the pressure the team was now putting on him. This was their shot to get Kennowich. A shot that had landed in their laps. Well, technically it had landed in Allyson's lap, but his team didn't consider that to be exactly pertinent.

They were all federal agents, and he figured that was what counted.

Vanessa's expression—the one she showed him behind Allyson's back—had a slight edge to it that he didn't have time to consider.

"Just tell me where it is, and I'll go pick it up."

If Allyson didn't like the pressure he was putting on this woman, that was fine. This "friend" of hers had been an accomplice to who knew what. For *years*. If she testified against Kennowich in an upcoming trial, then they could put her in witness security. After that, she might be safe but Allyson would never see her again, considering that keeping in contact would be a security risk that went against protocol.

Having physical evidence in their hands would mean that Vanessa didn't need to testify. Which would mean she didn't need to be given a new identity and moved to a new city. She wouldn't have to disappear.

Evidently Allyson hadn't figured that out—but she would, and then she would be less mad at him. Not that he thought she would thank him, necessarily. But a little gratitude for being here and being part of this wouldn't hurt. Would it?

He sighed, trying to soften his tone, "I know you've been through something unimaginably hard." He moved closer as Allyson turned back to her friend to be supportive. Or to guard her against his overbearing maleness.

He continued, "But you reached out to us so we could bring him down. In order to do that, we need to know everything you know."

After a minute or so of thought, and a glance at Allyson, Vanessa nodded. "Okay."

He looked at Allyson, willing her to figure out that what he was doing would turn out to be for the best. She knew he was right, even if she didn't want to admit it.

Sal's phone buzzed in his pocket. He drew it out to read the screen.

NICE SPEECH.

He unlocked it to text back.

SHHHH.

Sal hit the home button so he didn't text accidentally while talking. The call to Talia was still active, the line open between him and his team who were at the office. Listening.

He leaned against the end of the bed to take the weight off his aching leg. "Kennowich has a plan in the works?"

Vanessa hiccupped a breath. "It's why I couldn't wait any longer. I can't let people die, or get hurt." She spoke so low he wondered if the team could even hear her. "Not again."

"He's done something like this before?" Allyson rested her hip on the side of the bed again. "Or did you just mean that he's hurt you?"

"Yes." Vanessa shrugged one shoulder, the edge to her expression gone, now that she was looking at her friend and not him. "Both."

"You called me, and I'm here." Allyson seemed to feel the need to reassure her some more. "You're safe."

"When I realized what he was going to do, I copied the information to a flash drive and ran."

"And he had you followed?"

Vanessa nodded.

He'd caught up to her and recaptured her. "You managed to escape. Twice, right?"

She didn't look at him. "It was a miracle I was able to get out of the garage. I got over the fence, and then when I heard you talking in the back yard, I thought it was—" Her voice broke. "I hid. I knew if I ran they'd just chase me, and I would never get away." A tear rolled down her cheek. "You can't let him get me again."

Allyson said, "How many people were in that house with you?"

"Three…three men."

"Can you identify them, like if I get you pictures?"

Sal figured the men were looking for her. He'd been about to ask the same question before Allyson beat him to it. They'd found her once. Kennowich—or more likely those three men of his— were still in Seattle, and probably looking for her.

Vanessa said, "I think so. They were security guys I've seen at the office. But one was from Miami, I think."

Sal gave her a second, then got to the point. "Do you have the flash drive?"

She shook her head. "I hid it before they grabbed me."

"Where?"

Vanessa's hopeful expression dropped. "I don't know where I was."

"Could we retrace your steps?" Allyson suggested.

"Maybe. I came out of the bus station, and I was on a side

street. Like an alley. After that, they grabbed me and took me in the car."

"That's a great start," Allyson said.

Vanessa made a face. "It's not like I'm ever going to forget running."

Allyson nodded, and he figured she was giving her friend a sympathetic look.

They could show her picture around the area surrounding the bus station as well, see if business owners or any residents had seen her.

Getting that flash drive—if it really did contain everything about the plan Kennowich had in place—would be key to all this. The result they'd needed for months now. A way to get ahead of the man's plans for once. And maybe even stop them.

"I knew they were following me, so I hid it and then called Allyson."

The origin of that call was their starting point. "After that they grabbed you?"

She nodded.

"How did you manage to get away from the house?"

Allyson shot him another look, but he ignored it. Yes, he was asking repeated questions. But it wasn't to try and catch Vanessa in a lie. Often a witness remembered more details going over the experience a second or third time.

What he really wanted to ask was why they'd left her alone long enough for her to escape, but didn't think Allyson would appreciate that line of questioning.

He'd pushed her friend enough already. Knowing that flash drive was out there made him want to haul her to an interrogation room—even with what she'd been through.

They couldn't let it fall into the wrong hands if it could help save lives.

"One of the men got a call." Vanessa sniffed. "There were only three, so the other two must have gone somewhere with him.

I got out of the chair and managed to snap the ties." She lifted her wrist and showed him the red line.

Sal nodded. He'd done the same thing before.

"I ran out of the back." She winced like she was remembering the pain of it all.

He could empathize when necessary, and it seemed like Allyson had that part of this covered. What he needed to do was be a cop. Think like a judge, look at all the evidence and decide whether to issue a warrant.

Instead of this being simply about helping Allyson's friend now, it was also solidly a case they needed to see through to its conclusion. He and Allyson. Sometimes a case took months, which meant he'd see Allyson every day for the foreseeable future.

Even given what was going on and the trauma her friend had sustained, that thought invigorated him. He glanced at Allyson. Months working side by side with her, bringing down his team's greatest enemy. After that, he could retire to whatever career was next for him, satisfied he'd done everything he needed to.

Was this God's answer to his question? One last case...and then he could walk away.

A knock on the door preceded the rotating of the door handle. Two men walked in.

More than one badge was flashed in Sal's face. FBI. "We'll take it from here."

8

All along she'd been worried about the Northwest Counter-Terrorism Task Force stealing the case from her and shutting her out. Now it turned out that she should have been more concerned about an entirely different breed of feds.

The FBI had beaten Sal's team here. And they thought they, "had it from here"?

No way.

She and Sal both shifted. They came to stand side by side in front of the FBI agents, guarding her friend. She was determined not to allow them to take Vanessa with them. As for Sal, she figured he just didn't want his team shut out.

The first FBI agent shook his head. "We actually don't need your permission. This is our case."

"If it was," Allyson told them. "I'd have been called."

"Time is of the essence."

Sal lifted his chin. "I would've known you've been investigating Kennowich the minute I ran his name on my computer. Correct?"

He had a point.

One the FBI agent had no answer to.

"This is my friend." Allyson motioned over her shoulder. "You can back up and be a little less bargy. Then we'll talk."

Didn't mean she was going to give them squat. But being the bigger person, and at least sounding like she was prepared to come to some kind of arrangement—or compromise—would help people back down on occasion.

Standing shoulder to shoulder with Sal like this felt good. Almost too good; it wasn't something she needed to think about overlong. She could acknowledge it, and then she had to move on. Otherwise she was going to get entirely too accustomed to him being right beside her.

Allyson turned to Vanessa then and saw her friend's wide-eyed gaze. It was understandable that she'd be flustered. Maybe even a little scared and nervous. But Vanessa gripped the blanket, her knuckles white again.

This was exactly why Allyson had to not be distracted by Sal right now. Vanessa had to be her focus here, so she could make sure her friend was all right. Make sure these feds weren't Kennowich's men impersonating cops.

Allyson moved toward her. "It's okay, Vanessa." She wasn't sure what else to say, just studied her face to try and read what her friend wasn't saying. But she couldn't see anything more than basic fear.

While she tried to make Vanessa feel better, Sal faced off with the agents. "You guys new in town? Because I've never seen you before."

Allyson glanced at Sal's back. Did he also think they might not be who they said they were? What kind of person impersonated an FBI agent? That was just crazy, not to mention crazy illegal.

"We're out of Salt Lake. Heard over the wires that Ms. McNamara was here." The agent folded his arms. "This could be the break in the case we need. The chance to bring Kennowich's company down."

They needed to join the club if that was what they were interested in. Maybe this should be an interagency task force. Sal already had one of those, though it was unconventional to say the least. She didn't need many more people snapping their proverbial teeth at her case. Like Vanessa was the juicy morsel they all wanted a taste of.

"You got here quickly." They had to have found out right away that Vanessa had been located, in order to fly here that fast. It wasn't a long flight from Salt Lake City, but they'd made it in almost impossible time.

The FBI agent moved toward Vanessa. He stood at the end of the bed, completely ignoring Sal, who was now openly glaring at him. Like he'd completely ignored Allyson's comment just now. "We're prepared to keep you safe, Ms. McNamara. Anything you can tell us…or provide for us…that can help us get a full understanding of what his operation entails, can help us make this case."

"Join the club."

Sal's comment almost made her smile. Almost.

Allyson tried to figure out what they had already. What was their reasoning for looking at Kennowich and his operation? It was definitely something or they wouldn't have jumped at Vanessa being here. But it was obviously nothing they could make stick, considering they almost seemed desperate.

How long had they been investigating Kennowich, and they hadn't realized he had a missing person working with him? Surely they'd run background checks on all of his staff.

How many people had overlooked Vanessa, not even caring that she might be there under duress?

Probably fewer people had turned a blind eye to Vanessa's past than the number of innocent victims of kidnapping or trafficking that would never be located.

People bought and sold every day. Like Talia had been.

Allyson had joined the team that raided the house where Talia had been held. When she'd realized who the call referred to, she'd been unable to leave it alone. Even given how the team felt about her. Of course she'd helped, how could she not have? She'd just done it without Victoria even realizing she was there.

Vanessa grabbed her hand, jolting Allyson out of her

thoughts. "Don't let them take me. I don't know them. I only know you."

Sal shrugged. "I don't know them either."

Allyson lifted her chin. "FBI all start to look alike to me after a while."

She also felt like they traveled in packs. At least that was the way it seemed to her. The ATF was tiny in comparison. They worked closely with local police, and sometimes the marshals as well, but the FBI worked entirely different cases. Usually.

Allyson glanced at Sal. "If you don't know them, then I want to verify their IDs."

"Talia can do that."

"It doesn't matter if they are who they say they are," Vanessa said then. "I don't want to go with them. I want to stay with you guys."

Allyson turned to reassure her. "Of course you do. We aren't going to let these feds we don't know take you away, okay? Everything will be fine because we're going to *personally* make sure you stay safe."

She and Sal. His team helping. Her team providing assistance they might need.

Vanessa nodded. "Thank you."

Vanessa was clearly scared, but seemed to think they were… not bad guys. More like just strangers. But what if her instincts were right? Both she and Sal seemed to feel like these guys were "off" somehow…

Allyson intended to tread very carefully.

She twisted to face the FBI agents then. "You aren't taking this woman anywhere. If you'd like to talk to her, then you can contact his director." She waved at Sal, willing to trade on Victoria's reputation to get what she wanted done. "Victoria Bramlyn is who you'll want to ask for."

She was tempted to wish them luck, but that would be unprofessional.

His team wasn't getting her case. They could help, though.

She caught Sal's glance then and saw on his face how he felt about her throwing around his boss's name instead of hers. Amused. Slightly annoyed.

It wasn't like her boss was going to take this on. Daulton had no idea what this even was, or how it was connected to the Northwest Counter-Terrorism Task Force's ongoing operations. He'd probably never even heard of Cerium, or Kennowich. And he wasn't the kind of group supervisor who liked to wade in other people's messes.

Allyson said, "You guys can make that call, and then you can try again. Without the ambush next time."

They left, thankfully. But not without shooting dirty looks at both her and Sal. Allyson didn't much care about whether a couple of feds were happy or not.

She caught Sal's gaze then. "We need to get out of here."

He nodded. "We need to find that flash drive."

———

ALLYSON WAS in the back again, as she had been on the way to the hospital. Sal drove her and Vanessa, released from the hospital and now wearing a change of clothes Allyson had brought for her, to the first place Vanessa had mentioned she'd seen after leaving the bus station. A bowling alley.

Not too many of those around, and less that had a famous coffee house close by. So that was where they would start the hunt for the alley where she'd stashed the flash drive.

Sal's phone started to ring. He dug it from his back pocket, his other hand on the steering wheel, and handed it over his shoulder to Allyson. "Put it on speaker."

"Sure?"

Would he have asked her if he hadn't been sure? He figured if there was anyone with which he had nothing to hide, it was her. "Just answer it."

Vanessa was beside her in the back. When he pulled up to a

stop light, he glanced over. It seemed like she was sleeping. Or just resting her eyes.

A crackly female voice came through the phone. "Alvarez?" It was Victoria.

"I'm here," he called to the phone that Allyson held by his shoulder. "So is Agent Sanchez."

"Great." She almost sounded disappointed. Which of course made Allyson snort, like Victoria's opinion meant nothing but a source of mild amusement. "I got the rundown on those FBI agents. You don't think they came from Welvern's office?"

"They said Utah. Can you find out for sure?"

"If you've got badge numbers and names, then I can call their office right now. If you're going to make Talia pilfer security footage from the hospital and then run grainy pictures through facial recognition, that's going to take longer."

"Fair enough."

"So that's a 'no'?"

"There was no time to take photos of them," Allyson said. "And they weren't exactly handing over badge numbers, even when I suggested we'd need to check their credentials."

"So were they legit, or no?" Victoria's voice held an accusatory tone. She wanted them to make that judgment right now.

Allyson was the one who spoke next. "Why, are you about to hand your case against Kennowich over to them?"

"Of course not." Victoria let out a frustrated noise.

Sal almost smiled. Touché.

Victoria continued, "I'd like the witness brought to the office. She needs to be debriefed and kept safe."

"We're making a pit stop first. Trying to get the flash drive." He took a right turn. "No point in not picking up the evidence on the way."

There was a shuffling on her end. "I'll send backup."

"No need. Allyson is here." Sal pressed his lips together. He knew how that was going to sound and how Victoria was going to react.

"Fine."

Seriously, that was all she was going to say? He was almost disappointed—would have been without knowing there had to be a reason she'd stood down. Victoria never did anything without a reason.

Victoria didn't back down all the way, though. "If we could trust her, you'd have asked that she be considered for the open position back when we had one."

"Not when I knew she wasn't interested," he said, fully aware Allyson was listening to this. Probably intently. "All of our federal partners don't have to be brought onto the team."

It helped, but it wasn't necessary. Besides, he liked working with other agencies from time to time. It got him out of the task force bubble and doing something different. "That's not what this is."

Sal had always been on the edge of the team. He loved each of them and had protected all of them. Usually in his own way. On his own terms. But the result was the same. They were each whole and healthy, and in loving relationships. Two were engaged, and Dakota's wedding was coming up fast. They worked alongside their partners in work and life. More than ever before, Sal felt like the odd man out. Only in part because he was still single. He'd carved his own path, and they seemed to have accepted it.

"I'll call the interim assistant director at the Seattle office and find out if he sent anyone to the hospital." Victoria paused. "Then I'll call Salt Lake City. Between the two of them I'll find out who those agents were. And in the meantime, I'll have Talia get their pictures and run facial recognition."

He heard Allyson give a little chuckle behind him. Despite all her bluster, Victoria was going to do exactly what she'd said she would. What they'd asked for.

Allyson spoke then. "Can you find out if anyone at the FBI is investigating Kennowich?" She was quiet for a second. Then Allyson said, "Please."

He knew what it cost her to say that. Especially when she only thought she grasped the level of animosity Victoria had toward her. All because he'd been hurt on the job. Like that didn't happen to cops every day.

He shot her a smile then, in the rearview mirror, and she nodded. They understood each other, almost better than he thought the team understood him. At least that was true now that they all had significant others. Even Victoria, considering the way she and Welvern were with each other.

He and Allyson were both cops. The kind who beat the street. Knocked on doors. Tracked criminals. Built cases, and ultimately got convictions. He loved what Talia did, and it certainly had its uses. But Sal was old school.

"We're here," he told her. "Gotta go."

As he pulled over, Sal had to wonder if the thing between him and Allyson—he wasn't going to bother denying that there *was* a thing—was more than just them both being a similar kind of cop.

It had to be. After all, Dakota was the same kind of cop. And Niall. He didn't have with them what he had with Allyson.

Had he found something special with Allyson, or was she just a convenient friend? And why now? She didn't fit with his most current plan to leave the team and retire to the mountains of Wyoming.

Sal parked. He could hear Allyson rouse Vanessa from her rest.

They fit. Maybe he should quit trying to deny it and see what she thought about giving a relationship between them the green light. Did she even have feelings for him, other than as friends and colleagues? He wasn't sure but thought he might have seen something in her gaze a few times over the years.

The idea that it was too late now echoed in his mind, as it had already once today. Sal cracked the door and got out. He probably slammed it too hard because Allyson looked over. "What's wrong with you?"

"Nothing." Sal rounded the car to Vanessa. "Doing something like this can be scary. But we're not going to let you get hurt. Okay?" When she nodded, he said, "Think back to when you had the flash drive in your hand. Then look around. See if you can see anything familiar."

Vanessa wandered for a while, turned around and made her way back. Finally, she directed them around a corner. Her demeanor changed. She was growing more and more sure she was on the right path. He glanced at Allyson and saw that she was as excited at the prospect of bringing in both Vanessa and the flash drive as he was.

She had them walk another couple of blocks, then took a turn. "I think this is where it is."

Sal stared at the alley between two brick buildings. At the end, on the right, was the entrance to a basement-level parking garage.

Vanessa walked to a dumpster, rounded it, and crouched. Seconds later she looked up. "It isn't here."

Allyson moved to her and looked around, even crouching to see under the dumpster. "Someone got to it before us."

9

———————

"Seriously? Nothing?" Talia's stance was all attitude, practically barring the door to the task force office.

Then she saw Vanessa. She reached out, making a high noise from her throat. "Honey. Let's go sit down."

Talia pretty much pried Vanessa from Allyson, then linked arms with her and walked her to the kitchen area. "Let's get some tea. Do you like tea?"

Allyson couldn't hear her friend's response. They were too far away already.

Sal squeezed her shoulder and walked ahead and into the office. Leaving her standing there, doing nothing. Did he think she needed him to commiserate with her? She'd only come here because it made more sense than staying in an alley.

She was in their office—again—by protest, basically so they could regroup and Vanessa could rest. She would have gone to her own office if it didn't mean she'd have to leave Vanessa here. Which was tantamount to handing her over to Sal's team.

Sal headed in the direction Talia had taken Vanessa.

"Coffee pot is broken again." Dakota didn't even look up.

Sal glanced back at her, giving the Homeland agent a look Allyson couldn't decipher.

Niall—the only one she'd never met before—got up from his desk. He pasted on a smile as he made his way to Allyson. He stuck his hand out. "NCIS Special Agent Niall O'Caran."

"ATF Special Agent Allyson Sanchez."

He glanced over at Vanessa. "Is she doing okay? Do you think she needs to sit down?"

"She needs to sit down."

"How about you? Soda? Water?"

Ally shook her head. "I'm good."

All the while, Dakota stared at the back of Niall's head. Like he'd grown a second one during the walk from her desk to Allyson and was now waving it back and forth.

Ally decided she liked Niall. The young agent was personable. He didn't look at her sideways like some of them, and didn't just straight ignore her like she wasn't even in the room as the rest did. And Victoria wasn't even here. Niall seemed to think this whole situation was hilarious. His friends in the office evidently his source of amusement. There wasn't anything funny about Vanessa's situation, but she understood why he watched them all like this was a soap opera.

Sal glanced over his shoulder at her, the carafe and filter basket on the counter beside the coffee pot which he now had on its side. Because she existed, and so he acknowledged her. Sure it was probably more than that when she thought about it. However, now wasn't the time to overthink it.

Talia found a spot for Vanessa to sit.

"I'm sure Sal will have the coffee pot fixed soon enough. Do you want tea in the meantime?"

Before Vanessa could respond, Allyson had an idea. She asked Niall, "Do you have a pad and pen?"

Niall got them for her. Allyson moved to an open seat in the waiting area and lifted her foot to her opposite leg so she could lean the pad on her knee.

She wrote down everything she knew about Vanessa's disappearance. Then she flipped the first page over and wrote every question she needed Vanessa to answer, as soon as she could work through them with her friend.

What did you tell them when they held you?

She needed to have Sal get those photos. Help Vanessa identify who the men were. Her friend would need to look through mug shots and probably pictures of people who worked security for Kennowich.

"Talia." She called the NSA analyst's name across the room. When she had the woman's attention, she said, "Are you looking through Kennowich's financials to see if he paid anyone under the table—or otherwise—recently?"

That might clue them in as to who these men were. Someone he'd hired to find and capture Vanessa. Which could lead this team to successfully track the men and capture *them.*

Which could, in turn, result in the missing flash drive. Assuming they were the ones who had taken it from the alley. Perhaps that was why they'd all left the house with Vanessa in the garage. They'd gone to get the evidence she'd stolen.

Talia tipped her head to the side. "Of course."

She might as well have said "Duh." Talia didn't wait for Allyson's reaction to her answer. She just turned to her computer and got back to work. Vanessa sat on a couch at the far end of the room, sipping from a steaming mug.

Still apparently busy fixing the coffee pot, Sal observed each of them. Allyson. Talia. Even Dakota and her sideways looks. What had he thought would happen when he brought her here again? He knew what the deal was. Or did he hope that one day his friends were going to magically forgive her for "letting him get hurt," as they describe it?

Allyson's phone chimed with a new email. One more message to add to the bunch she had yet to read.

But the subject line caught her attention. She swiped through and read the email, standing up as she did so. "Another smash and grab at an FFL."

Sal turned around. "Like the one last night?"

"Yes." She stowed her phone. Looked at the pad of notes on the chair beside where she'd been sitting.

"FFL?" Niall asked.

"It's a Federal Firearms Licensee. Like a gun shop." She glanced at Sal. "Someone drove another rental truck into the side of one and ran off with every gun and box of ammo they could carry." Again.

Dakota leaned back in her chair. "So you've gotta go?"

Any other time she'd be out the door already, except for the look on Vanessa's face. "*This* is my case." And this was where she would stay. No matter that they didn't want her here.

She sat down, hardly able to figure out why they seemed to still hold her responsible for what had happened to Sal. Or, at least, Victoria's interpretation of what had happened with her and Sal at the courthouse. Who knew exactly what she'd told them?

The alternative was that he'd told them the story himself, and they came to these conclusions on their own. Either way, the consensus was that it had been all her fault. She was the one who had messed up and allowed Sal to get hurt. He'd nearly been medically retired from the marshals over that attack. Sure, she'd been hurt as well. Badly. But not like him.

She felt the sting of guilt every day and woke up sweating to the memory of seeing him go down.

Maybe she should go to that FFL and look around. Work with her team, not his. Her boss followed up the news about the robbery with an email. She was authorized to be here. He was fine with her looking after her friend, so long as she kept him up to date. He knew she was working on the Kennowich thing with the task force and with Vanessa's help.

Maybe she should give that up and let this task force work on it, go back to her regular job…maybe it was for the best.

Then she locked eyes with Vanessa again, and all the guilt welled up again. She hadn't been able to find her. Hadn't been able to prevent her from being taken in the first place. Hadn't kept her from harm years ago, or since she had first called.

Just like Allyson hadn't stopped the attack that led to Sal getting hurt.

Her gaze locked with his, and he shook his head. She knew then that she was in the right place. He didn't want her to doubt herself.

When had she come to rely on his opinion so much? It wasn't like she needed his approval. But being with him felt right, even if it was just about work.

She was going to have to deal with this case for the time being.

And then she would go back to her team.

Her office.

Her life.

———

SAL FINALLY GOT the coffee going. "Whoever made the mess that clogged this up is going to have to answer for it on Judgment Day."

No one laughed. He wandered back to his desk and sat.

Vanessa was still sipping her tea. Allyson had gone back to whatever she was writing on her notepad. He hadn't been surprised that she'd wanted to go to the scene of a robbery. After all, hadn't he just been thinking in the car about how they were both cops? The kind of cops who were *cops.* Something that might not make sense to many people. Except for cops.

His team was a whole different breed of federal agents. He wasn't surprised they acted frosty to Allyson. They were insulated at the best of times. It came with the territory, working on the fringes of what government agents did.

They might have been standoffish with her, but they were professionals, weren't they? Niall had even introduced himself.

Victoria wasn't there. Though, she likely knew they were here. Maybe she would stay away. Do boss things elsewhere, so she didn't have to see Allyson. So she wouldn't be tempted to tell her —again—how she was responsible for what happened to him.

As if Ally was to blame.

But no matter how many times he'd told them, they wanted someone to be culpable. They wanted a place to put the guilt they all felt about not being able to stop bad things from happening. To *him*. That insular way of doing things. The same thing that kept them so tight knit also meant outsiders were treated like just that. As though they didn't belong. The team had worked together for years. They could collaborate, and had, with the FBI and Secret Service.

For some reason, however, Allyson seemed to rub them the wrong way.

His email chimed. A message from Dakota, one single word.

CORNER.

He looked over at her and shook his head. He was not going to walk to the corner and "chat" with her where no one could hear them.

She typed on her keyboard, angry stabs of her fingers. Sal's email chimed a second later.

IT'S NOT ABOUT HER.

She got up and walked over there, getting a drink from the water dispenser. Sal sighed but followed. On the way, he shot Allyson a reassuring smile.

Dakota gave him a look, lowering the tiny paper cup from her lips. "I told you I needed to talk to you."

He waited for her to tell him what it was.

"It's personal."

"So spit it out." He folded his arms.

Her expression changed, and he realized it really was personal.

He'd been sighing a lot recently and felt the need to do it again. "What is it?"

Maybe there was something wrong between her and Josh. Or she'd developed an allergy to Neema. Were there problems?

Dakota crushed the paper cup and tossed it in the trash. When she turned back, it was a second before she lifted her gaze to his. "Will you give me away, at the wedding?"

"Like the *father of the bride* thing? That stuff?"

She shrugged, and he saw a lack of surety she'd never possessed before. Proof that emotions clouded a person's judgment. But she seemed to be fine with it. *No, thank you.* He wasn't interested in being overcome by feelings. He had work to do, so he could get on with his life.

"You really want me to do it?"

She shrugged again, realized what she was doing, and stepped back. "Who else am I going to ask? You're, like, my oldest friend."

"Wow. That's kind of sad for you."

She didn't laugh.

Would he really be able to do it? Give her away. Let her go. Gift her to someone else so that she could move on and go live her happy life. The loss was palpable. In a way he hadn't anticipated.

Sal lifted his free hand and rubbed at the ache in his chest.

Dakota crossed the couple feet between them and clasped his elbows. "Please? I don't want to walk down the aisle by myself." *I need you.* She didn't say it, but the words hung between them nonetheless. She might even be a little bit scared.

You're my oldest friend.

Sal touched her shoulders, leaned down, and planted a kiss on her forehead. "Sure."

Dakota let out a whoop.

"He said yes?" Talia asked.

Niall grinned over at him. "Never had a doubt."

Sal walked across the office again, where he poured him and Ally coffee. The rest of them could get it themselves, for all the emotional upheaval they put him through.

As he walked back to Ally, Talia tapped a tablet on the edge of her desk. "It's ready for you."

He handed Ally the cup of coffee, then motioned for her to go with him. Sal grabbed the tablet he'd had Talia load with pictures. Only some of them were mug shots. The rest were headshots from the employee page of the website for Kennowich's pharmaceutical company.

He pulled over a chair for himself. Allyson sat with Vanessa on the couch. "I'm going to show you a series of pictures."

He showed her the first photo.

Vanessa giggled.

Sal looked at the screen. It was a picture of him from high school—at a bull-riding championship if he wasn't mistaken.

"Can you tell me if you see anyone in here who was at the house where you were held?"

Vanessa nodded.

Ally leaned close but otherwise didn't interfere. As though she trusted him to be careful with her friend.

He saw the second Vanessa recognized one.

"Him."

He shifted the screen so he could see it. "Can you confirm for us whether this was the man?"

"His name is Peter Tines." She shivered but nodded. "He is the leader. He's also Kennowich's head of security."

Sal turned back to Talia. She nodded and got to work. The NSA analyst would look for him, find out where he'd been recently. If they could place him at the house somehow, they could probably get a warrant for his phone. But then they would have to go before the judge and convince him this was worth pursuing.

They had two big issues right now. First was the flash drive, and the second was what Kennowich was planning.

"Can you tell me what Kennowich is planning?"

Dakota strode over. "Telling us is your best course of action. Because the alternative is that we need the flash drive. And the fastest way for us to find out if they still have it is for you to get taken again."

Allyson shot to her feet. "You want to use her as *bait*?"

Dakota shrugged while Vanessa glanced between them.

"I cannot *believe* you just said that to the victim of a kidnapping." Ally fisted her hands by her sides. "If anyone's going to be bait, it'll be a federal agent who looks like her."

Dakota's gaze hardened. "Of course, that's what I meant."

Ally rolled her eyes. "Yeah, right."

Sal didn't believe it either. But he also didn't need them fighting. Especially not if it meant he'd be in the middle of it.

Ally sat back down. "Please tell us what Kennowich has planned. What is it that he's going to do?"

"You don't think I can be bait?" Vanessa frowned. "You'd catch them, right?"

Sal said, "It wouldn't be you. It would be a decoy." Neither he nor Allyson would risk an untrained innocent.

"They'd never fall for that." Vanessa swallowed. "Peter knows me too well."

Sal figured that with him and Allyson working together, they could make it work with a decoy. It was an out-there plan, but Allyson was good at that kind of thing. And it would be a chance for his team to see what a valuable asset she was. Then maybe they'd see what was so obvious to him. They were all entirely too quick to believe the lie that she somehow could have prevented what had happened to him.

Vanessa lifted her chin. "The only way they'll believe it is if they see me. You can be close by, and then move in."

Allyson was already shaking her head, before Vanessa even finished. "No, I don't want to risk you like that. I lost you once, and I don't want that to happen again."

"I know." Vanessa nodded. "Then keep me safe, because I want to do this."

10

______

Even as much as Allyson strained to see, she couldn't make out the inside of the other SUV. The one where Vanessa was being wired up. Ready to be sent out to face the same wolves who had held her captive in that hot garage.

On top of not being able to see, Allyson had also been stuck with Dakota and her almost-family. "I don't like this."

"Did anyone say you needed to like it?"

She didn't turn from the window. Not even to shoot her the evil eye so Dakota would know she was mad, even though otherwise not bothered. By Dakota, or how she'd decided she felt about Allyson.

"So you'll needlessly risk an innocent person just to get a result on a case?" Allyson pressed her lips together, then said, "Good to know that's the kind of team you have."

"Victoria signed off on it."

"I'm well aware of that, considering I was standing there when you put her on speakerphone to tell everyone the same thing. That doesn't make it right." Allyson huffed without a sound, so Dakota didn't hear it and think she was immature, or something. "If she says jump, do you all ask how high?"

"Yes."

Allyson turned to her then. Yep. She'd heard the right tone in Dakota's voice. On top of that, the woman sat in the front seat and had a totally straight face. "Vanessa has been through enough already. You saw as much for yourself. This is too much."

Not to mention it wasn't right. No matter that they were following the orders of their boss, they were still risking Vanessa. Dakota didn't seem to even care that a woman would be in danger. Whatever it took to get the result. Was that who they were?

She needed to ask Sal. There had to be extenuating circumstances or security protocols she wasn't seeing. Something they hadn't clued her in on that would justify this recklessness.

He was here somewhere. In fact, so were the rest of Sal's entire team—minus Victoria.

Allyson glanced again at Dakota. "Don't you guys have other open cases?" As soon as Victoria gave them the word, it was like they had nothing better to do than get in the middle of her thing.

"This is the biggest case we've ever worked."

"So you'll risk *everything* to get a result? Even someone's life."

Dakota stared her down instead of answering the question.

Just because this woman, and her colleagues, were so sure about it didn't mean Allyson had to approve. Vanessa was barely out of the hospital and now they were putting this on her. Yes, she volunteered. But wasn't it, in fact, their job to keep her safe, regardless of what she wanted?

Sal understood that. She knew he did. He was a US Marshal and knew what it took to adequately protect someone. But he wasn't here to argue about it with her. He was in the car with Vanessa, Haley, and Niall. She was here with Josh—in the front seat—and Dakota. And the dog, asleep behind Allyson's seat.

The dog was ignoring her, as Josh had said she would. Because she was not part of Neema's pack, and neither was she a threat. Apparently, those were the only two reasons for the animal to pay attention to her.

All the dogs Allyson knew were bite dogs. She'd seen them

train and didn't like the idea that Neema might suddenly *decide* she was a threat. Like maybe because Dakota indicated she was. She liked dogs. Cute ones, like the little retriever her father had found in the churchyard. Thin and injured. It had snarled at him until he'd won it over.

Allyson didn't want a dog that was aggressive. She also didn't want something that couldn't defend itself. Which meant stalemate.

She was still on the fence about the whole thing. Maybe she should ask Sal. *No.* She made a face to the window again. She didn't need to confer with Sal every time, about everything.

Besides, tonight was about getting Vanessa safe. Finally.

"Did you know this was all about an internship?"

Vanessa had escaped, been abducted, and then escaped again. What more did she have to go through before this was over? It was past time for her to be free of this man for the first time in nearly a decade.

"What?" That was Josh. He twisted in the front seat to look back at her.

"Kennowich had her interning for him in college. Then he basically lured her to full time." Allyson blew out a breath. She didn't want to say it, but they had to understand the stakes. "Who knows what he employed to persuade her—or force her—to be loyal."

Dakota turned in the front seat and glanced at her. "You know, it's pretty hilarious that you don't want to risk an 'innocent' right now. Especially considering how fast and loose you usually play it."

"You mean four years ago, the last time we worked anywhere near each other?" It wasn't possible that she'd changed since then? That day at the courthouse had flipped her life inside out. She would never forget seeing Sal go down and realizing it could result in the worst outcome, fast.

"We know you, and the kind of cop you are."

And apparently, they didn't like any of it. "I guess you do."

Allyson wasn't going to bother arguing with her. The whole group of them had made their minds up about who she was and that it had all been her fault.

She'd thought long and hard about that day at the courthouse since then. It was the last time she'd spent more than one night at her dad's cabin. Not coming down off that mountain until God had given her an answer. Absolution. Forgiveness. Direction. She'd been like Jacob, wrestling with the angel. But instead of refusing to let go until he blessed her, she hadn't gone home until he gave her an answer.

There were a number of things she did differently now, regardless of the commentary from other agents—ATF or marshals. Safety was a top priority. It came second, right after coffee. She followed the rules now. Even ones she'd put in place herself.

"Just funny to me that you'd object. Considering."

"That's so nice for you. I'm glad you're enjoying this." Allyson cracked the door and got out, not wanting to participate further in the conversation.

The front door to the other SUV opened and Niall climbed out. He let Vanessa exit the back and said something to her.

Vanessa nodded. Then she saw Allyson. They shared a small smile. Vanessa knew that Allyson had her back. Which was exactly what Vanessa had asked for, and why Allyson followed her from a distance as Vanessa made her way through the park like she was tired of police protection and needed to stretch her legs.

If Allyson had been given any time at all to prepare for this, she'd have changed into running clothes and grabbed her air pods. Much easier to blend in at a park if she looked like she was working out. Not so much, dressed as a cop. So she found an out-of-the-way spot where she could watch and keep hidden.

"I see something." Niall's words came through her earbud connected to the comms radio.

Allyson had been surprised they even gave her one, but she figured it was a kind of insurance so they didn't get hurt by something they didn't know was going down. Rather than just to keep her in the loop.

She heard Sal's reply of, "Copy that."

Allyson stuck with Vanessa long enough she wondered if any of Kennowich's men would even show. And then she heard someone behind her.

Allyson turned, half assuming it was Sal.

———

SAL STARTED to wonder if they would even show. He walked through the park, headed for the spot where Allyson was to locate cover and keep watch.

Kennowich had to be motivated to find her. They'd put it out on the wires that the team needed extra police presence so Vanessa could get a walk. Like her getting to stretch her legs was a high priority.

Not exactly standard procedure for the US Marshals on protection detail. He was mostly banking on the men believing that the marshals didn't realize who they had. That this witness was far more valuable to Kennowich than the task force thought she was to them.

The radio was quiet for long enough, Sal said, "Report."

"False alarm," Niall said. "I've got eyes on the target. All clear so far."

Niall and Haley had set off a few minutes ago, jogging together through the park. Their assignment was to approach from the west. Get line of sight on Vanessa. The team would keep an eye from all angles.

Up ahead, Sal spotted something on the side of the path. The sun had gone down hours ago—good cover for a witness to stretch her legs, but with the dim lamplight, he couldn't see what it was.

As he approached, he saw it take shape. "Contact. Man down."

He didn't say more than that until he'd crouched by the man.

Unconscious. Sal took in the state of his clothes and then reported in. "Maybe a homeless guy. He's been hit over the head."

The man stirred.

"Dazed, but he's coming around."

Dakota replied then, asking for his position. He told her, and she said, "I'll call an ambulance and relieve you to maintain pursuit."

"Copy that."

Sal didn't like leaving the guy. Not even for the minute or two until Dakota could get there. But they were shorthanded. And this was too much of a coincidence.

It might not make any sense that a random passerby had been attacked, but he and Dakota both knew how the other felt about coincidences. He continued to follow Vanessa's predetermined path.

Talia radioed in that all was still well. She had Vanessa in sight, watching from a network of cameras she had set up earlier in the evening.

There was one person who hadn't responded yet. "Special Agent Sanchez, report."

When she didn't reply, he said, "Anyone got eyes on Ally?"

He didn't care what it sounded like, him using her nickname.

Dakota replied. "She got out of the SUV. I don't know where she went."

"Ally, check in."

He waited.

"Agent Sanchez."

No response. He needed her to respond so that he could go to her and make sure she was all right.

"Talia?"

"I'm watching the target."

Which meant she couldn't split her focus trying to find a trained federal agent. And he didn't want her to take her eyes off Vanessa.

Talia said, "Target is maintaining position. She hasn't moved since she stopped. Not a great angle, but I can see her shoes by the tree like she sat down and put her back to it."

Good. He was glad that she was safe, and not just for Allyson's sake. Allyson probably had eyes on her too. Maybe she wasn't in a position to be able to make noise and give her location away. If only she'd reply, then he would know.

"All of *us* are where we should be. And on comms," Dakota said. "I mean, all of the task force team members."

Sal bit down on his back molars. He really needed to talk to them about this "us vs. them" mentality they had going on. Dakota should be ecstatically happy. She was getting married soon, so she should be busy. Or at least have too many other things to worry about than Allyson—where she was, and what she was doing.

Sal passed a couple of regular folks and nodded to them. They reacted like he was a threat, picked up their pace and hustled on. He shook his head wondering when the world had forgotten basic manners. That was something he preferred about small town life. People might all know your business, but they also cared.

He spotted two guys up ahead of him. Jeans and thick jackets. One had a ball cap. Their clothes could disguise weapons being carried. He couldn't be sure if they were the men Vanessa had pointed out, given how far he was from them.

He saw one motion to the other, though, and so picked up his pace to close the gap. Just in case.

The two men headed for where Vanessa had been told to plant herself. Exactly where she should be. Like they knew precisely where she was sitting, even now.

Before the two men could close in on her, Sal called out. He didn't want them to get near her.

The two men pulled guns even as they spun around. The second they spotted him, they opened fire.

Sal dove to the ground and rolled. The impact jarred every joint in his body, but he got behind the cover of a trash can beside a bench.

The men kept firing.

He drew his weapon and waited for a chance to shoot back. They never stopped firing for even a second so he could lift up and squeeze one off. Pretty soon one of them would…

There it was. The telltale click of an empty magazine.

Sal lifted up, aimed and took a shot.

The man moved at the last second, and Sal missed. If they kept this up, someone was going to get caught in the crossfire.

He ducked back down as the shots started up again. They needed to box these guys in. Sal got on the radio. "Do the aquarium thing."

"Copy that," Dakota replied, breathy from exertion.

Josh said, "Copy."

Niall and Haley both replied as well. Niall would help, but Haley was headed to where Vanessa and Allyson should both be.

Sal spoke a quick prayer for all of their safety. They had new team members since the aquarium, but he figured their significant others could explain what they'd done. Or they would get the idea fast.

Sal lifted up a second time and managed to get off two shots. He caught one guy in the leg, and he went down.

As he did, Sal spotted Niall and Josh creeping out with their guns drawn.

"Police!"

"Put it down! Put that gun down!"

Together they arrested the men.

"Target is on the move."

Sal glanced in the direction where she should be. "Haley?"

"On it." Her voice sounded breathy as well now.

"Gun down!" Niall's voice rang with an edge of frustration. He'd been laid out only a few days ago, left unconscious by men who had taken Talia. No concussion, thankfully. Just a bad headache.

One of the men made a break for it. Sal chased the guy, but

Dakota lifted one arm just as he closed in on her. The man slammed into her arm and she laid him out on the ground.

When she flipped him and put a knee in his back in order to put on cuffs, she looked up. "Why do I always get the stupid ones?"

"I need to find Allyson."

Sal walked away to check the spot where Vanessa was, walking faster than his body wanted to go considering that tuck and roll. On the way, he asked Haley for a sit rep.

He saw her before she could reply, standing by a tree off in the grass. Their office manager saw him approach. "Vanessa is gone, and I don't know where."

"Talia, where did she go?"

Haley said, "I was just about to ask her that."

Talia replied. "To the northwest."

"By herself?"

Haley shrugged. "I have no idea."

"Go after her." Talia sounded mad.

Sal knew she would do everything she could to get her back in their grasp. Not leave her to the gunmen.

"What about Allyson?"

"North side of the park." Talia barked the word. "Now."

Sal took off running, Haley with him every step. She was actually faster than he was, but they only got there in time to see Vanessa and Allyson getting shoved into an SUV by three men.

"Ally!"

The van drove off before he could reach them.

11

———

Allyson blinked and saw the linoleum floor. Both her arms were at funny angles, her shoulders bent back. She was moving.

Or being moved.

Legs dragging behind her, she was carried down a hall to a room. A house, like the one where they'd found Vanessa out back?

Vanessa.

The noise that emerged from her thick throat sounded guttural. Like she had strep…or like someone had smashed her throat. The tingling in her extremities told her she'd also been stunned.

She blinked again, and the floor was different.

One of the hands on her arms let go and her body tumbled. Thrown down. She rolled and the back of her shoulder hit the wall. Allyson let out a breath and another moan.

The last she remembered, she'd been in the park.

Told you all this was a bad idea.

Too bad none of them were here for her to actually say, "I told you so." And wasn't that a crying shame? Allyson took a breath and tried to swallow. Her throat was swollen and painful.

Allyson shifted to sit up. Twinges in various places caught her attention, but she wasn't going to think about how she'd gotten them. Falling. Being thrown around. Landing on things that had been in her pockets, like her phone and the cred pack that held her badge. What had they done with her badge, tossed it away? That meant that at least these people knew exactly who she was—and that she wasn't just Vanessa's long lost friend.

She splayed her fingers on the floor. They hurt like they'd been twisted the wrong way. As much as she could figure how it all played out, a punch to the throat, gun twisted out of her hands. They'd disarmed her fast, took her gun and phone, and tied her up. Subdued. By the way her pants looked, she'd been dragged to a vehicle and then driven here. And again dragged into this room.

Dust and debris on the floor. Spider webs on the window. It looked like an abandoned house.

This wasn't good. She screamed at the voices in her head that said she would never be found. She doubted she would see her phone again, or that it was even in any condition anymore to track her. But she had to remember that Sal and his team would be looking for her—they were professionals and this is what they did. They found people. They made things right.

Allyson tried to remember if Vanessa had been taken the same time she was. She thought she had. But why both of them? Hadn't they only wanted her friend? It didn't make sense that they grab her too, considering she was hidden away and watching. Surely it would have been easier to just take one of them.

Unless there was a reason they needed Allyson as well.

Her body shuddered. That was the only acknowledgment of the fear she allowed. There was no way she could fall apart right now. That wouldn't help her figure out how to get out of here—or how to stay alive until someone came for her.

Anger burned hot in her middle. That was good, it would help her focus. Keep her alert when someone came into the room and forced her to fight for her life. Dakota's face flashed in her mind. That antagonistic tone, and those accusing eyes. *All your fault.* Allyson was happy to take the blame whenever, but what if this had been Dakota's plan all along? She had wanted someone to be bait.

Now she and Vanessa were both in danger and it was all his team's fault.

From far away, a sound ripped through the otherwise quiet. A woman. Screaming.

Allyson's whole body felt like it turned to stone. Was it Vanessa making that sound? If it was, then she was being tortured. Tears filled her eyes. Fear for herself, and for her friend. Allyson had told her she was going to protect her. Vanessa had felt better knowing Allyson had her back.

The screaming stopped. Then, a minute or so later it started again.

A sob worked its way up Allyson's throat. She needed to keep it together. Like fighting back these tears instead of letting them fall while she wondered what they were doing to her friend. Hearing it was worse than seeing it. Then everything went quiet, and Allyson decided that silence was worse than screaming.

A short time later, the door opened. A man entered, carrying with him a chair. His knuckles were bruised and bloody. Peter Tines, Kennowich's head of security. She'd seen his picture back at the task force office. In real life he had a military bearing. A hard face that was craggy, with stubbled lines. Eyes that painted a picture of a man prepared to do anything. As if she couldn't figure that out from the state of his hands.

Peter set the chair down in the center of this otherwise empty room. Then he hauled her to it by her armpits and sat her down. Her hands were bound in front of her, but he did nothing to secure her to the chair.

"Good." She lifted her chin. "I have a few questions."

Peter Tines blinked, then laughed. It had a hollow sound to it.

"First, I'd like to know that Vanessa is still alive."

"She is." He answered the question, but it was in no way a concession.

What state she was in was a different line of questioning entirely. "Is this what working for Kennowich is about?"

He shrugs. "Pays the bills."

"I'm sure it does." She didn't want to pigeon hole him as a heartless ex-soldier. A mercenary. Maybe he had other sides to his personality, but she couldn't see them right now. Maybe he had a cat that he loved more than anything, or he took care of his aging mother.

Probably she would never know the answer to that.

"What is Kennowich's plan?"

"You haven't figured it out yet?" He almost looked disappointed in her. "I'd have thought you'd put the pieces together by now."

"I'm a little busy right now." She tried not to let annoyance bleed into her tone at the idea that she should have been cleverer. She'd been taking care of her hurt friend. *Excuse me for putting a person in front of the job for a few hours.*

She saw the tensing of his body. The shift of shoulders and hips that came before his fist to her face. She dipped her head to the side, too fast, which hurt even before he punched the side of it.

Allyson blew out a breath.

Then he hit her collar bone. Her sternum. A couple of punches later, he untucked his shirt. Everything in her wrenched and her stomach threatened to deposit the last meal she'd eaten on the floor.

But he just tore a strip of material from his undershirt and wrapped it around his hand.

And kept hitting her.

Not trying to get information out of her, it seemed he was just enjoying the chance to hit a woman. *Two can play that game.* It took a minute, but eventually he got in the right place. Allyson slammed her foot up into his crotch.

Peter doubled over, laughing.

Allyson spat blood on the floor. "Where's the flash drive?"

They had to have it. But why did they need her and Vanessa? Was this about luring the task force to them?

How long was she going to have to wait until Sal showed up with the cavalry? Surely they saw the abduction, pursued the vehicle, and were even now outside. Ready to breach the house and get them back.

Yeah, right.

Still, Allyson was ready for help to come. If it *was* coming.

She just prayed it wouldn't end up a trap.

———

Nothing. That was what they had.

Sal paced the spot in front of the coffee pot. It brewed its second pot in the last hour. That was how long Allyson and Vanessa had been gone. Hours. Not minutes. Every one of those minutes felt like years of his life.

All night he'd been trying to find them.

He grabbed the edge of the counter and leaned forward. It would look like he was trying to stretch the muscles in his back, but anyone watching would know the truth.

He was at the end of himself. Despite running after them, Allyson and her friend were gone. He'd been about to do it, too. Just take off in a run down the middle of the street in pursuit of the vehicle, like some dog chasing a car. But before he could set off, Josh had pulled him back.

Sal had told Neema to go after her.

Josh and Dakota, both with him by then, had looked at him like he was crazy, before Dakota explained, "That's not a command."

When he made a move to run again, she'd grabbed his arm. "She's gone."

Sal hadn't wanted to hear it then. No more than he wanted to think about it now.

He had wanted to lash out but held himself back. He had to

do the same thing now, just thinking of Josh's reaction. Hearing the man's voice in his head.

"Take a breath and calm down, dude." He'd even stood partly in front of Dakota. Defending her from Sal's frustration. The dog had barked.

Realizing that they'd had no choice but to ask him to stand down. He'd crossed a line. Become the aggressor.

Sal turned and leaned his hips against the counter. When would the coffee pot be done? "Anything on the license plate?"

Talia's fingers stilled, hovering over the keys. She looked over. "Not yet."

The whole team was on this, Josh and Dakota at their desks and working the problem. Dakota was on the phone. Talia continued typing away at her desk. Niall had gone with Haley to the hospital so the homeless man could get seen to, and they could ask him some questions about what had happened. Even Victoria was out conferring with her sources.

The whole team was on this. Yes, he was repeating that to himself, but he would lose it if he didn't keep reminding himself that they were capable—of all the things they'd achieved as a team. What they'd accomplished. Most of the time it had been against all odds.

Somehow. Some way. They were going to get answers.

Sal blew out a breath and tried to figure out why that didn't make him feel better. Because his tendency was to leave, to go it alone to get a problem figured out? He was the one who went undercover and worked the case from the inside. But he couldn't do that this time. Just like he couldn't hit the streets without a lead.

He walked to the window and stared at the mountains on the horizon. He reached out to the faith his father had instilled in him. Took a moment and prayed.

Allyson had faith, but she also believed in herself and her own abilities. They both had things they needed to grow in. Stuff God wanted to talk to them about. He hadn't been able to do anything except encourage her. She'd mentioned her dad getting away to pray at his cabin. It was something Sal wanted to do.

Location didn't matter all that much when it came to prayer, but it was definitely easier to listen without the distraction of people and noise.

"The vehicle is registered to Kennowich's company."

Sal strode to Talia's desk. "So he's not even hiding his involvement."

"Or he doesn't think he will get caught." Dakota replaced her phone's handset on the base at her desk. "Like he's above the law."

Josh leaned back in his chair, tapping his pen on the desk. "I'm kind of starting to hate this guy."

"Wow." Sal shook his head. "It's brazen, but at least now we know for sure who we're looking for." He turned back to Talia. "So where is the van now?"

Talia didn't answer. Her computer speakers chimed with a new notification. "Victoria just got a warrant for the security guy's phone."

"Peter Tines?"

Talia nodded. "Now we can dig into his entire life, not to mention track where he is." She typed the whole time she talked. "Right now it's switched off. But when it turns back on, I'll let you know."

Sal didn't want to hear that. The last thing he wanted was to have to wait longer. He was itching to go after Allyson. But they all knew that. He didn't need to say it.

He was halfway to the door before he even realized he'd moved.

"Incoming," Dakota called out.

He spun to her just as the door opened. It was Allyson's boss and a couple of coworkers from her team. Daulton, Carl and... Sal had forgotten the third guy's name.

"Where is she?"

"What happened?"

Sal explained everything, including what Talia had just told him.

"That was a dumb idea, putting them at risk like that."

Sal folded his arms across his chest. "We had it covered."

"Obviously." Carl made a face. Not happy. "So this is all about her friend that she found?"

Sal nodded. Carl should join the club.

Allyson's boss blew out a breath. "We just came from the FFL robbery. That's two now, which means it's a pattern. A string of break ins."

Carl took up the explanation. "We've got some tire treads from a different vehicle leaving the area, but we figured it likely won't pan out to a vehicle distinct enough to locate it."

"You still have to work it."

Carl nodded.

"We're finding Allyson and Vanessa." Sal motioned to his team. "All of us are on this."

Daulton said, "And you'll let the ATF know if you require additional resources?"

"Will do."

If there was a breach involved in getting them back, the ATF would absolutely be able to help. Their SWAT-type team was skilled at breaching houses.

"I'll put our tactical team on standby. They're still in the area from the operation to get Yewell at the warehouse."

"Thanks. We'd appreciate that."

"If this goes on more than a couple of days, they'll probably all make their way home."

Sal knew their tactical teams were spread all over. If needed, the Washington ATF personnel would be joined by agents from Alaska all the way down to California.

Daulton continued, "We'll do everything we can to help."

"That's right," Carl said. "If you're working to get Allyson back, then we want to help."

"We can use you." Plus Sal wasn't above accepting help from

wherever they could get it. Especially when it was high-quality, trained help. But mostly, because it was Ally. He needed her back. Safe. First they had to find her, though. Which would prove to be more of a problem with every hour that passed.

The longer it took to find her, the lower the chance they had of getting her back.

"I'll confirm with Victoria, just so it goes through official channels." Her boss held out his hand and Sal shook it.

Sal asked him, "How is your guy who got hurt at the warehouse?"

"He's—"

Alarm bells started ringing. The office security system.

Sal yelled, "Down! Everyone down!"

They all hit the floor. And waited. Nothing. He lifted up from behind his cover to see what was going on.

A drone hovered outside the window. Gun mounted on top.

Aimed right at them.

"There's a—"

The drone opened fire.

12

Allyson was tired of waiting, all alone in that room. Had it been long enough? Minutes or hours, she wasn't sure. But what she did know was that it had been dark, and now it wasn't. Maybe she didn't care anymore if she'd waited long enough for the team to find her. She just wanted to get out of there, preferably before he came back.

Was Peter Tines going to come back? What was he waiting for? Allyson wasn't sure she wanted to hang around and chance finding out. It would likely hurt as much as their previous conversation had.

Despite the questions, trying to get her to tell him what exactly the feds knew, she couldn't help wonder what he had been waiting for.

Now she was the one waiting.

What was she waiting *for*? Allyson gritted her teeth and stood. Breath hissed from between her lips as pain rolled through her head. Her face throbbed. Her ribs…

She squeezed her eyes shut for a second and sucked air in through her nose. Stifling air. There was no breeze, and the window had been boarded shut.

Allyson moved toward the door, making no noise with her

work shoes. She stood to the side of the door and just listened for another minute. Was she really going to try this? Mostly she figured she had no other choice, considering she wasn't going to sit around waiting for rescue anymore. It probably wasn't coming, anyway. There came a time when everyone had to stand up and take control of their own life.

Metaphorically and literally.

She also had to figure out a way to get free of these plastic ties. If she'd been awake when they bound her, she'd have made sure to turn her wrists inward. From there it would have been pretty easy to slam her hands toward her body, pulling them apart with the width of her hips. Snap. The ties would be off. It would hurt when the skin broke around the wrists, but she'd done it before and knew it would've worked. Unfortunately, whoever tied her up had stacked her wrists one on top of the other.

Which meant she had some ability to use her hands, but not a whole lot. And unless someone cut her free, it wasn't likely she would be able to break the thin plastic.

Allyson used one hand to twist the handle, praying it didn't squeak. And that no one was on the other side to hear.

She peered out the door and looked both ways. She had no idea how long it had been since Peter left. And he hadn't gone to Vanessa's room—at least Allyson hadn't heard anymore screaming.

The hallway was long. More so than a regular family home. Though she figured this was a house.

A sharp *snick* preceded a door down the hall. Ally shoved her door almost closed again. She left a tiny gap so she could look out. Peter Tines exited another room and walked in the direction away from her, tucking his shirt in as he went.

Was that the room where Vanessa was being held? Allyson wanted to vomit at the implications of him leaving and redressing himself. She prayed for Vanessa, praying that she hadn't been hurt in that way; that since he'd ripped his undershirt earlier, maybe he'd just been changing in there. She also had to thank the Lord that Peter hadn't violated her.

Maybe Vanessa wasn't even here anymore.

But there was only one way to find that out. So Allyson let herself out of the room and wandered as silently as she could over to the other room. She twisted the handle with her other hand this time.

And hissed out at the pain. She winced. Had she sprained her wrist somehow?

She moved into the room and saw Vanessa also righting her clothing. Her face was not happy.

"Oh, honey."

Vanessa glanced over at her. It took a second for her to realize that Allyson was there. Then she started to cry. Before she could crumple to the floor, Ally walked over to her. She took in the rumpled single top sheet on a bare mattress and the state of her friend's clothes and hair. It was clear what had happened here.

Allyson hugged her for a while. It was on the tip of her tongue to say, "It's okay," when it very much wasn't. And maybe it wouldn't ever be after something like this. What was she supposed to do, or say, now? They had to get away from these men and this house.

Vanessa pulled back and said, "How did you get out?"

"They didn't tie me to the chair. Just this." She lifted her hands. "And the door wasn't locked."

Vanessa nodded.

"You're not even tied up." Allyson wandered to the window and looked out at the morning sky. The sun was rising, but not up yet. "We need to at least try and get out of here."

"What's out there?"

"Nothing but trees." She didn't recognize the landscape. "We must be out in the middle of nowhere." She turned back and saw Vanessa shiver.

"How are we going to get out of the house?"

"I don't know, but we have to try right?"

"Where will we go outside? We could die out in the middle of nowhere."

They certainly weren't dressed for hiking. The temperature was probably low, given it was morning and the high temperature for the day wouldn't be for hours yet. "We won't get anywhere if we don't at least try. I refuse to give up. Ever."

After all, if she quit then she wouldn't be the woman she wanted to be. The brave, strong female ATF agent she had trained to be, and the woman of faith her father had taught her to be.

They were both there because of what Vanessa knew about Kennowich's plan. And because they'd needed a way to get the flash drive back. It had to be a big deal of some kind, a transaction. Vanessa hadn't yet explained what it was, and they hadn't been able to have that conversation.

Her friend had tears in her eyes. Allyson wanted to help her but there was going to be a chance to sit and take time to process the emotions later. Right now they had to get moving.

Allyson moved to the door. "Come on. We can't stay here."

Who cared about a flash drive when they needed to get somewhere safe. And quickly.

Together they worked their way down the hall to the stairs. Allyson descended first so she would meet any attacker before Vanessa, listening intently for any sound. At the bottom she could see a door.

They stepped off the bottom step. Allyson could hear a voice talking low in another room. She tugged Vanessa to the back door and eased it open. When she didn't see anyone outside, she stepped through. Vanessa moved, looking behind her toward the voice, and clipped the frame.

She let out a small cry.

Before Allyson could react, someone called out, "Hey!"

She tightened her grip on Vanessa's hand. "Run!"

They tore down the driveway and onto the grass. She had to get to cover and put distance between them and the men now in pursuit. They could go for a phone, maybe at a neighbor's house, or in one of the cars parked in the drive. The cars were a risky option, considering they'd need keys as well.

The urge to get out of there and reach safety fueled her aching muscles. Then they could work on what was next.

They ran far enough that they couldn't hear their pursuers anymore. No sound but their own sharp breath, nothing around them but trees.

They slowed to a lumbering walk.

"What are we going to do?" Vanessa's voice was high pitched, full of complaint and fear. That didn't help Ally figure out what they were supposed to do.

"Aren't we supposed to follow a river?"

They were really in the middle of nowhere now. "Do you see one?"

"No, but isn't that what you're supposed to do when you're lost in the woods?"

"For now we just need to keep moving. Then we can worry about getting to a road and flagging down a ride."

———

WHEN GLASS DIDN'T SHATTER, Sal started to move. His leg didn't like being in this position. As he shifted, he saw one of the ATF agents move to stand. "Get down!"

Bullets slammed against the window.

The agent frowned. "The glass isn't breaking."

Sal glanced over the top of the desk. "Talia, turn off the sirens!"

A second later the noise quit. It was like sudden hearing loss. The drone hung in the air outside. Gun mounted on top, firing semi-automatic bursts. Three rounds each. The glass was cloudy now. Circles of impact overlapped each other as that muted rat-tat continued.

Sal stood up, then. He was still nervous, and he should be considering there was a gun pointed at them, firing rounds—even though the glass was doing a fine job of keeping the bullets from hitting them. Dakota's head came into view for a second. Josh lifted up. "Not yet."

She disappeared again, and Josh met Sal's gaze over the desktops. He looked equally as confused. It seemed no one had known about the glass.

"Victoria."

Sal half expected glass to start flying at any moment. That the window wouldn't hold, and they would be sitting ducks with nothing but air between them and the barrel firing rounds. Sal turned to the ATF agents. "You guys good?"

Daulton lifted up to survey the scene. His intent gaze that of a man who'd seen a lot, and had just realized he was still capable of being surprised.

"Talia, you okay?" She'd turned off the sirens, but he hadn't seen her face yet. She lifted up above her desk. He caught her gaze with his. "Good?"

She nodded.

Daulton, the ATF group supervisor stood. "You guys have bulletproof windows?"

"I seriously had no idea." Maybe that made him sound dense to not know, but it was also true.

He'd been in the hospital those first few days when the team relocated from Portland to Seattle, so he hadn't been present for any remodeling. He'd been busy recovering from being shot in the leg during Niall's thing at the college.

He had actually escaped relatively unscathed, which was no small thing given that they managed to take down Yewell and his Secret Service assistant director accomplice. Well, at least in the grand scheme of things. Still, those old injuries weighed on him. Most had only happened in the past few months. Barely time to recover in between.

Dakota stood then. "Victoria had it put in when we set up the office here. I thought it was weird then. Now I think I'm going to get her a gift card."

One by one, they all stood.

The ATF agent whose name he didn't know stared at the window, shaking his head.

Talia shrugged, standing but also typing on her keyboard. "We got the idea from a house we uh…visited."

Sal shot her a look. He'd heard about the hacker locking them inside that smart house. He hadn't been there; he'd been with Yewell at the time, getting into his operation with the help of an undercover ATF agent. They told him all about it only recently because they'd been trying to distract him from thinking about Allyson being missing with no leads to get her back. He hadn't been reassured, hearing about a time when they'd been trapped with no way out.

Talia muttered, "Great." Then louder, she said, "Someone from the accounting firm upstairs just called 9-1-1. We'll have visitors soon."

Dakota turned to look at her. Talia glanced between them. "You guys should get out of here. I'll take care of it."

Yes, law enforcement was on the same side as them. Talia would tell the responding officers the truth about who they were and what they did here. It wasn't a secret. But they also didn't want the whole team—or all of them who were there right now—tied up answering questions.

Josh pulled open a drawer and pulled out a dog leash. "Who is it that got dispatched to the office?"

Talia mentioned two names while Neema got up out of her crate where she'd been sleeping. She shook, stretched, and wandered to Josh's side. He clipped the leash on. "Good." Then he looked at the rest of them. "Let's get out of here. We can use the back door in case that drone is waiting for us to hit the street."

So whoever controlled it could kill them? There was a pleasant thought.

Sal had no interest in being in danger when what he *should* have been doing was finding Allyson. "Get me a location on where she is," he told Talia. "I want her found."

Talia snapped a salute. "Yes, sir." There was no humor in her eyes, however. She knew he was scared for Allyson. And also for all of the rest of them. "I'll send what I have to your phone."

"Copy that." He grabbed his gun and badge and headed for the hall.

"You guys aren't big on people knowing who you are, are you?"

Sal shrugged in answer to Daulton's comment. He knew ATF agents weren't either. "Fewer questions means we have to make up fewer answers. No one wants anyone curious enough to knock, showing up at the front door to 'see what we do.'"

His phone chimed. Sal looked at the screen and read what Talia had sent. "I've got an address where one of the guys who works with Peter Tines checked into a motel. He's there now."

Daulton gave him a blank look. Sal said, "The man we think took Allyson and Vanessa. This guy works for him."

Carl chimed in, "Do I want to know how on earth she knows who he is, or where he is?"

"However she does it, that's not ATF business." Daulton gave his guys a stare. One nodded and the other smirked. "Our business is Allyson. So call when you get a solid lead. Yeah?"

"Copy that." Sal headed for the stairs instead of the elevator. He needed to bleed off the energy and adrenaline that had built up inside of him. The ATF agents followed behind. He didn't blame them for wanting to be there to get her back, but he hadn't thought Daulton wanted anything to do with Vanessa. Or Kennowich. Which made him wonder if the guy was a plant.

Great. This all had him questioning everyone's loyalty. There was no way a federal agent had been bought off. Not any of these guys. He shouldn't be so cynical in his old age, but it appeared he was getting jaded. That meant this was likely the time to retire.

Sal watched for the drone but didn't see it. The gunshots had stopped now.

He drove to the motel, assuming the ATF guys were going to go back to their gun store robbery case. Part of him wondered if one of them would show up again before he found Allyson. But to expect betrayal meant he wasn't focused. He was waiting for something that might never come when he needed to concentrate on what he knew—and what he needed to do.

When he pulled into the motel parking lot, he spotted the room number Talia had given him along with the guy's picture.

Just then, what appeared to be the same man from the picture rushed out of his room and swung a duffel bag into the back of a pickup truck. He had a military haircut but pulled a ball cap on right after he started the engine. Then he backed out of his parking space, one hand holding a cell phone to his ear.

Sal followed him, praying he would lead the way to Allyson.

13

Allyson's leg muscles burned and shook like that time she'd tried spin class. She was in shape because she had to be for her job. This was killing her though. She glanced behind her, back at Vanessa. No, they were going to live.

The trees around them brushed and swayed. A rustling, kind of like forest music. It had to be midmorning, but the sun was only a dim orb behind a cloudy sky, making the world around them muted.

"Is he gone?" Vanessa was not quite out of breath, but a sheen of sweat had formed on her hairline. Maybe she liked spin class.

Allyson walked to her. She put her hand on her friend's arm and looked over Vanessa's shoulder. "I don't see him."

But that didn't mean Peter Tines wouldn't show up again soon enough. They'd been seeing him every few minutes through the trees, ever since they left the house. Sometimes five, sometimes it was much longer. Every time Allyson thought they were finally free of him, she'd catch a glimpse of him.

He never approached. It was almost like he was taunting them. Always ahead of them, like wherever they turned, he knew exactly where they were going.

Allyson hissed out a breath between clenched teeth. "Let's just keep going."

The air turned colder as the sun rose, the sky darkening. The tree branches began to sway with purpose, the wind whipping at their hair and clothes. Allyson reached a fork in the trail. She stood staring at it, no idea which direction to go. They needed to get out of this forest, not spend more time walking around aimlessly. They had nothing: no supplies, no cell phone, no weapons. No flash drive. Disappointment that they weren't able to look for the flash drive back at the house where they'd been held burned a fiery hole in her stomach.

Allyson prayed for direction. As though a beam of light would emerge from between the clouds and show her the way. She prayed some more through the silence. Then a wolf howled. Another called back to it. Then another after it. Maybe the whole pack.

Was that her answer? She wasn't super clear on the "how" of God speaking to her. Usually it was just a nudge that required she be quiet long enough to notice. Right now she was so tired, her head so full of questions, that she had no idea what to do. Or where to go.

Vanessa whimpered.

"We have to keep going." Allyson took her arm, helping her despite her own aches and pains. As long as they stuck together, they would survive this endless trek through whatever forest this was. Vanessa walked slowly, like the more injured one of them. And maybe physically and mentally she was. But Allyson was having to push hard to get her body to keep moving.

Allyson's body said no with every step. But she forced it to keep moving. Eventually one, or both of them, would be unable to continue. And then what would they do? Neither was in the right state to carry the other one.

Over to her left, between two trees, Allyson spotted a flash of movement again. This time it was gray, unlike the jacket Peter Tines wore. She studied the spot as they continued up the path.

Had they taken a wrong turn—were they now being stalked by a wolf?

"There's something behind us." Vanessa's whisper sounded overtly loud after long minutes of no talking.

Allyson glanced back. A predator tracking them. On two legs, not four. It was him. Peter had found them again.

"How does he *keep* finding us?" She spoke aloud more to herself than to Vanessa. "It's like he's got a tracker on us."

Everything that was happening made zero sense.

Vanessa stopped and patted her pockets. "Do you…" She pulled the thumb drive out of her pocket. "Could it be this?"

"Is that the flash drive we've been looking for? The one with Kennowich's company on it?"

Vanessa nodded.

"Yes, that could be the tracker. How did you get it?" So they did have the flash drive. Frustration boiled up in her like water boiling over in a pot. All it did was make a mess everywhere. "You didn't say anything."

"There wasn't time. We were running."

They needed to be running right now. Allyson said, "When did you get it?"

"Earlier." Vanessa's eyes filled with tears. "When he was…in my room. I took it out of his pocket when he was in the bathroom."

"Why didn't you tell me?" She wanted to throw it away and run, but it was a key piece of evidence.

"Is this how he's tracking us?" She looked so sad. And sorry, even if she didn't say it aloud.

Allyson had to admit it likely was. She sighed and said, "Probably."

She fought the feelings of irritation and anger that Vanessa had kept this from her. That they needed to take it with them still. That Peter needed to just *show up instead of lurking around.* Then she would have someone to vent her frustration on.

There had been faults in their friendship years ago. Things

she'd spent years thinking on. Secrets. Misunderstandings. Assumptions. Allyson had helped Vanessa out of a couple of situations, and now she was back doing the same thing.

Were some of those old tendencies cropping up into their relationship now? The things they'd never gotten the chance to resolve, or work on—because Vanessa had been taken—seemed to have a similar tune. Allyson hadn't thought it was necessarily either of their faults, considering they'd both neglected what would have been good boundaries.

It was a shame their issues were coming up now, so soon after being reunited. Her tendency to help more than she should. Vanessa's need to control what she could and acting helpless when she couldn't.

But what kind of person would she be to argue with Vanessa right now, after everything she'd been through?

Vanessa sniffed. "We couldn't find it before, and you were so disappointed. I didn't want to get your hopes up unless the team was able to get something off it." Her voice was a high-pitched whimper. "Now it's probably making it so Peter can track us."

"We need the information on that flash drive."

"But I can be a witness, remember?"

Allyson took a second to think. "We could hide it and come back, but they'll probably take it before then."

Vanessa waited for her to make the decision.

"Let's just keep going. Maybe we can find a spot to man a defense." If she could subdue Peter, then she could get his phone. Assuming he was carrying one.

Where was Sal? She wanted to call him. Desperately. To hear his voice and have him come get them. She was beyond tired. Beat up. Exhausted and in pain. For the first time in…forever, she wanted to sit down and cry about it. Maybe even ugly cry. And when was the last time she'd done that?

Allyson located a tree branch, thick like a baseball bat. She picked it up. *Perfect for swinging.* She needed to hole up somewhere;

have Vanessa hide as well. Then when he showed up and finally quit toying with them, she would take him down.

Maybe even hunt him herself.

"Keep the flash drive and find somewhere to hide." She set her hand on Vanessa's shoulder. "I'm going to get him before he can touch you. That's my promise to you. No matter what, he's not going to touch you again."

Vanessa nodded and headed for a hiding spot. Allyson crept away to hide elsewhere and watch.

Gun or not, she was going to get Peter's phone.

———

SAL EASED down on the brake slowly, so it wouldn't squeak. His fingers gripped the wheel as he stared out the side window through the trees.

The vehicle he'd been following for almost an hour now pulled into a driveway and parked near the sidewalk at right angles, blocking in a white beater. The pickup's occupant climbed out and slammed the door.

The other side of the drive was occupied by a huge truck, lifted up beyond what was legal with huge mud guards.

Lights were on in the house, though the sun was now high. It glowed orange behind the clouds. He couldn't use the cover of darkness, but he still needed to get close.

Was Allyson here? A rush of adrenaline surged through him at the idea he might be close to her, especially after not knowing where she had been all night and into today. There was no time to waste. Waiting for night to fall again would mean even more time spent as a captive. His brain began traveling down that slippery slope trail to all that might be happening to her.

He shut off the thoughts, pulled his car closer into the trees and got out. No neighbors. These people—whoever they were— didn't have to worry about people being nosy, or complaining about the noises that came out of the house.

Another thing he didn't want to think about.

The front door slammed, much the same way the guy had shut his car door. Sal heard yelling. More than one person. He made his way around the outside of the house. The back door flung open and two men spilled out.

"Just get out there and help round them up," one told the other. "The boss is going to expect a report at check-in so we better have something to tell him, and it better not be that we lost them."

Lost?

As in, Allyson and Vanessa had escaped? That sounded promising.

Sal felt the corners of his lips curl up. *That's my girl.*

Another thing he wasn't going to think so much about. He just needed to find her and her friend. That, and possibly locating the flash drive, were his only priorities right now.

"Is the tracker still active?"

Sal peered around the back corner of the house and immediately recognized the man. He was one of the FBI agents who had tried to question Vanessa at the hospital. But she hadn't recognized him as one of the three men in the garage, so he was either a newcomer or maybe he had kept his identity hidden during the stint where she was held captive.

The man giving orders, the fake FBI agent, answered his friend. "Should be."

"Okay." The man pulled out his phone, then turned, jogging off toward the trees.

A tracker? They had somehow bugged either of the women and now they were able to locate them. Or "round them up" as that man had said.

The one who would be reporting in when the boss required him to.

Allyson was alive, and he would find her. Which meant he needed access to that tracker. For whatever reason he wasn't going to admit to yet, he was more concerned with Ally's well being than her friend's. But wasn't that understandable? He would work to get them both back, and of course track down the flash drive too, but Allyson was the one he cared about. The one whose fate had caused his gut to be tied up in knots since he helplessly watched that van drive away.

The back door slammed shut. Sal sprinted full out in the direction the man had gone. He would make more noise going fast but prayed he'd be able to get the drop on the man before he was heard.

He rushed at the man, dipped his head forward and tackled the guy's middle. They both went sprawling. The man let out an "oof" as they landed on the ground, then rolled so Sal was on the bottom. Sal kept hold of the guy and kept rolling. When he was on top, he lifted up and punched the man square in the jaw.

The guy went limp, unconscious.

Sal grabbed the guy's phone from the ground where it had dropped and used the man's thumb to unlock it. He went into settings, changing the length of time before it timed out and locked again.

From the man's phone he sent Talia a text. Then he used the guy's belt to tie him to a tree, so he'd be secure for at least a while. The team, or the local sheriff, could pick this guy up and get him to a holding cell. Or Sal would come back for him. He figured the guy had outstanding warrants. Likely someone in a police station or federal office somewhere was looking for him. Or he owed back child support. He'd learned from experience as a marshal that it was highly unlikely someone involved in a kidnapping had a completely clean record.

A cop somewhere would want to talk to this guy.

Sal was more than happy to take someone like him in. Get the local sheriff to process him into the system so he could answer for whatever he'd done.

He sent another text and told Talia about the guy in the house, and the check-in from the boss that was supposed to be happening soon. He also asked her to find Allyson, using the information found on the phone.

He saw the second she began to do her thing. The screen turned black, then green text scrolled down it. Like a program initiating.

Sal started walking in the same direction the man had been going. He'd keep on that path until he was told by Talia of a more specific location.

A high-pitched scream rolled down the mountain like a flash flood. He paused, assessing what direction it had come from.

High in the mountains, someone was in distress. Not an animal. A human.

Sal set off running. Talia came through and the phone vibrated. Same general area. Their tracker and the scream. He ran nearly two miles before hearing anything else.

A lump rose in his throat. Sal swallowed it down. He was not supposed to be having this reaction to the fact Allyson was in danger. Possibly hurt. He'd been determined to walk away from her and start a new life.

It wasn't like she would never be in danger with the line of work she was in. He would leave, knowing she could be killed any minute on the job. She was a cop, and it was part of that life. Investigating crimes and her part-time work—as many ATF agents took on—as a member of one of their breach teams. Serving warrants. Getting right up in the faces of violent criminals.

Sal had to stop just to breathe. Sharp pains rolled through his chest. Just a stitch. Nothing to do with thinking about what he would do if Allyson was killed.

The phone buzzed.

Quarter mile, eleven o'clock.

How Talia knew that he had no idea. But he decided to just go with it. He heard a scuffle then and moved to get a better sight of the area where the noise was coming from.

Sal found Allyson in a vicious fight with a man. Vanessa stood a few feet away, a look on her face that he couldn't decipher. He had no time to assess it and understand what her expression even meant.

Sal drew his weapon and yelled, "Police! Freeze!

The man twisted to face him. Allyson punched him in the kidney while he wasn't looking. The man grunted and stumbled to the side.

"Hands up."

Beyond the man, Allyson plunked down, shaking out her hand. Chest heaving with each inhale. "Vanessa, you okay?" She took a step toward her friend and stumbled.

"I think so."

The attacker didn't back down. He drew his weapon and shifted with intention. Sal squeezed his trigger and put two bullets into the man's chest before he could kill someone.

Vanessa screamed.

Allyson paled and then collapsed on the grass.

14

———

"Ally!" She heard Sal call her name.

Now he'd decided to call her by her nickname? Maybe he had before, she couldn't remember. She tried to sit up.

"Easy."

Allyson blinked and saw his face close to hers. She squeezed her fingers together and felt the material of his shirt.

"You okay?"

"I think so." What had happened? She spotted the dead man on the grass behind him and shivered. "He's dead?"

Vanessa raced past her. She stepped on the side of Allyson's shoe, stumbled, and nearly went down. She collapsed beside his body, crying full out now.

"Peter!" She wailed his name as though, if loud enough, she might call him back from the dead.

Why would she react like this?

"Can you stand?" Sal grasped her arms.

"Thanks." Her legs shook, but she managed to get upright with his help.

"Okay?"

Enough for him to let go? She wasn't sure she wanted that, whether her legs would hold her or not. Allyson looked up at his face then, and they stared at each other while Vanessa cried and exclaimed over and over the name of this man who'd kept her captive.

"Uh…Vanessa." She stared at her friend grieving over a dead man who had hurt her…okay, wait, what had he actually done to her? Had he hurt her? Was this reaction an indication there had been a relationship, or was Vanessa just going through some kind of mental breakdown? "Come away from there. We need to go, okay?"

She glanced at Sal and saw him frown. "Is she…"

"I have no idea."

Sal squeezed her elbow. "I'll call in reinforcements. Get us a ride out of here, and protection."

Allyson nodded, then made her way to her friend. She touched Vanessa's shoulder. Her friend's muscles tightened under her hand. She twisted around, launching up as she moved.

Before Allyson even realized what was happening, Vanessa tackled her.

Caught off guard, they fell back onto the grass. Allyson landed on her back, a rock at her left side. She hissed out a breath.

Vanessa grasped for her.

Allyson batted away her hands. "Are you trying to strangle me?"

Her friend whimpered as they struggled, forcing her to fight. Allyson had no desire to restrain her, but Vanessa was intent on causing damage. She had to defend herself, and that meant she would need to subdue her.

Allyson pushed off the ground, grunted and rolled. She flipped Vanessa onto her back. Before she could recover from the surprise, Allyson subdued her like a suspect. "Calm down." She exhaled. "I'm sorry, but you need to calm down, or I'm not going to let you up."

Sal stood three feet away, gun still drawn, on the phone.

Vanessa hissed at him. "You killed him!" She screamed the words.

Allyson had to yell just so Vanessa could hear her repeated orders to calm down,

Vanessa pushed out a breath. Allyson held onto her, but allowed her to clamber to her feet.

"Talk to me," Allyson pleaded. "Tell me why you're so upset."

Vanessa's shoulders sagged, and she whimpered again.

"This man hurt you. He would have killed you, or one of us, if Sal hadn't eliminated the threat." If she wasn't so tired, Allyson probably would have been able to word it better. But in a pinch she figured she did okay. "This man hurt you." And yet, Vanessa obviously had strong feelings for him. Whether they were true, or simply twisted, she didn't know.

"Peter loved me!" She screamed the words in Allyson's face. "And I loved him!"

"Vaness—"

Her friend lifted both hands and shoved her. "Don't talk to me. I *knew* this wasn't going to work, but I didn't know you'd *kill him.*"

Everything in her sank. It was a wonder Allyson didn't just collapse again on the ground. No strength. No will to carry on. "What are you—"

"I *told him* you would be the one who screwed it up. Guess I was wrong about that, since it was the lone gunslinger over there." Vanessa's gaze shot daggers at Sal. She stomped around in a rage, barely containing her fury. Like it might spill out at any moment.

Sal watched. Phone put away. Gun still aimed, loose in front of him. Ready to be used at any second if Vanessa did something he didn't like.

Allyson spoke very carefully, her fatigue making her thoughts coalesce slower than she'd have liked. "You've been working with him all along, haven't you?"

Vanessa glanced over. As though Allyson was an ant...with half a brain. About to get squished.

"Is there even a flash drive?" Except there was. The second

she said it, Allyson remembered Vanessa had pulled it from her pants pocket. "Does it have any evidence on it?"

"You were right about it being the tracker." Vanessa smirked. "About the only thing you were right on."

"What about your coworker? Did you kill him?"

"Does it matter? That's hardly the point here." Vanessa waved one arm around, unaware of Sal moving to face her. She might have forgotten he was here. "Even if you bring charges against me, Kennowich will still get what he wants. I'm just one cog in a giant machine. We are all both dispensable and vital in our own right."

Useful and disposable at the same time?

Allyson wanted to consider everything. Too bad her brain seemed to have gotten stuck on the fact she'd been played. And to this extent. The sting of betrayal cut her like she'd been stuck with a hundred needles at once. She tried to swallow down the idea but it got stuck in her throat, and her eyes filled with tears.

She'd trusted this woman.

Allyson had put her reputation and well-being on the line to protect her. And now it turned out that everything Vanessa had said or done had been a lie.

And boy had Allyson fallen for it.

The Northwest Counter-Terrorism Task Force could come in from here. They were determined to solve their case, and with the way she felt right now, they could have it. They would blame her for this too and probably shut her out.

Fine by me. She just wanted to get out of here.

"Put your hands in the air, Vanessa." Sal's voice was calm. Steady.

She was so glad he was here.

"I'm walking out of here."

Allyson shook her head. "No, you aren't. You're going to come with us to an interrogation room, where you'll answer every question we have." They needed to know why Vanessa was back now. Why she had drawn Ally into this and strung them all along?

Was it all just a huge diversion tactic so Kennowich could do something else under their noses?

Vanessa reached behind her back.

"Don't!"

They both reacted, knowing what was coming. She'd gotten Peter's gun after he was killed. Before Sal could shoot her, Allyson rushed toward her former friend. She bypassed her hand, which was stretched out, holding the gun, and tackled Vanessa the way her former friend had tackled her only moments earlier.

If they killed her too, they would lose all their intel. That thought was what energized her as she fought for possession of Peter Tines's gun.

Sal yelled something she couldn't understand. He'd called her Ally again, though. She heard that.

Vanessa rolled her. Allyson twisted. Pain flared in her back and she rolled again, finally grasping the gun tight.

Her head hit a rock. The gun fell from her fingers.

Lights sparked across her vision, and then everything went black.

———

Sal winced at the dull thud. She'd struck a rock. Now Allyson was completely unconscious. He didn't hesitate.

Sal grabbed Vanessa's arm and pulled her off Allyson. She swiped up the gun and moved to aim it at him.

"Enough!" He yelled the word loudly in her face and then hauled her a few steps away from Allyson, one hand wrapped around her wrist of the hand holding the gun.

He gritted his teeth. He had no cuffs and backup wasn't here yet. Should he use Peter's belt to secure her? A belt had worked once already today.

She shifted the gun around, trying to twist free from his grip. He said, "Don't. That won't go anywhere good for you, so drop the gun!"

She cried out in frustration but let go of the weapon.

Sal needed to get to Ally and make sure she was all right. He also needed to call Talia and get a medical chopper, or at least EMTs up here with a stretcher. That could take hours. In the meantime, Allyson could bleed into her brain and die.

He wanted to shake Vanessa.

"I'm not going to tell either of you anything." Her body shook as she tried to wriggle out of his grasp. "I have nothing to say." She paused, then said, "Not without a witness protection deal."

"No way." That was what he wanted her to get—nothing. Whether he would get his wish was a different story entirely.

He still couldn't believe he and Allyson had both been so thoroughly duped. He'd felt like something was off, but never would he have guessed this. And on top of it all, Vanessa had been in love with a man who had kidnapped her. Used her, just as they were using Allyson.

How twisted up did she have to be for that?

It turned his stomach. This was no friend of Allyson's, not now and maybe not even years ago. He was sad for Allyson, knowing she had to have also come to that realization. She'd genuinely been hurt over the loss of her friend, and then was so glad when Vanessa showed back up again.

Now it was all wrong.

He looked at her, lying on the ground. The steady rise and fall of her breath.

"Kennowich got to you, didn't he?"

Maybe Vanessa had been a victim at one time, but she wasn't one now. She'd walked the road that brought her here, and it hadn't been as someone who wanted to get out. She was here as an emissary. Kennowich's hands and feet.

And what a horrible thought that was.

In love with one of his men. Sent to lure Allyson, and maybe the task force to her as well, so that they were running in circles trying to figure out the truth. They'd probably planned every minute of this to keep everyone confused.

Which meant Kennowich could very well be enacting whatever plan he had in the works at this very moment.

Shooting up the office.

Keeping them all distracted.

At the end of the day, everyone had to choose who they represented. He tried to represent good. His Savior and his earthly father. Justice. Rightness. Some people only represented themselves or, like Vanessa, they did everything for someone else. Kennowich, or Peter Tines. Or both. All in league with each other, or she played them against each other.

Sal tried to have faith for today and hope for tomorrow.

Faith. That was what his dad had said he carried with him. Allyson would need her own faith to navigate the fallout of this. Could he be there to help her? He'd never done that with another woman, but she was definitely different.

One of a kind.

"On your left!"

He spun around, still holding on to Vanessa.

Dakota and Josh emerged from between two trees, Josh's dog padding along behind them.

Sal nearly sagged with relief. "Take her. Get cuffs on her." There was no time to explain. As soon as they had a hold of Vanessa, he raced to Allyson.

Please don't be dead.

They already needed to process one body and get a coroner here. He didn't want to have to do that with Allyson as well.

He sank to his knees and touched her face. Felt for the pulse in her neck. Weak, but it was there.

"She okay?"

"No, she got knocked out." Why would Dakota ask such a dumb question? Allyson wouldn't be on the ground unconscious if she was okay.

"Geez, you don't gotta be mad."

He glanced at her. "Call for Life Flight."

Josh lowered his phone. "Already done. Talia will get them on their way. She's also sending the coroner and the local sheriff."

Sal nodded, grateful for the other man's help, then turned back to Allyson. "Hey." He patted her cheek. "You probably don't want to wake up right now, but I'm thinking it's a good idea."

She didn't rouse, but he wasn't surprised. The woman was exhausted. He'd seen it when she'd fought Vanessa. Fatigued. Running on fumes, as it were. Plus, on top of that, there was the emotional upheaval of realizing her friend had lied to her. She'd been kidnapped. Had hiked all the way up here.

She was out of energy, had hit her head, and now her body had shut down. Preserving the strength it would take to heal.

Sal didn't envy what she was going to wake up to. He gathered her in his arms and stood. When he turned, he saw a look pass between Josh and his fiancé.

Dakota still held onto Vanessa. "Are you going to carry her two miles back down to the house?"

He nodded and started walking, then remembered to ask Josh, "Did you guys detain the man in the house, or the one tied to a tree behind the house?"

"There was no one there when we got to it." Josh shot him a look. "In, or behind."

Dakota said, "You need to wait for a stretcher."

"She can't wait that long." He motioned to Vanessa with a tip of his head. "Who's going to interrogate her?"

"The task force, obviously."

"She knows what Kennowich is doing. What he's up to." And Sal was going to trust his teammates to find out what that was.

Vanessa smirked. "You think I'm going to tell you all my secrets?"

Allyson stirred then. He set her down and saw her eyes flutter open.

"Hey."

"So sweet," Vanessa drawled.

Sal glanced at her and Dakota. "Get her to the office and start the debrief."

"Copy that." Dakota's voice had a tone he ignored.

Allyson's eyes filled with tears. He imagined she wanted her former friend out of her sight. She probably couldn't even look at Vanessa right now.

"You'll wait for the coroner?"

Josh nodded, a curious look on his face.

"Can you walk?"

Allyson stood, only swaying a little. "I want to get out of here."

"Take it easy. That's a nasty bump on the back of your head."

"Okay." She didn't nod, just kept her head still. She also held onto his arm with both of her hands, leaning some of her weight on him as they slowly descended the mountain.

He wanted to talk with her about Vanessa, but her head probably hurt too much to take on such a heavy conversation. He knew she could have peace and hope with Jesus, even in this. But how did he say that and have it not sound like a total cliché?

He knew what the answer was. And he was working on how to put it into practice in his own life. He'd been kind of dissatisfied lately, but maybe a little of that was all right. It forced you to grow.

Down the mountain, a gunshot rang out.

A moment later the dog ran past them. Then Josh, sprinting full out.

15

———————

"Go." Sal ignored her. He kept going, moving faster now. She said it again, "Go."

"What are you—"

"Dakota is down there, right?" He barely nodded before she said, "So *go*, Sal. I'm okay."

"I'm not leaving you here by yourself, Ally."

"I'll walk down slowly. You need to go help Josh."

"If there's danger, I need to make sure you're safe."

"What about Dakota?"

"She has Josh."

It was like he didn't even know what she was talking about. "Probably wouldn't hurt to have you help her as well."

"I already responded to that."

Josh and Dakota might be engaged, but that didn't mean they didn't need additional support. He was going to stay with her, like a stubborn, pigheaded *man* while Dakota could be hurt somewhere out here?

Sal's eyebrows rose. "Pigheaded?"

Uh, she'd said that out loud?

The expression that crossed his face was unreadable. A multitude of emotions that moved too fast for her to register all at once. "I'd tell you to stay here, but I doubt you'd listen."

He touched her cheeks, leaned in and kissed her forehead.

He let go and turned away.

Allyson swayed.

Sal raced down the hill ahead of her. Her head thumped while she tried to figure out what had just happened. He'd kissed her. That was "what." Obviously. She wanted to smack the side of her head, jog her thoughts back to running at regular speed.

That wouldn't be good at all.

She started walking. Deep breaths. Focused on the ground. One foot in front of the other and all that. She needed to get down the mountain to the house.

He'd seemed pretty intense about protecting her. Did that mean he was interested in protecting her the same way he thought Josh protected Dakota? Those two were engaged. That didn't mean she and Sal were going to plan a marriage.

Sure, she'd been crushing on him pretty badly since they'd met. So pretty much for years now. Had too much happened since then for them to have a relationship?

She'd always thought part of him agreed with his team's assessment of her actions. Did he not?

Another gunshot rang throughout the hillside.

Sal. She glanced in all directions to make sure she wasn't about to get caught off guard. That wouldn't be good. She was unarmed and injured. Who was firing, and at whom? She prayed quickly that Dakota was all right, and that everyone else there would be as well.

Vanessa had betrayed her. Attacked her. And she'd been in love with Peter Tines.

She closed her eyes for a second, listening to the world around her while she just took a moment for her thoughts and reactions to catch up with what was happening.

When Allyson set off again, toward the house, she had to swipe a tear from her cheek. She glanced up at the sky. *I don't know how to do this.* Sal was with her, though—at least, he would be as soon as she got to where she was going. *Is that why you brought us together?*

She didn't want to get into a big mental debate about timing, but she also didn't believe in coincidences either. That meant the timing here counted for something. Not nothing.

Sal saw her coming as she walked down the path. He broke off from his huddle with Dakota and came to meet her, pulling her to him for a hug. "How's your head?"

"How is Dakota?"

"Well now," the woman herself said. "I didn't know you cared, Sanchez."

Allyson would have shot her a look, but that would involve throwing up because of the pain. Probably wouldn't have quite the same impact. "What happened?"

Sal turned her to face him. She didn't like the look on his face, but she knew what it meant. Allyson said, "Vanessa is dead?"

Then she saw the woman lying on the ground.

Dakota said, "Rifle shot. A single bullet caught her between her bicep and her heart, far enough she took a minute to bleed out on the grass instead of dying instantly. Josh headed out to look for the shooter."

She didn't take her gaze from Sal's the entire time his teammate spoke.

Sal said, "I'm sorry."

Dakota shifted into the edge of Allyson's field of vision. "She was a traitor, right?"

Allyson twisted in Sal's hold and faced her. "She also had valuable intel." Something Dakota would understand they should have safeguarded. Allyson exhaled out a long breath. "I think I need to sit down."

Sal led her to the back porch and a dusty patio chair. Ally sank into it.

"You need an ambulance."

She wanted to shake her head but didn't. "Evidence collection. Paperwork." Her mouth opened involuntarily, and she covered an eye-watering, jaw-popping yawn with her hand. She might be exhausted, but she doubted she'd be able to get any sleep at all.

Every inch of her body felt like it had been pounded into oblivion.

A car pulled up. Josh strode around the house and said, "Looks like feds."

She looked at Sal. "As in, the ones who showed up at the hospital?"

He shook his head. "These better be different because those ones worked for Kennowich." When she just stared at him, he said, "One of them was the man I followed here to find you."

Two men strode around the house. Shiny shoes, nice ties, and dark gray suits. Badges were flashed. They both had the same hairstyle. Probably had the same brand of phone as well. "We're here because a federal agent was kidnapped. ATF Special Agent Daulton called us."

"That would be me." Allyson raised her hand. "The one that was kidnapped." She gave them her name.

One made notes into her phone as she explained it all. When she paused to think through the last part, what happened since the moment they'd run from the house, Sal cut her off. "She needs to be seen by a doctor. If you're done taking her statement, we're going to leave."

"We need to speak with each of you," the one closer to him said.

"We're happy to give a statement." Josh's arm was still around Dakota.

The FBI agent didn't seem super hyped at that idea. "Fine."

"We should search the house for evidence as well." Although, thinking about it now, Allyson wasn't sure she wanted to go in there.

Which probably meant she absolutely should go in there.

Therapy. The chance to face her fears, and maybe find some evidence Vanessa had left behind.

Like that flash drive in her pocket.

Allyson got up and walked toward her dead former friend's body.

Sal crouched beside her. "Hey—"

Allyson waved him off, then dug in Vanessa's pocket.

"Is that evidence?" One of the FBI agents leaned over to see.

"If it is—" Sal helped her stand. "—then it belongs to the Northwest Counter-Terrorism Task Force."

Both FBI agents' hands flexed. Toward their guns.

What on earth?

"Allyson and I are leaving now."

The dog growled at the two men she didn't know. Sal led Allyson away from the group and around to a car parked down the street. He held the door and she got in. Slowly.

When he got around to his side, she had her eyes shut.

"Okay?"

She didn't open her eyes. "I could use Ibuprofen."

"I meant about Vanessa."

"Am I supposed to grieve over someone who betrayed me multiple times? Because my head really hurts."

"I figure you'll end up grieving over the loss of the friendship you should have had, or could have had, more than the death of that woman."

"It's nice that you're trying to help. But my head really hurts."

What she wanted to do was push everything away and get back to work. Sal squeezed her hand. She heard the brakes as he stopped at an intersection. When she opened her eyes, she saw him facing her, twisted in his seat. He touched her face.

"Sweet and everything, but you know, it doesn't mean as much. Because I know you're only being affectionate to me because Josh and Dakota aren't around right now to see."

———

FOR THE SECOND time in as many days, Sal paced the hallway outside a hospital room. This time it was Allyson being seen to, while her friend lay dead on the forest floor. He'd found the closest medical center in a small town about fifteen minutes from the house. Allyson had been poked and scanned. Now she was getting the split in her scalp glued shut.

The doctor knew what he was doing, even if this was a small town, but it still seemed odd to use glue.

You're avoiding the issue.

It was almost Dakota's voice in his head, but that wasn't exactly right. He couldn't remember when she'd said that to him, but it was what popped in there. A nudge from the Holy Spirit.

He'd screwed up. She thought the only reason he'd been sweet to her in the car—or tried to be at least—was because Josh and Dakota hadn't been able to see? Was that what she'd thought about his kiss on the mountain?

He'd been so overcome that she was okay. Walking, talking. Not slurring her words. That she could actually escape a concussion despite everything was just astounding.

There was time to fix this. For him to explain to her how he really felt, and that he hadn't even thought of Josh or Dakota either time. In fact, when he looked at her…it was like…like there was no one else there at all. He only saw her.

Sal's phone rang. He pulled it out. "Alvarez."

"It's Weber."

He found the nearest chair so he could lean his head back against the wall while Josh gave him whatever update there was to know. "Hit me."

"You sound exhausted."

Sal huffed out a laugh. "Because it's true." He'd been going full throttle all night looking for Allyson.

"We got a couple of cell phones. One from our dead guy, Peter Tines. The other was left in the house."

"You think Talia will be able to get anything off them?"

"Whether she can or not, we'll know soon. She's already on it."

"Good."

"How is Agent Sanchez?"

Why did that question have a *tone*? Sal stared at the baseboard between the wallpaper and the linoleum floor. "Getting looked at. He's going to *glue* her head back together."

"Yep." Josh sounded like he was laughing. "The vet did that to Neema last time she got cut. It's good, Sal."

He made a face Josh wasn't ever going to see.

"You should ask her out."

Sal said nothing.

"Her friend just died, and she found out she's been betrayed. She needs the distraction. You can cheer her up."

"I don't even know where to start." Sal crossed one leg and put his boot on the opposite knee. "There are so many problems with that—too many to point out."

Josh actually laughed. "Stop thinking about it and just do it. You've slow-played this thing long enough. It's time to act."

"And the fact that Dakota and Victoria, not to mention everyone else, hates her?"

"They don't." The humor dissipated from his voice. "You know how you're always hauling them out of trouble and helping them with problems? They're just as protective of you. In fact, I'd put money down on the fact they are scared thinking they might lose you. They reacted badly and boxed themselves into a position. And they're women, so it's not like admitting they are wrong actually comes easily."

Sal had always thought it didn't come easy to anyone, no matter the gender.

They both said nothing. He was quiet for so long, thinking it over, that Josh finally broke the silence. "Thank you for agreeing to give Dakota away. She was worried you'd think it was dumb."

"Sure." There was a weight to the word, one neither of them missed.

"Dakota is processing the friend's body."

"Pretty sure you can stop calling her that," he said. "Vanessa wasn't Allyson's friend when she died, and I doubt she has been for years." Maybe even never. "The woman was seriously messed up. I'd have liked to know if she had some kind of Stockholm syndrome, or what."

"Or if Kennowich had leverage over her."

Sal nodded, even though Josh couldn't see him. "Could be that he had some, given she was in love with Peter Tines."

"What I don't get is how he got away with it. I mean, you can't just go around kidnapping interns and keeping them for years. What's that about?"

Sal said, "It's like she was happy to follow him everywhere like some lost puppy, or someone who'd been brainwashed. She stayed under the radar for years and let everyone in her life believe she was dead."

Josh was quiet for a second then said, "Huh. Kind of sounds like a gang initiation. Like she did something for him, and he hid her as a gesture of thanks. Or a bargain. Either way he had information on her that could be used against her. Somehow he persuaded her it was all necessary."

Sal shook his head. "All I know is the whole thing sounds bizarre." And Allyson was caught in the middle of it. He hated that she'd been so tugged around, here and there, through the entire ordeal. He squeezed the bridge of his nose. "Any luck finding the shooter?"

Josh would be motivated since his fiancé had nearly been killed. The man said, "No, but there's a truck still here in the driveway."

"Pickup with a gun rack?"

"That's the one. When you saw it, was the gun rack empty?"

"No, it was not," Sal said. "The gun was there before—did he use it to shoot Vanessa? Was he aiming at Dakota?"

"She says no. One shot, clean kill on the not-friend."

"And the other shot fired?"

"Her saying, 'hi' back."

Sal worked his mouth side to side. "The truck belonged to the man I tied to the tree. So the other guy from the house could have let him go. Or he heard Dakota coming and hid. Either could have been the shooter. Lucky break he got, taking out Vanessa."

"Maybe."

Sal said, "I'll take a look at the mug shots we showed Vanessa. See if I can figure out who it is." That was how they would have to track the shooter. And likely that was the key to this case.

Sal told him about the other vehicle that had been in the drive.

"I'll get Talia on the lookout for the truck since it's gone. If it was at the house, then one, or both, might have taken it when they left."

"Okay."

"So do we believe Vanessa, that there is some kind of threat about to play out?"

"If Kennowich is up to something, we need a way to find out what it is." Sal usually tried to color within the lines of legality, but he wasn't opposed to stretching those limits if he had to. Especially if it saved lives. But how could they find out what they needed to know?

"Could be on that flash drive Allyson pulled out of her fr— that woman's pocket."

"If there's even anything on there."

"Wow, you're in a mood this afternoon."

Sal huffed into the phone. It beeped in his ear. "I'm getting another call." Before Josh could answer, he hung up. "Alvarez."

"It's Daulton. Did you get her back?"

"Yes, sir. She's with a doctor right now getting patched up."

"Copy that." Sal heard a rustling. "I'm sending you an address. Get over here as soon as she's done."

Sal opened his mouth to object, not really sure what he was going to say.

Daulton had already hung up.

The text came through seconds later.

FFL Robbery #3. All hands on deck.

Underneath was the address.

The door opened a second later, and she peeked her head out. "Did Daulton text you?"

"Yep."

"Good." She strode from the hospital room with her shoes in one hand. "Let's go."

Behind her, the doctor stood holding a needle.

She breezed past him. "Time to leave."

16

______

Her head hurt, but she hadn't let the doctor give her that shot. Like she wanted to admit to him that she was freaked out by needles? Better to leave. And she would add extra money in Daulton's office birthday card this year for his amazing timing.

Allyson buckled her seatbelt like she didn't hear the audible rumble of her stomach.

Sal glanced over. He looked as wrung out as she felt. "You need food?"

He probably just wanted a quick win. An easy problem of hers that he was able to fix. "Sure." She shot him a wry smile. "Along with three ibuprofen, a shower and about eighteen hours of sleep."

"Reminds me of the Mittenmast case. All those long days at the courthouse?"

She nodded. "That was killer. I think I lost three houseplants during that case. Good thing I don't have a dog."

He pulled into a chain pharmacy, beside which was one of those hole-in-the-wall, fast-food burger joints with a drive-through, no inside seating, and the *best* fry sauce.

"Chocolate milkshake."

Sal chuckled. "Cheeseburger? Fries? Onion rings?"

"Yes."

He cracked his door. "Wait here."

She watched him walk inside the pharmacy and come out a few minutes later with a grocery bag hanging from one hand. He strode to the drive-up window and spoke to the teller, pulling out his wallet. Before stepping back, receipt in hand, he turned and pointed at the car.

When he opened the driver's door again she said, "Aren't we driving over there?"

"Sure. But I wanted to order first." He drove to pick up the food, and they settled in to eat in a corner of the parking lot.

"Daulton is expecting us, right?"

"Sure." He wiped the corner of his mouth with a napkin. "I'm keeping him updated. He said he'll see us when we get there."

"Okay." She figured he could have eaten while he drove. She'd even seen him do it before on occasion. "So why are we taking our time?"

"Because you were just kidnapped, and a woman you thought was your friend is now dead. I want to make sure you're really okay before I take you to work."

Well. There was a lot there. Most of it Allyson didn't want to think about. Later, she would cry over a pint of ice cream. Probably in the bathtub if she was honest with herself. Did she want to talk about it with Sal?

She dipped a fry in her milkshake and pointed it at him. Thankfully the milkshake was so thick it didn't drip. "I want to know if you blame me for what happened at the courthouse."

"No. Of course not." He kind of looked offended. "Why else would I defend you to my team?"

"But they still don't like me."

"That's what you're worried about?"

She shrugged.

"I can't really help how they feel. I could talk until I'm blue in the face, but it's like working with a bunch of wild mustangs sometimes."

She smiled. Pretty apt description, if you asked her. "You miss the mountains?"

"Of course." He took a sip of his drink, swallowed, and then opened his mouth again. As though intending to say something. But didn't.

"What?"

"I'm thinking about finishing out my tenure as a marshal and going home."

He was thinking about retiring? She couldn't believe it.

"Maybe I'll get a PI license."

Quit his job altogether? "Maybe you should just transfer to a Marshal's office in Wyoming. Keep the job, take a slower-paced assignment, right? And you'd be close to home." Hadn't he thought about that?

"I've looked into it."

If he did that, he'd probably never come to Seattle. What would she do if he was gone? Saying she'd miss him didn't quite cover it.

Maybe she would go and visit him. All that wide-open space sounded good. She was more comfortable when she wasn't surrounded by a crowd of people. Not antisocial as such, but she'd seen what humans could do to each other. The worst side of life. Enough to make an introvert out of anyone just out of self-preservation.

Maybe for her next vacation she would go to a small town. A place everyone said, "Hi," and where she could go hiking. Make coffee over a fire. Sleep under the stars.

"It's okay if you don't want your team to know we're… friends." Or whatever they were. "I understand wanting to keep personal things from your coworkers. Mine gnaw on stuff like they're dogs with a bone.

Sal just glanced at her with that unreadable expression. She'd thought she could read him pretty well, but lately it seemed like she had no clue what he was thinking.

"Whatever I'm going to do next," he said, "there's no way I

can leave the team until this Kennowich thing is figured out. They're good on a personal level, most of them engaged to be married. They don't need me to watch their backs so much. Now we just need to be done with this case."

And then he would be gone.

"How about you?"

She scrunched up her nose. "I've thought about being done with the ATF." She could take some cool vacations. Get to work on that bucket list. "I do want to have a family, and I wouldn't want to work this job when there's a chance of getting pregnant. It's too risky." She shrugged one shoulder. "I could take a desk job."

Except that sounded so boring it would be exhausting. Sitting around with nothing to do was more tiring than having a busy schedule.

Allyson shut her eyes. It was pretty pointless thinking about marriage and family when she didn't have a man in her life. At least not one who had told her how he felt.

The car stopped.

Allyson blinked, realizing she'd fallen asleep. Sal put the car in park and glanced at her. She said, "How long was I out?"

"Almost an hour."

So basically the whole drive here. Sal had a soft look on his face.

"Do I have those creases on my cheek from sleeping?"

He chuckled. "You're presentable enough, considering you were kidnapped earlier and we stopped at a medical center on the way here so you could get your head glued."

"I'm not a nursery rhyme character who needs to be put back together again."

He didn't respond to that. "We're only here because Daulton and the rest of the boys want to see for themselves that you're okay. Then I'm dropping you home so you can get more sleep."

"Copy that." She shoved the door open, but he put a hand on her arm.

"Hold up. I'll come around."

So he could help her out of the car? As if she'd let "Daulton and the rest of the boys" see that. Allyson climbed out. Carefully. When she could be sure she wasn't going to topple over or collapse, she shut the door.

Sal frowned but said nothing. They walked side by side to the gathered crowd. Two detectives, a uniformed Seattle PD Sergeant, her boss and the boys.

"Whadda we got?"

They all just stared at her. Someone muttered a curse under their breath.

Allyson planted a hand on her hip. "Do I really look that bad?"

Carl said, "Yes."

"If I had something to throw, I would throw it at you."

He chuckled, walked to her, and pulled her to him in a loose hug. He'd never done that before. None of the guys had, for that matter. Now they all wandered over one by one to give her a squeeze. Daulton held out his hand, and she shook it. "Good to see you, Sanchez."

She squeezed his hand, then let it go. "Good to be seen."

He nodded.

"What's going on here?"

"Same old," Carl said. "Rental van. Getaway vehicle. Too many similarities to the other robberies, clearly the same people."

"So it's a crew, and they've found a method they think will keep working."

The police sergeant said, "Until it doesn't, and someone gets seriously hurt."

Basically everyone nodded.

"By now they have a pretty big stash," she said. "Are we thinking they'll offload them in one big sale, or in a bunch of single-item cash transactions?"

"Sir!"

Everyone turned to see a uniformed officer trot over with a

plastic evidence bag hanging from his grip. Inside the bag was a cell phone. "This was found in the rental van."

Daulton said, "We'll get that back to our lab, find out who—"

"That won't be necessary."

"Sanchez?"

She gritted her teeth for a second. "That's my phone."

———

SAL HAULED a folding chair out from the gun store so Allyson could sit down. "This better not take long."

Daulton shot him a look but didn't argue. He also didn't agree with Sal's assessment.

The detectives and their Sergeant crowded around, asking a whole lot of questions about why an ATF agent's phone was in the rental truck that had rammed into the side of this gun store. Daulton started at the beginning and told them about Vanessa showing up.

Sal flashed his badge and finished the tale, updating them all on Vanessa's death at the house. "We got the flash drive back, but we could be back to square one."

Not to mention the FBI's interest now, and the fact Allyson—along with the rest of them—could very well be in danger.

The Sergeant folded his arms across his expansive chest. "This guy's plan isn't the point right now. The point is that we have a bunch of stolen guns, not to mention the fact that Allyson is somehow caught up in it."

Sal said, "It makes a connection between the kidnapping—which we know Kennowich was behind—and the gun store robberies."

"Discounting the fact the only common denominator is this agent." The detective gestured towards Allyson.

She said, "This agent has a name. It's Sanchez."

"Well then, Sanchez. You'll need to explain how you're suddenly all caught up in this."

Sal watched as Allyson elaborated on Vanessa's disappearance and the life she'd lived since then—and her betrayal.

"That's one crazy story."

"It's not a story." She shot the guy a scathing look. Past the end of her energy, even with the nap she'd taken in the car. He was glad he'd stopped for food and pain meds. He figured if he'd asked her then, she probably would've told him she'd rather do this first. His way was better, especially considering how she looked now. No doubt she'd still swear she's improved.

The ATF guys shifted, ready to jump to her defense. They'd have to get in line behind him. Everyone was on edge.

"This does more to expose your severe lack of judgment."

Sal took a step toward the detective. "Now, wait a moment—"

Allyson touched his chest, gently moved him back and stepped in front of him. "Thank you for your time." Like she'd been the one asking for a statement, or explanation. "I need to be going now."

"Good idea." Sal grabbed her hand, not caring how it looked. "Let's go."

They both turned, ignoring the local cops' expressions. Daulton held up a hand. "Tomorrow morning I want you at the FBI office. You'll need to make a statement and explain everything you just told these fine officers."

Allyson started to object.

Daulton continued before she could. "This isn't our case anymore. It's being given to the FBI."

"Because of me?"

"It's a conflict of interest, regardless of the why or how your phone ended up here."

Allyson pressed her lips together.

Daulton had made the right call, though. They both knew it. He couldn't have one of his agents caught up in all this and keep working it.

Even though his team did that all the time.

This guy was by the book, something which had the tendency

to rub off on his agents. Allyson had pushed against that before, which had led to that one-in-a-million scenario where he'd been hurt. She had as well, something everyone seemed to have forgotten.

But that was years ago now. Despite the fact they'd gotten the suspects back under control and had even concluded it had been no one's fault, she seemed to still be hung up on the fact his team blamed her.

Sal wasn't sure she knew she'd been muttering in the car, with her eyes closed.

Now she was more like her boss. By the book, a stickler for the rules. Probably in large part the reason why Victoria continued to dislike her. Or at least was rubbed the wrong way by Allyson and her convictions and attention to procedure.

This was going to be a blow, even being looked at as possibly part of this. Allyson had a good explanation. Any accusation wasn't going to hold water. But it would still linger.

He tugged on her hand, and she walked with him to the car. Sal glanced over at her. "Okay?"

"During any other week you wouldn't need to ask me that."

"Maybe." He pulled the door open for her. "But I'd want to."

She climbed in, frowning at him as she did so. Sal rounded the car. His phone rang, so he climbed in and put it on speaker.

"Alvarez."

"Don't come back to the office."

"Talia?"

"Who did you think it was?" She sighed, exasperated. "Listen, you need to lay low for a few hours until I figure something out. Don't log onto your computer and definitely don't access any work files from your phones. I'm also alerting Daulton and his agents who were with us."

Sal felt like he'd arrived late to a party. "What are you talking about?"

"The drone that opened fire on our office—"

Allyson shifted in her seat. "The one that didn't even break the windows?"

He'd told her the story before she'd fallen asleep.

"Hey. Sanchez. Good to hear your voice." Talia paused for a second. "But yes. While the drone was firing on us, it also hacked our network."

"The hacker is dead." Sal frowned. "You told me that."

Talia's sigh blew against the speaker. "There are other hackers in the world, Sal. Kennowich has obviously hired another one to get into our system. I told Victoria, and she's working out the plan."

"You think she'll do it?"

"The fourth day protocol is kind of nuclear. I'd rather not if we can avoid it."

Allyson said, "The fourth what?"

Sal explained, "It's all based on the story of Lazarus." He paused. "Jesus wept, right? He knew He was going to resurrect his friend, but He still grieved anyway. The heart of God was moved."

Talia said, "This is different, but we're playing off that and have designed a backup plan where we basically pretend we're down for the count. Destroyed. Boo-hoo, Kennowich has won. It's all very sad. But it should throw off his attempts to take us out should we go dark. Then we get the chance to regroup, so we can focus on catching him in the act."

"Huh."

"Which we just might be able to do," Talia said. "Because Kennowich is at a hotel in downtown Seattle."

Sal shook his head. "There's no way that is a coincidence."

"I agree," Talia said, "I'll keep you posted."

"Copy that." Sal hung up and tossed the phone in the cup holder.

As he turned on the engine, he took a minute to let all the pieces settle. Vanessa. Kennowich. Allyson. The gun stores.

Weapons sales. All of it was tied together, and Kennowich held all the strings.

Sal didn't like this at all. He was tempted to go dark and hunt this guy himself. He could go undercover, get Kennowich to trust him. Or sit the guy down and force him to explain what he was up to. Would going rogue be the only way to uncover what was really going on?

He had to make sure no one got hurt.

Allyson squeezed his knee as he drove. "Talia will figure it out."

"Sure." But would it be in time?

"Keys?"

Allyson dug them out of the front pocket. She handed them over, still astounded that her backpack had been in Sal's car the whole time she'd been held captive.

Then she realized what she'd done. "I can open my own front door."

He glanced at her. "I know." Then stepped inside. "Stay here." He even held out a hand, like she'd seen Josh and Dakota do to get Neema to "stay."

Allyson stepped in her apartment after him, glad she'd actually tidied up yesterday. She didn't want to know what Sal would have thought if she'd had clothing draped over the furniture, junk mail on the counter, and dirty cereal bowls in the sink.

Sal emerged from her bedroom a second later.

She set her hand on her hip. "Find anything interesting?"

He didn't react to that. "It's clear."

Oh. That was what he'd been doing. "Thanks."

Sal shook his head, a slight smile on his face. "You're welcome." Then he just stood there.

"Uh… Do you want a drink, or a sandwich or something?"

"I'll get it." He wandered to the refrigerator, but she saw him glance at his watch.

"You don't have to stay if you have somewhere to be."

"It'll keep."

She wandered to the breakfast bar and sat at one of the stools, elbows on the counter, chin in her hands. She exhaled, actually feeling the stress of the last few days bleed off. Not to mention wondering whether she'd left piles of laundry on the bed when she went to work…however many days ago that was.

He turned from the fridge then. Sausage. Bell peppers. Tomatoes that were in desperate need of being put to use. Half an onion she'd put in a storage bag, and a small container of crumbly cheese. "Omelet?"

"How do you feel about Italian?"

"Sure."

She hopped off the stool and came around to retrieve a packet of pasta shells from the cupboard. She set him up with a cutting board and knife. Better to face the fact he'd be a distraction, and she'd end up cutting her finger, and just let him do it.

She set the water to boil for the pasta and got a skillet. Herbs.

"Do you need the cheese?" He shook the container.

She grabbed it. "Always."

Sal barked a laugh. One that made her smile. She stirred. He chopped. When the water boiled, she dropped the pasta shells in.

"From memory, from scratch?"

She glanced at him and shrugged one shoulder. "I like what I like, and I make this regularly. I guess I remember how to do it. Plus, I don't make anything that takes longer than twenty minutes to cook, unless I'm putting it in the oven."

Despite that being a smile-worthy statement, the humor that had been there in his gaze a moment ago was now gone. Allyson turned and leaned the outside of her hip against the counter. "What is it?"

"Kennowich is in town."

Her whole body flinched.

Sal closed the gap between them and touched her cheeks. "He's not going to take you again. He's not even going to touch you."

"Why am I so scared of someone who probably doesn't even know who I am? And he definitely doesn't care enough to target me."

The skin around Sal's eyes flexed. She wondered if he agreed with her, because it seemed like he wasn't sure that was true. "I want to walk up and put a bullet in him for what he did to you."

"You don't catch a guy like this by going in fast and hard; you need finesse."

It went without saying that he wasn't actually going to kill the guy.

"Are you saying I don't have finesse?" He lowered his hands to her shoulders, chuckling.

"Of all the task force members, you're probably the only one who could do something quietly and effectively. The rest of them are more about brute force." Allyson made a face. "Except maybe Victoria." That woman honestly scared her. And that was before she even considered what Victoria might be capable of.

"Are you really okay about Vanessa being dead?"

Allyson touched his sides so he would stay close for longer. "If I wasn't, it's not like I could change what is."

"So you just need to accept reality?"

"I want more answers than I have." She glanced to the side for a moment. "Why did they take me? Why did she call me? Why taunt us with the flash drive, why leave my phone at the robbery?"

"You think he tipped his hand."

"Didn't he?" She shrugged one shoulder. "I mean, we had no idea the gun store robberies were connected to Kennowich until my phone was left there. The phone that the kidnappers took."

His jaw worked side to side. "Maybe I'll ask him instead of shooting him."

Fear ran through her. Like swallowing cold liquid and feeling the sensation all the way to her stomach. "Please don't do anything reckless."

She understood his need to move forward. She didn't like feeling powerless, or helpless. They were cops. That wasn't their natural state.

He grinned and gave her a squeeze before he pulled away and moved to the food. Probably all stuck to the pans by now. "As opposed to what?"

She stirred the skillet. "I think when we wrap up this case, I'm going to take a vacation."

"Anywhere nice?"

"I think I'm going to rent a motor home and drive to Wyoming. I've heard it's nice." She didn't look at him.

"It is."

They settled in to eat, Sal beside her at the breakfast bar. After a few minutes of quiet, he said, "What else do you want, apart from fantastic sausage pasta?"

He thought it was fantastic? She didn't want to damper that, but had to respond to his question, "To catch Kennowich."

"After that."

"A vacation."

"You've already said that." He leaned back in his chair. "What about farther out than that."

"A family." She shrugged. "Though, I can't seem to make something work long term with anyone. If I knew why maybe I'd be able to figure that out."

"The DEA agent?"

How did he know about her ex? "He's back in his hometown now, retired. I seem to have that effect on male federal agents I'm close to. They all seem to want to quit and go home."

His gaze softened.

"Vanessa's father was the closest thing I've had to family in years." Since her father had died when she was a teen. Her mom had passed away not long after she was born. "What about your mom?" She knew all about his father.

"Soon as I left for college, she just…dropped off the map. Didn't call me. I went by a few times, but we just…grew apart I guess? She ended up moving to California." His voice had a layer of gravel to it.

"But you had your dad."

He nodded.

They'd both been blessed with invested, spiritually-strong fathers. "That's what I want for my kids. The kind of father I had, plus a mom who is there." She picked at a piece of pasta with her fork. "Not that you can plan to not die, but…"

He squeezed her hand. "I know what you mean." There was so much promise in his gaze, but she didn't know what to say about it. Possibilities hung in the air, unspoken. She had a good life here, but Allyson wondered if she couldn't move toward something better.

Him.

When this case was done, when he left the task force, could she risk everything on a "maybe"? On the *chance* that this might work?

Allyson wanted to think she was brave, and in a lot of ways she was.

But about this?

She wasn't so sure she had the courage to take that first step.

———

AFTER THEY BOTH FINISHED EATING, Sal rinsed their dishes and added them to the dishwasher. Seeing her yawn several times was what had clinched it. But he still didn't like leaving her unprotected.

She ended up shooing him out the door with a smile.

But not a kiss.

Sal figured she might have been open to the concept. She was also wrung out emotionally and physically—a crazy couple of days. It would have been taking advantage to press for a goodbye kiss tonight.

He had made her promise to call him if she had a nightmare or any other problem.

Sal buckled up and turned, not in the direction of the member's only campsite where he left his Airstream full time. Instead he turned toward downtown and the hotel where Kennowich was checked in.

Two warring thoughts vied for supremacy in his mind. One, could he change Allyson's mind from a motorhome to his Airstream, pulled by his father's truck, for her vacation. And two, what on earth was Kennowich doing in Seattle.

Sal wanted a future. And it was looking clearer that it might be happiest with Allyson in the picture. And a few kids running around on his land. That was the dream he wanted, not the life he lived on the road right now. Despite how he felt about the trailer and the ability to be mobile anytime, it was wearing on him that he was never "home."

And though it would be painful to be back on his father's land, it was also his land. That was the only place he wanted to raise a family.

Sal wanted to get back to it finally. He had thought that his restlessness was just about getting a break and going on vacation, or getting a job somewhere with the same feel as home. But it wasn't. It was about being home. Permanently.

And maybe convincing Allyson to go with him.

Sal turned the corner onto the street where the hotel was located. Why was Kennowich here? The man's business was located in San Francisco, and all over. But not Seattle. And yet, Vanessa had come here. Half his security force was on the run.

Had Kennowich heard that Vanessa showed up here—on the run from him supposedly—and followed in order to retrieve her? Or had he come here for some other, probably nefarious, reason? It was a bold move. And would make it plainer to those surveilling him if he committed an illegal act. The man was most likely here to oversee the sale of those stolen guns.

The only reason the task force thought an operation was in

play was because Vanessa had told them about it. But she'd been playing them. So was there even a supposed threat, one they needed to stop? Or were the robberies something else entirely?

It was way too tempting to go by the hotel and see for himself that Kennowich was really there.

But thinking about Allyson, and what might happen in their future, was a good distraction. He couldn't kill the man, had no cause to arrest him. Aside from walking up and asking straight out what he was up to—destroying the illusion of surprise—there wasn't much Sal could do.

He wanted to be done with this case. Not that he also wanted to be done with the team, but there was a threat and he wanted it over with. In fact, if it wasn't for the bulletproof glass in the office, one or more of them would no doubt already be dead.

But they weren't, and the task force was going to take down Kennowich once and for all. They just needed to figure out what he'd done—or was about to do—that could give them the evidence they needed to make it stick. Could they tie him to Allyson's kidnapping?

Sal pulled up on the opposite side of the street. He'd just put the car in park when his phone rang.

Talia calling.

He swiped to answer it.

"What are you doing?"

"Hello to you, too."

"How was dinner?"

Sal shook his head, even though he was sitting in the car in the dark, and no one could see him.

She tried asking another question. "Is this really what you want?"

"To be sitting here, trying to do surveillance?"

"Is *she* what you want?"

Sal's jaw tightened. "Did anyone ask you that about Mason?"

"You know what I mean. This woman is the reason you got

hurt. She's the reason you're in lingering pain, and I just don't think she's the right choice for you. That's all."

"You don't even know her, not really," he said.

"I know enough."

"Because of what Victoria told you?" he asked. "Ever think that might be a version she wants you to believe?"

"Why would she do that?"

"Why does Victoria do anything?"

"Look, I know she's unorthodox—"

Sal barked a laugh devoid of humor. "There's an understatement."

"I just want you to...count the cost. That's all."

"The cost of being with Allyson?" He twisted in his seat to watch the front doors of the hotel. If he was going to be here, then he might as well actually do surveillance. "Do you think Mason did the same before he got into a relationship with you?"

"What—"

He wasn't sure if he cut her off, or if she just didn't have more to argue with him but he said, "You hacked the Secret Service office. You're part of an off-book task force with a reputation for being apart from normal channels. Some might even say that we're rogues. Mason is a straight-laced Secret Service agent on the fast track to a stellar career. Can he really afford to be linked with an NSA analyst tied up in too many shady things?"

She was quiet for a long time. Long enough he was worried she might be upset. It was hard to tell with women, especially when he couldn't see their faces.

"What I want isn't that dissimilar from the rest of the task force. Only I don't need Allyson to join the team. I actually am looking at—" It was his turn to hesitate. "Retiring."

She gasped.

"I want to go home. I want a family. And it's still early yet, but I think I might want all that with Allyson. She's a good woman. Someone with steady faith, who understands the stresses of this job and the toughness to weather them. Yet still manages a softness about her."

"Wow."

"I would imagine a lot of that is what Mason sees in you. What Josh sees in Dakota, and what Niall sees in Haley."

He heard her inhale a hitched breath.

"Are you crying?"

"No."

"Liar."

"You really like her."

Sal said, "I'm happy for you. I'd like you to be happy for me, no matter what choice I make."

He gave her some time to compose herself, then changed the subject back to work. "Is Kennowich even in the hotel right now?"

"GPS on his phone says so."

"Do I want to know where you got that information?"

She didn't answer that question, and instead said, "Do you want backup? No one else is close by, but I can call someone and get them there to be your number two if you want."

"It's fine. I just want to get a feel for the guy." Unless the situation escalates. "I'd like to see what kind of man this is who seems to be fixated on our team enough to send a long-lost woman on his behalf."

"And a drone."

"Yep."

She said, "I know what kind of man this is. We all do because we've experienced it firsthand."

"You most of all. That's why I'm the one here."

He was going to make this better. Not just for her, but for the rest of them. For the fear and pain they'd been through over the past few weeks…months. As Sal's last case with the task force, he was going to ensure this case they were building against Kennowich brought down the full weight of the law on his shoulders. No way would Sal allow him to get away with what he'd done, and all the people he had hurt.

The front doors of the hotel slid open and Kennowich sauntered out like it was two in the afternoon.

Traffic sped past between them, and Sal lost sight of him for a second. When he got an unobstructed view again, Kennowich had a woman beside him. Her back was to Sal, but she was slender. Blonde hair tied up in a bun.

Kennowich spoke to her, then the woman turned to leave and Sal saw her face.

It was Victoria.

18

———————

"Thank you for coming." The FBI agent had a soft smile, flanked by laugh lines. Probably from time spent with his grandchildren. "I'm Special Agent Miller."

She shook his hand. "Sanchez."

As he turned to lead the way, Allyson saw a slight limp in his gait. He glanced back over his shoulder. "If you'll come with me. This won't take long."

She followed him to the conference room where they were going to take her statement about why her phone was found in the rental van. The order to report this morning to this specific agent had been in her email inbox when she woke up.

She hadn't even had time to get a new phone, so she brought her laptop here with her just in case she got the chance to check in.

Miller tugged out a high-backed, leather-looking chair, then took another. She sat, and he placed a file on the table as he did the same. On top was a plastic evidence bag.

While he got settled, she said, "Is there any update on Assistant Director Welvern?"

Miller's boss had been shot a matter of days ago, outside Talia and Haley's apartment. Allyson didn't recall if she'd heard how bad it was, but the man had been in the hospital for longer than she'd have thought he'd be if it wasn't serious.

It was clearly serious.

"We're anticipating his recovery." Miller smiled, polite but the lack of warmth was evident. What was that about?

Before she could respond he slid the evidence bag across the table and turned on a recording device that he set between them. "Agent Sanchez, can you please confirm whether or not this is your phone?"

"Yes. That's mine." She motioned to it. "May I?"

When he nodded, she touched the screen. It illuminated her lock-screen image, a tent in the woods under the Northern Lights.

Now that she looked at it, she had to wonder whys she'd chosen that picture. She'd never been camping. As a kid, they'd always stayed in her dad's cabin. Was it just the lure of something that sounded restful, peaceful, or beautiful when the rest of her life hadn't been? She'd been drawn to the idea of that level of freedom, certainly. Like renting a motorhome and just…driving. Of course she'd have to stick to the contracted number of miles so as to not get charged extra for going too far.

"That's your phone?"

She nodded.

"For the recording, please."

"Yes, that's my phone."

And she had more to ponder later, when she was back at home and not so exhausted this time.

She wanted peace. She wanted to love and be loved, probably more than anything else right now. Maybe even more than her career.

She'd been going through the motions for years, waiting for life to happen to her. Waiting for Vanessa to show up again. Waiting for a relationship to come along.

Maybe she needed to go out and get what she wanted. To seize that day, and the rest of it.

The rest of her life.

"This cell phone was found in the cab of a van stolen from a chain rental lot. It was used to commit a robbery that appears to be one in a string of several." He looked up from his files. "Any idea how that could be?"

Allyson explained the whole story about Vanessa and the kidnapping, the task force's investigation into Kennowich. "The last time I had my phone, that I'm aware of, is at the park. Right before I was stunned and thrown in a van. As far as I can tell there are two explanations: Either the men who kidnapped me are also the gun store thieves, or I dropped my phone in the park and the thief somehow found it and then left it in the van."

"We'll come back to that in a minute." Miller made a note in his file. "Who is able to corroborate your statement about the kidnapping?"

A dead woman, for one. For two, "The agents of the Northwest Counter-Terrorism Task Force. And the FBI agents who showed up at the end, after Dakota was shot at."

Miller should be able to see something had happened to her. There were red marks on her wrists, and a host of other visible bruising. Why did her story need to be corroborated? "The agents that showed up at the house are out looking for the shooter who killed Vanessa, right?"

"I'd have to look into that." He pulled his phone over and typed on the screen, asking her for the address. She gave him as much detail as she remembered about the location. How would she know what street it was on without going online to that Home's For Sale website and looking up the address like she looked up anyone's address?

Allyson blew out a breath and tried to rein in her thoughts, and her frustration. "The full report should be with the task force."

"Let's table discussion about this kidnapping for a second in order to get back to the robberies." Miller sat back in his chair. "Your team at the ATF is investigating these incidents?"

She nodded, then remembered the recording. "Yes. Are they

agents from this office who showed up at the house where I was held?"

He blinked, a blank look. "I'm not aware of that. This is a substantially-sized FBI office."

"Okay." What was she supposed to say to that? "All of this is tied together. The robberies, Kennowich, and Vanessa."

Maybe it was up to her to figure it out. But how could she do that, when they hadn't any luck catching Kennowich doing something illegal? Could they uncover who was behind the drone attack? Maybe charges could be brought for that.

Allyson continued, "If you'd like confirmation, I'm sure Victoria Bramlyn could answer any further questions you might have."

Miller knew who she was, judging by his reaction. "I've always wondered why a state department director who doesn't work in any of the visible channels is the head of a task force."

Allyson shrugged. "I have no idea how that came about. Maybe she can tell you."

"A little above my pay grade, I'm afraid."

She'd thought their two offices were interlinked more than this —that they worked together often. Was this not the case? She and Sal had met fake FBI agents, and now here was one with such a singular focus that he had no idea what was going on outside of that. Maybe he really only needed her statement, and nothing else would come of this.

"It's all connected."

"All I know," Miller said, "is that the four robberies we've been asked to investigate are connected."

"Four?"

"And now they involve you."

Four? That is the first she was hearing of there being four robberies. Through the window she spotted Sal, standing, talking to another of the agents.

"Special Agent Sanchez!"

She was already out the door and halfway to him when she heard Miller scramble to follow. "There were four robberies?"

Sal cut off what he was saying to the agent and turned to her. "What?"

"Gun store robberies." She wasn't going to repeat herself anymore. Then she caught the look on his face. "What is it?"

"I'll tell you later."

Sal and the other FBI agent walked off, heading to Welvern's office where the door and blinds were both closed.

Something was going on, but still she couldn't help wonder if she'd come on too strongly. After all, she basically insinuated she'd follow him to Wyoming.

She hadn't changed her mind, but did he feel the same? She was ready for more than just a simple kiss and dreaming—separately—about their futures.

————

SAL COULDN'T EVEN THINK about Allyson or all she was going through right now. He wanted to help, but not since he'd seen Victoria shake that guy's hand. The memory of his boss with Kennowich was burned in his brain.

Sal asked the FBI agent about Welvern and how he was doing.

"What is up with you guys asking about him?"

"He's a good guy, and the task force was there when he got hurt."

"That's right." The agent nodded.

Sal didn't tell the acting assistant director that Welvern had done them a lot of favors the past few months. Welvern had backed them up plenty of times. Not to mention that he clearly had something more than a friendship going on with Victoria.

But right now Welvern was in the hospital, and Victoria was shaking the hand of the man they were trying to catch.

The acting assistant director took Sal's statement about the kidnapping and what he knew about Allyson's phone having been found in the van. A few minutes later the agent had him pause. "Clarify for me how the NSA agent on your task force was able to ascertain this man's connection to the kidnappers." He leaned back in his chair. "After all, the man was in a hotel room. Its sheer luck that had him leaving there in his truck in time for you to follow him to the same house where Special Agent Sanchez was being held."

Sal shrugged. "I prefer to call it providence."

"Does that happen to you a lot?"

He stayed quiet for a minute. It wasn't like he manufactured leads out of nowhere, and he wasn't spinning a tale. "There's a reason I was in my car doing surveillance while Talia was at the office on her computer. I just don't understand all that stuff. She's tried to explain how it works, but I'd need a degree to grasp it." He shrugged. "I'm not wired that way."

"US Marshals, in my experience, have their own individual skill sets. It's what characterizes that agency."

Sal nodded, pretty sure that might have been a compliment.

"And I've also found they don't readily admit to having the wool pulled over their eyes."

"I'm not ignorant of what's going on around me." How could he be? He'd seen Victoria with his own eyes. "Just trying to make sense of it."

The acting assistant director nodded slowly, his assessing gaze unwavering.

Sal continued on with his statement. What he saw, and what the two men at the house spoke about. Relief settled over him once again as he recalled what had happened. The realization Ally wasn't there and having to race after her. Peter Tines. Vanessa. Both were dead now.

"Do you think Allyson was a target in all this?"

Sal considered the question.

The FBI agent said, "After all, they're implicating her in the robberies now."

"If that's their intention, they've done it poorly. No one will believe she was part of it."

"We might have if your team hadn't retrieved her so quickly," the agent pointed out. "Not to mention their intention was likely to keep that Vanessa woman's secret from being revealed at that point."

It had only come out because of Peter's death.

"She was devastated that her friend betrayed her. Being used on top of also being lied to is something she'll have to learn how to move on from." Not to mention learning to trust her own judgment again.

The FBI agent wasn't fooled by Sal's loose tone. He sat back in his chair and studied Sal.

With that one comment he'd revealed his personal stake in this. He cared about her, much more than the simple concern of one colleague for another. Sal was concerned with what happened to her. Especially if Kennowich's intention was to single her out.

Sal got them back on the point. "Whatever it is, this definitely doesn't have to do with the robberies. At least not in its entirety."

"You think there's a larger plan at work?"

"It's the only thing that makes sense." Especially considering the drone attack—both with bullets and the simultaneous cyber breach. "Agent Sanchez is a good cop. I'm sure if there's anything she can do, she'll help. Same for my team."

"Noted, and appreciated." The acting assistant director shook his hand, and walked Sal back to the main office.

Allyson strode to meet him in the middle.

"You're still here?"

"You said you wanted to talk."

Sal was about to suggest they go somewhere else when the elevator doors opened behind her and a familiar face walked out.

Allyson must have read his expression. She spun around, reaching for her weapon as she moved. She didn't draw it though.

Neither did he, though his fingers reached for it.

"Whoa. Easy." The acting assistant director strode up to stand by them as Kennowich stopped and looked around.

An older agent approached him.

"I'm here to speak with the person in charge of this office."

Sal reached for his phone and fired off a quick text to Talia, telling her Kennowich was there, asking if they should clone his phone.

Whether they did or not, Sal wanted to be in the room when Kennowich had this conversation with the acting assistant director.

Talia's reply came quickly.

TURN ON YOUR BLUETOOTH.

As soon as he did, his phone blacked out. Then it started acting weird.

The man who'd interviewed Sal introduced himself to Kennowich, and they shook hands. "Let's talk in my office."

Only it wasn't his office, it was Welvern's. Was he gunning for his boss's job while the man was in the hospital? He was recovering from a gunshot wound, sustained by sniper fire. Maybe this guy assumed Welvern wasn't going to come back at all.

"Thank you." Even Kennowich's voice dripped wealth. The San Francisco businessman dressed in accordance with his net worth. Shined shoes that looked like Italian leather. A power suit. A silk tie and folded handkerchief sticking out of the breast pocket. He wore a gold ring on his right pinkie finger, some kind of stone in the center of the signet.

What on earth had he been talking to Victoria about?

Sal strode over. "I'd like to be present."

Maybe that conversation last night was what brought him here this morning. If it was, then Sal wanted to know everything this man was going to say about Victoria.

Kennowich flinched and spun to face Sal. He reared back, like Sal was bearing down on him, almost tripping over his fancy shoes.

Sal stopped short of the two men.

"Sir?" The acting assistant director stepped between them, his body turned so he could glance between Sal and Kennowich, now pale faced. "If you'd take a step back, Deputy Alvarez."

Sal did so, just because it might get him in the room. Meanwhile, Kennowich continued to act like Sal was a threat to him.

Sal said, "Is there something I should know?"

"I'll ascertain that." The FBI agent waved him away toward the elevator. "Thank you, Deputy." He led Kennowich to his office, dismissing Sal.

"I'm sorry," he heard Kennowich say. "It's just that the death of my employee has hit me so very hard." He even glanced over his shoulder to look at Allyson. "And there are a group of federal agents harassing me and my business."

Sal felt his eyebrows rise. His security guys abducted Allyson, but *they* were the ones harassing him? He heard Allyson's intake of breath and saw out the corner of his eye that she had moved to storm after them.

Sal spun. He banded an arm around her waist and caught her to him, face to face. "Don't." He whispered the word in her ear. "Let the FBI do their jobs."

"You really trust these guys?"

"I'm hoping Talia got us what we need for right now."

His phone buzzed.

No, go. Someone is already accessing his phone.

"Great." Sal shook his head. "We have nothing."

19

———————

"You know that invading his personal device would be completely illegal, right?"

Sal shrugged as he followed her off the elevator outside the task force office. "We skirt a lot of gray areas. Victoria smooths over the ruffled feathers, if there are any. Besides, we didn't get into Kennowich's phone."

She shot him a look.

"We have an arrangement that we established with a US attorney after we saved his daughter from human traffickers." He shrugged like it had been no big deal, even though the look in his eyes said otherwise. "That gives us the leeway we wouldn't have otherwise, and as recompense for his help, we prove it was a good bargain for him to make—just one look at our results shows that. Our conviction rate vs. that of other agencies? It's sky high."

Allyson wasn't sure what to make of that, considering it sounded like an under-the-table deal had been made.

"I was surprised you didn't slap me back there." A small grin curled up the corners of his lips. "I thought you were going to fight me to Kennowich."

"I thought about it." She stood to the side while he punched in the code. "The man *kidnapped* me." He pulled the door open and she followed him in, still speaking. "I wanted to scratch his eyes out just for that. I wasn't even thinking about the rest of it."

Haley blinked. "Remind me not to get on your bad side." She turned back to her computer monitor, a tiny smile on her face.

Talia chuckled. "Right? Who knew." She glanced sideways at Allyson. "Our friendly neighborhood ATF agent has hidden depths."

Allyson stopped in the waiting area and folded her arms. "Don't kidnap me and we won't have a problem."

"Yeah…" Dakota said from her seat at her desk. "We're not going to make that promise."

Because they might not be able to keep it? Allyson wanted to actually smile at her, but that was the last thing she would give Dakota. The woman might take it as an offer of friendship when Allyson much preferred this antagonistic push and pull. It gave her something to focus on instead of the crushing grief of betrayal and the lingering fear from the abduction.

"At least tell me you guys got *something* from hacking Kennowich's phone."

"It wasn't a hack," Talia countered. "I just copied everything on there since I couldn't clone his device."

Sal muttered something about not understanding women, and moved to his own desk. "Who else was in there?"

"No way to tell," Talia said.

Allyson dragged a chair over from the waiting area and sat in the center of the aisle between all their desks. "What about the drone? Is there a way to prove that attack was Kennowich?"

Talia shrugged. "I'm not convinced it was him. At least not by what I'm seeing. Still, the fact he could get past our firewall at *all* means he hired someone serious to attack us. Someone maybe even better than me."

Haley gasped.

Dakota chuckled, then said, "Yeah, right."

Allyson said, "What about the hunt for the sniper?"

Dakota sobered. "The FBI hasn't found him yet—or the friend Sal tied up."

"So we've two men in the wind," Allyson said. "No evidence as to where they've gone, and now Kennowich is complaining to the FBI about you guys. Is that everything?"

"We're aware we need more leads." Haley shifted in her chair.

"I'm just processing aloud." Allyson raised both hands and showed Haley her palms. "Making sure I've got it all straight in my head."

Talia rolled her chair to the edge of her desk and held out a cell phone. "New one, for you. All your contacts and everything from your old phone has been copied over."

"Do I want to know how you did that?"

"Don't ask, don't tell. Isn't that how it is?"

"Not as far as I know."

Talia laughed and slid her chair back. "Fair enough." She tapped a few keys on her computer. "Kennowich's phone has mostly business stuff on it. If I had to guess, I'd say it's 'too' clean. Like it's been sanitized, just in case we got our hands on it. There's nothing incriminating to find unless you count his taste in music." She shuddered.

"So he knew we would look."

"We?"

Allyson ignored Dakota's question. "Which means he knows we're expecting him to do something."

"Which means," Haley interjected, "that he's probably not going to do anything."

Dakota said, "Or what he's planning is so covered no one will ever be able to trace it back to him."

"That's what I don't get about my phone." She turned to look at Sal, who had his head in his hand, watching her. How long had he been doing that? "Why leave it in that van? It connects the two things."

"And leaves us with the stolen weapons, no other ties to Kennowich, and something that may or may not be in the works."

She nodded, not liking how subdued he seemed. He was really bothered by the turn of events on this case, as though it hit him harder than he'd expected.

Allyson logged on to her work server from the phone Talia had given her, even though that probably gave the woman a back door into the ATF's computer system. She pulled up the files for every theft—a copy of which had been provided to the FBI so they could continue the investigation. It would likely come back on her that she'd accessed them, but she made a note in the file log that she was reading over the information in case anyone called her on it.

She had nothing to hide.

If the thieves had covered their tracks thus far, that meant they knew what they were doing. Maybe they even had a way to sell the guns under the table. A buyer waiting? Vanessa had mentioned a threat, but it could just be the weapons sales. And yet, why would Kennowich, a man rich from his pharmaceutical company, want to get in the middle of petty weapons sales?

It made no sense. Unless he was broke or something, and looking for a quick score.

"What about Kennowich's financials?" she asked Talia.

"That's what I'm looking at," Haley said. "And Niall went to California to do some boots-on-the-ground work. We're trying to figure out if it's all above board. There are a lot of subsidiaries and other parts of his business. It's hard to straighten it all out, but it doesn't look good. He seems to not have a lot of net worth, despite everything going on. He's leveraged to the teeth and behind on payments right now."

So he could be broke. They just didn't know for certain yet if that was why he'd opted to rob gun stores. She chuckled at the idea the smug rich guy was actually bankrupt. There was some satisfaction in that thought. Sal glanced over at her, and they shared a smile.

"Guess you had to be there," Dakota muttered.

Allyson looked around. No one else was smiling at them. She wasn't part of their team, and she wouldn't ever be. She had a connection with Sal, and that was it. She was only there now because she'd been dragged into their case by Vanessa.

These people were so confident in how they all felt about each other that they could bicker because it didn't change that.

It wasn't that the ATF had no camaraderie. It just had the normal amount. They were work friends who hung out on occasion after hours.

She probably needed some non-work friends, like at a book club. But when she'd done that before, they only wanted to read thrillers that sounded like overly-sensational versions of her day job. Or women's fiction that made her want to fall asleep.

Allyson shifted in the chair to get comfortable for what would probably be an hour of reading case notes.

Maybe Kennowich would get an incriminating call. They could surveil him and see where he went. Who he met with.

Then there was that exchange earlier with Sal. How he said he had things to tell her, but still hadn't.

Allyson's email buzzed a notification on her new phone, along with an awful chime. She flinched, thinking she heard Dakota chuckle.

She read the email. "One of the guns stolen during the first gun store robbery was used in a shooting last night. They ran the bullet through our system and got a hit that connected the two. The guy rolled over on his friends."

Sal said, "The source of the stolen weapons?"

She stood. "The ATF is going to go round up the buyers."

THERE WAS a buzz in the air at the ATF office that Sal knew well. The second the elevator doors slid open, he dropped her hand and stepped into the hum of activity.

Not just because it would become clear something was happening. They weren't dumb. They'd probably figured it out. However, she didn't need her coworkers seeing her holding hands with him. There had been enough of that ribbing between the women at his office, bantering with Allyson while they worked on the case.

Daulton caught sight of them. "You're not here."

Allyson raised both hands. "I got the email. Did you bring them in?"

"Just the one guy." Daulton motioned to the hallway at the end of the open plan office. Sal spotted a handcuffed suspect getting walked to where he knew the interrogation rooms were.

"Who is he?"

"Local gangbanger." Daulton looked down at the tablet he held in one hand. "Couple of stints for breaking and entering. A grand theft auto charge from when he was a kid."

"So he's hooked onto a crew that's organized."

"Looks like it."

Allyson said, "And we didn't give this to the FBI?"

"We don't know if it's related yet." He gave her a pointed look.

Allyson answered with a short nod.

The ATF wasn't going to hand this guy over to the FBI until they knew for sure his arrest was connected to the gun store robberies. They wanted to hand over proof along with the suspect.

"Which means you are *not* here."

"Copy that." She turned to Sal. "Coffee?"

"Yes, please." Sal watched her go.

"If this goes on much longer, she'll have to be permanently attached to that task force of yours."

He turned back to Daulton. "I'm not sure that's a job she would take."

"I'm sure you'll think of something."

"You wanna get rid of Agent Sanchez?"

Daulton gave a short shake of his head. "I never thought that girl belonged here. Don't get me wrong, she's a great agent. It just seems like she should be doing…more than what we do." He shook his head again. "I'm not explaining it right."

Sal waved him off. "I think I know what you mean."

He'd seen something in Allyson as well. An indication that she didn't belong here. Not in an exclusionary way. It was more like she could have…better than this. He'd just never thought that involved him before.

Did it now?

"I'll let you guys listen in." Daulton wandered off.

Allyson came back with two full mugs of coffee, and they headed to the viewing room where they'd be able to hear the suspected gun thief being questioned.

"… the streets." The young man's face was smooth, but his eyes were years older than his skin. A hard life, one that started young.

Sal figured he'd shudder if he heard about all the places this man had been. All the things he'd seen, and done.

Carl was the interviewing agent. "You got the guns from who?"

"A guy." The young man flashed white teeth. "I didn't get his business card."

Carl pushed a photo across the table. "Know this guy?"

The young man peered at it. "Sure, I think he's friends with my cousin."

"I guess we'll have to pay your cousin a visit, then. Let him know you shot his friend. Twice. And then left his body behind a dumpster."

The young man swallowed. "Maybe it isn't him."

Carl said nothing.

"It was self defense. He was gonna kill me. My lawyer's gonna prove it."

Carl didn't offer to call the young man's lawyer, and the young man didn't ask. "Where were you two nights ago, around eleven p.m.?"

"With my girl."

"That something she can confirm for us? Assuming she wasn't with *you* perpetrating a robbery on that gun store on the corner of Allumbaugh and Front Street."

The young man worked his mouth back and forth. "You gonna pin that on me?"

"That and three other jobs. After all, it's where that gun came from."

He started to shake his head. "Nah, I didn'a have nothin' to do with any'a that."

"Sure?" Carl sat back in his chair.

"You think I don't know what I did?"

"It's advisable that you do. That would be my suggestion." Carl paused. "Unless, of course, you didn't knock over those gun stores. But maybe you know who did?"

"You think I'm gonna rat someone out?"

"I think you don't want a life sentence that has you gasping for free air until you're sixty. You want to be some crusty old guy just out of prison, trying to get his life back with nothing to show for it but two sleeves of prison tattoos and a bunch of scars you don't want to talk about?"

"I ain't scared of prison."

"Different this time." Carl let that sink in. "A lot different. You're an adult, for one."

"Yeah, but I ain't a rat."

"So you got on a crew all about the smash and grab and hit a few gun stores. Probably just wanted to keep some of the merch for yourself, right? Couldn't help it. Sticky fingers."

A short while later the guy admitted he at least knew the crew, though he seemed to be scared of them. It didn't take long after that for Carl to get him to give up an address where they might find some of the guns. The murder he'd committed wasn't part of the robbery scheme, but he'd used one of the stolen weapons anyway.

"If this pans out, and we find who is behind the robberies," Carl said. "Then we might be able to talk to the judge. See what we can do about the fact you have an outstanding warrant on a domestic violence charge."

"That's bogus. My girl freaked out and attacked me and I was just defending myself."

Carl flipped the file shut. "The offer still stands nonetheless."

"Doesn't matter." Fear flashed across the young man's face. "I ain't goin' nowhere near those guys."

Carl tried to get more, but the kid shut down. He gave Carl only the information as to where the guys he'd bought the gun from hung out. Whether the weapon had been lifted from the batch of stolen guns, or given to him, they didn't wait around in the interrogation room to find out.

The agents in the office got a warrant to search the house expedited from the judge. While they were waiting, they put together the operation.

Daulton turned to Allyson. "An operation that you are not authorized to be part of."

She didn't look happy, but she also didn't have much leverage to argue with his order.

Two hours later, Sal was at the back of the group of federal agents when the lead man pounded on the front door.

"Police with a warrant! Open up!"

No one came to the door.

The man at the front blew a small charge, enough to break the lock, and then kicked the door the rest of the way in.

The living room and kitchen were full of people, men and women in various states of dress, all on the move. Drug paraphernalia littered every available surface.

Chaos reigned. Running. Talking. Shouted orders. Pleading voices.

A young woman tried to run past Sal. Skimpy clothing, no shoes. Curled hair that was probably clean a week ago.

He ordered her to halt, but she kept going. At the last second he saw her arm shift. Then the flash of a knife.

"Stop!"

She didn't.

The knife sank into the skin between his belt, and the bottom of his protective vest.

Sal collapsed just as the woman ran out of the front door.

20

———————

Allyson saw the woman land on the front step and try to make a run for it. The bloody knife she held wasn't a good sign.

"Drop it!" She aimed her gun on the woman.

But the woman didn't stop. Her eyes were glazed now. Allyson braced her weight, fully at liberty to shoot the woman if she tried to swipe that knife at her. Acting first, she grabbed the wrist and squeezed hard. She used her grip as leverage and flipped the woman over her shoulder. She landed on the grass.

Breath expelled from the woman's lungs and she let go of the knife. Allyson flipped her to her stomach and put cuffs on her.

"I need a medic!"

She looked back down the hall inside the house, where Carl now stood. "We have an agent down." He yelled so loudly into his radio, the whole area could hear him as he carried Sal from the house.

She ran to him, bracing some of Sal's weight against her even though it made her head pound.

Four cars screeched up to the curb and doors slammed. Dakota. Josh. Even Talia and Haley, followed by a Secret Service agent…a whole group of them.

They ran over. Dakota tried to take Sal from her, but Allyson didn't let her.

"Let me see him," Josh reached for Sal.

Carl said, "Let us lay him down." Through her earphones, she heard a call come through the radio, but it was Carl who said, "Ambulance is two minutes out."

Sal's head lolled back on the grass.

Dakota jabbed her shoulder. That was when she realized she was breathing hard, seeing spots at the end of her vision. She grabbed Dakota's fingers before she could shove at her again, and pushed them away.

"Back up."

Allyson didn't move.

"Let me *see* him."

Lord. It was bad. Blood seeped from the wound in his side. How deep had the blade gone?

She was so distracted by the sight of it, she didn't realize Dakota was moving her until Allyson had already been dragged to her feet and shoved out of the way.

She caught Dakota's elbow.

The Homeland agent spun and got in her face. "What?"

Allyson reared back, not sure why they were fighting. She was trying to help Sal. Wasn't Dakota also doing the same thing?

She opened her mouth to say…she didn't know what. Didn't matter, because Dakota got in her face. "You dragged him into this."

"He got stabbed!" Like that was her fault?

"You think I can't see that?" Dakota shoved at Allyson's shoulder.

Her head swam, but she forced herself to remain upright.

Talia appeared by Dakota's side. Then Haley.

"What happened?"

Allyson shook her head. "That woman." She pointed to the handcuffed lady Carl now dragged away to a car, and a huddle of agents. More agents spilled from the house, walking out hand-cuffed men and women.

Crime was equal opportunity.

But would they find guns in the house? Or something to link all this to Kennowich?

That seemed farfetched. And probably… "A waste of time."

"What did you say?" Dakota closed in. As though she hadn't been close enough already. "This is *your* fault. Just like last time, and now it's happened all over again."

She motioned with an outstretched arm at the handcuffed woman. "*She* stabbed him!"

Talia set her hands on her hips. "He was only here because of *you*."

Now both of them were ganging up on her. Allyson glanced at Haley. Her gaze was a little more assessing, where the other two were reacting based on their emotions. Getting in her face when she should be helping with Sal's wound. Holding his hand.

"You need to put pressure on it."

Josh looked up at her.

Dakota moved between them. On the offensive, because that was the way she'd been trained. To have a command presence at all times, in all situations. "They've got this. What you need to do—"

"Dakota." Josh's voice cut across her tirade. "What Sal needs right now is for all of you to calm down."

The Secret Service agent stepped forward. "We all know you're scared for Sal. But calm is what's needed right now." Geez, up close the guy was huge. And super cute. His caramel eyes glinted, he turned to Talia. His gaze softened with affection.

Josh finished, "Not all of you ganging up on the woman Sal cares about."

Dakota huffed.

Allyson said, "This is happening whether you like it or not."

"Just because you know we don't like it?"

"No." Allyson shook her head. "You know Sal. How can you *not* know why I have feelings for him?" She figured it was remarkable that one of them hadn't fallen for him a long time ago. But then, the men they were in love with seemed their perfect matches. The calm to their fire. The steadiness and strength they relied on.

She could have that with Sal, and she hoped they would, but they were still trying to figure it all out.

Allyson's energy ebbed. She ran her hands down her face. "Look, I know you care about him."

The women all started to talk.

"Do I have to tell you all to shut up?" Allyson asked. "Because I will."

Dakota pressed her lips together. Talia huffed this time. Haley looked vaguely amused.

Allyson said, "You care about him, but so do I. And we're *all* worried."

The EMTs raced over from their ambulance, and Josh explained what had happened. After they hauled Sal away, Josh came over to them. "He needs to go to the hospital so they can see the extent of the damage and get him stitched up."

Dakota shot her a scathing look. "If something serious happens to him, it'll be your fault just like it was before."

"We all know the risks of the job. Do you think Sal doesn't?" Allyson paused for a second. "Or that he even blames me in the least for what happened at the courthouse?"

Haley said, "I figure Sal would rather be doing this than anything else. Even with the risks."

"That's not true." Allyson didn't want to be the one to point it out to them. She didn't want to tell them that he'd rather be on his mountain, or that he was ready to quit the team and leave. Sal would tell his team when the time was right. "You're all just scared for him."

Dakota folded her arms. Josh slung one arm across her shoulder, pulled her to his side and kissed her forehead.

"We're not enemies," Allyson said. "Despite the fact you seem to think we should be."

"Your problems got him hurt."

"I'm not going to be your easy target just because you feel Sal pulling away and you want to blame me." She barely got the last word out before she had to take a breath. Her head was pounding.

Haley said, "Are you okay?"

Dakota glanced between them. "Sal is the one who's hurt."

She shut her eyes. He'd looked so pale. Was he going to die? Such a dumb way for a man like him to be killed. Some stupid woman with a knife, and he hadn't spent time on his mountain like he so desperately wanted.

And despite her rebuttal to Dakota's accusations, she *would* feel as though it was all her fault.

"Sanchez!"

She spun to find Daulton making his way to her. "Go home. You look awful."

Dakota snorted.

"I'll probably go to the hospital."

She got to the curb before realizing Sal had the keys to the car.

"Need a ride?"

She turned to see Haley approach. "Sure."

Haley beeped the locks to an SUV behind Sal's car. "Let's go."

———

At least he had his pants on. Sal was just missing a shirt when Dakota flung the door open and strode in. She saw the white bandage, low on his left side, and pulled up short. She looked like she was about to faint.

Sal blinked and looked at the ceiling. "I'll be out of here before you know it."

"Sure," Dakota said, arms crossed and chin lifted. For any other woman, that was a solid, hands-on-the-hips death glare, but she was way too much of a cop for that. "And then weeks of pain while your stomach muscles heal. You're just lucky it didn't nick anything vital."

"It wasn't luck." He looked around for his shirt.

"You know what I mean."

"Do I?" He watched her eyes fill with tears. "Go. Find Josh." How else would she feel better?

Instead of doing that, Dakota turned and sat on the edge of the bed. She hung her head, her back to him. He watched her torso expand as she sucked in a full breath and pushed it out. Finally she looked at him. "You almost died."

"I'm not sure that's true."

"I was horrible to her."

That probably was true.

"Oh, God. You agree." Dakota brushed hair off her face. "She'll hate me forever, and then I'll be your kids' godmother and it'll be super weird because they'll *know* we don't get along."

"Did I miss something while the doctor was stitching me up?"

"She's halfway in love with you."

He froze, having found his shirt on the chair in the corner, then glanced at her. "Ally?"

Dakota rolled her eyes. "Who else would I be talking about?"

She was in love with him? Even halfway was good. He just had to get out of here and go find her. Or was she outside, in the hallway? He didn't put it past Dakota to shut everyone else out and be the first to see him.

"Are you going to marry her?"

Sal scooted to the edge of the bed and tried to distract her so that she wouldn't notice he felt ready to pass out. "Will you stand up at the wedding and object?"

Dakota narrowed her eyes, a gleam of mischief there. "Should I?"

Someone knocked on the door, and this time he got the chance to say, "I'm not decent," before they barged in. Dakota was in here, so unless it was Josh, there would be questions to answer. "Hand me my shirt." He waved at it.

As soon as he was mobile, he needed to find out what the hospital staff had done with his phone.

She handed him the shirt. "Are you going to go after her?"

He slid his arms in and then paused before tucking it over his head. "She isn't outside? Also, why would I need to 'go after her,' Dakota?"

A guilty expression washed over her face. "Well…"

"You guys shut her out."

"She got you hurt. Again."

"All of you need to let that go."

"But you're our 'Sal'. How can we do that?"

He pulled his shirt the rest of the way on, not sure how to even begin to answer that. "Where is she?"

Dakota sighed. "You're not going to let me be their godmother are you?"

The door opened and Victoria strode in. "Good. You're dressed."

He stood. The world swayed, but he planted a hand on the bed until the sensation passed. The skin around the stitches tugged a little, but with the medication they'd given him, it didn't hurt much. He was just aware of it.

Victoria handed him a bottled water.

He downed the whole thing. "Where's Allyson?" Sal tossed the bottle at the trash can. He also needed his shoes.

"I'd have thought you'd want to know the outcome of the raid, as well as the movement on the FBI and ATF's investigations. The ones that aren't our case." Her voice had a tone he understood.

"Doesn't mean I can't help if I'm able." And he had, only it had gotten him hurt. "This was my choice."

Kind of like her meeting with Kennowich.

Sal wanted to believe it had been above board. But if it had been, then Talia would know about it. She tracked all of their phones, and she hadn't said one word about a meeting between Kennowich and Victoria. Or an operation. Which meant Talia didn't know.

So the boss didn't have an above-board reason for meeting with Kennowich.

The only alternative was that it had been a fishing expedition. Maybe Victoria hadn't mentioned it because she hadn't been certain she could get anything useful. And when it failed—he'd have heard if the outcome was otherwise—she kept it quiet that she'd tried.

He held her gaze long enough she figured it out. He didn't know how, but he'd long thought there had to have been some spy work in her past.

Victoria gave him an infinitesimal shake of her head.

"What just happened?"

Sal glanced at Dakota. "Nothing. Where's Allyson?"

He really needed her to explain to him what had happened with the team and Allyson while he'd been injured and unconscious. Something between the house when he'd gotten hurt, and now.

He said, "Last time I didn't know where she was, it was because she'd been kidnapped. So cut me some slack and *explain*."

Dakota made a face.

"What is it with you and her?" he asked. "She's a good cop, and my friend."

Victoria said, "She's an easy target?"

"That's probably not something you want to admit."

"This job is stressful," Dakota said. "We have to bleed off the tension somehow."

"By picking on Allyson?"

"We're sorry, okay?" Dakota's voice was a high whine.

"Wow, way to convince me you actually feel bad."

Victoria wasn't about to apologize. "I heard that when you got hurt she responded by being even more anal than normal."

Sal glanced at her. "Because you're maverick, and she's a

stickler for the rules?" Or just procedure in general. *Like not telling your teammates that you're meeting with the source of the threat.*

"Rules aren't what keep people safe," Victoria said. "Things are almost never black and white."

"I don't agree," he countered. "You've played things loose before, and the situation erupted. People got hurt. It's just a fact of life that things go wrong. You can't place the blame on someone who was just doing their job, it's not right."

Victoria couldn't argue with that. Or she just didn't bother.

Sal said, "I need to go."

"Because you're going to find her?"

He turned to Victoria. "Isn't that why I'm here? It's personal this time."

"It's always personal with you." Before he could object, she continued, "It's because you care. That's why you're such a good marshal. You understand the value of family, and you needed one. This team needed a patriarch, and that's you."

"Family doesn't lie to each other."

Dakota said, "What's he talking about?"

Victoria ignored her. "Friends *always* need love and support from each other. This could be more like a family who gets together on the holidays, right?"

"So you can send a card with a hundred dollars in it instead of showing up?"

"I'd only not be showing up because you wouldn't want me there."

Dakota glanced between them. "What is she talking about?"

Victoria shook her head. "Allyson Sanchez is really your choice?"

"My choice is just that," he said. "*My* choice. Like going back to my mountain and actually having a life. Being with a woman I respect and who I'm already in love with."

The door opened again and three additional people spilled in. Haley, Josh, and Talia.

"I just got a notification." Talia held up her phone. "The task force is being implicated in a huge weapons sale. It makes it look like we're the ones who took those guns and set the whole thing up —that we were just trying to incriminate Kennowich to throw everyone off."

"How?"

"That's the information coming in from the people who were picked up at the house raid. They're all pointing at us as the ones behind it all."

And Allyson's phone had been left in that rental van. Which meant she would be accused along with the rest of them.

Talia's face paled. "The FBI is about to show up here and at the office. They've already got a warrant to go through everything, and they're looking for us. We're going to be arrested."

21

Allyson kicked the door to her apartment shut behind her and dumped her backpack on the floor of the hall. It felt like days since she'd been here, even though it was just hours ago.

She got some water at the sink, guzzled the whole glass and set it down. She warmed up leftovers from days ago that was probably ready to be thrown out.

While it heated in the microwave, she reached for her phone in her back pocket, remembering almost instantly it was not hers.

It was the phone Talia had given her.

She hadn't even looked at it since leaving their office. Would it be weird if she used it to call now and ask if Sal was all right? It wasn't like the hospital was going to give out that information.

Allyson got the phone from her backpack and dialed Talia's number.

No answer.

She set the phone down and ate standing up. No point sitting, a single diner in the quiet. Usually she put a podcast on her stereo just for background noise.

Tonight she didn't feel much like doing that. All she could think about was…fork halfway to her mouth, Allyson stopped.

She set the plate down and moved to the sink, where she spat out the little that was in there. Then she rinsed and spat again.

He could have bled out on the concrete. The knife might have nicked something vital, and even while being cared for in the hospital, he could have died. He could be dead now, but it's not like anybody would even think to tell her. Allyson was kept totally in the dark because of his dumb team that he cared about so much. And if he was dead, where did that leave her? Not on a mountain, living some fairytale dream life that wasn't going to happen anyway, that was for sure.

Was he dead?

Figure out what you want.

Ugh, that sounded suspiciously like something her ex had said to her a couple of years ago, right before he walked out. He'd dropped her off after a particularly excruciating date where they'd tried to talk about all those things that seemed to come so naturally to her and Sal.

So now that she had figured out what she wanted, what was she supposed to do about it? He was all she could think about. Worry for him was what consumed her, along with the headache she still had from hitting her head on that rock.

She looked at her phone.

Would one of them call?

The doorbell rang then. Allyson moved to the end of the kitchen counter and stood there. It wasn't like it was a friend. No one just "stopped by" these days. That wasn't a thing anymore, even though she recalled people stopping by like that when she was a kid. Neighbors, parishioners. Widows bringing dinner.

She stared at the closed door long enough that whoever was on the other side got impatient and rang the bell again.

Were they here to tell her that he had died?

Allyson set the phone down, walked over to the door, and looked out the peep hole. Standing in the hall were at least three FBI agents, one of them was Miller—the older agent who had interviewed her—and one was a female. The third she didn't know.

If she hadn't recognized one of them, she would wonder if they were even real agents—more fake cops. She had learned long ago that you couldn't trust just anyone, and she was versed to check credentials if necessary.

Before, she'd had someone with her. At the hospital, she'd been the one to defend Vanessa from those fake FBI agents from Salt Lake City. At the house, they might have been real but she didn't know for sure. The agent who had given her the most pause had been Miller. But that guy had taken her statement at the office.

Now no one was here with her. She'd have to stand up to them alone when she didn't feel it. Facing off with feds was the last thing she wanted to do right now.

Allyson opened the door. "Can I help you?"

The woman stood in front. One agent alone was disarming, or at least less intimidating to most people. Behind her were the two men, a younger guy—probably a rookie—and Miller. The only people who thought a female FBI agent was "less intimidating" didn't know squat about female law enforcement agents.

Miller nodded. "Special Agent Sanchez. May we come in?"

The female smiled politely. "We'd like to talk to you about the recent developments."

"The raid, or the gun store robberies?"

"All of it." Her smile remained, like her face just got stuck that way and she couldn't turn it off. "We're also looking more closely at the task force and their part in this."

"I'm not with that team."

"No, but you are involved." The words were spoken with a distinct tone. What exactly was this woman trying to insinuate by saying it like that?

Allyson wondered if she'd been sent here for an attempt at girl talk. She almost laughed, considering she was about as good at that as she figured Dakota probably was.

She looked at Miller. "I've already given the FBI my statement about the phone in the van. I have no idea what their intention was of leaving it in the rental van, aside from connecting my abduction to the thefts in a serious way." She shrugged. "Whoever is doing this pretty much shot themselves in the foot with that move. They wound up putting more suspicion on them than on me."

The smile turned brittle. Female FBI lady said, "We'd like you to come down to our office and talk it through with us."

"Again?"

"We would like to know everything you know about the task force. That's all, just an unofficial request for any information you can provide that might help us."

"You're investigating the task force." And she was being forced to help? "I'll have to call my group supervisor. Make sure he's up to speed on what I'm doing."

"I'm sure Special Agent Daulton will authorize your assisting us. After all, it's all very informal."

She knew Allyson's boss?

"If you could come with us right now, we would very much appreciate it. This is a time-sensitive matter."

Apparently she wasn't going to get to finish her dinner. Not that she probably would have anyway.

Allyson grabbed her backpack, and they walked her to their car. The two men got in front, the younger one driving and the female agent in the back. She buckled up next to the agent, stuffing her belongings between her feet.

She shot the female agent a smile, but the woman didn't return it. She only sat straight in the seat and didn't make eye contact with Allyson.

She figured an attempt at conversation might be good. So Allyson said, "If you have my phone from the gun store robbery, then you know I'm not connected to Kennowich."

No one said anything, or moved.

Finally Miller said, "We'll make that determination for ourselves."

Were they looking at her as well as the task force? Sure, she'd hung around them the past few days. But it wasn't like she would ever actually work alongside them.

The driver didn't signal. He pulled onto the freeway on-ramp, headed in the opposite direction from the FBI office.

What was along this road…aside from everything east of Seattle? Which was ninety percent of the country.

All she knew was that they weren't headed where they'd told her they were going.

Allyson tried to formulate a plan. She was going to play it cool. Not let on that she was suspicious. What was going on?

She glanced over and shot the woman a smile like everything was fine.

When they turned into the airport, Allyson got ready to finally make her move. She twisted to find Miller holding a gun on her. "Hand over your weapon. Slowly."

Allyson swallowed.

It really was too bad she'd left her phone on the counter in her kitchen.

———

"We have to assume Allyson is a target as well." Sal glanced at Talia. "Can you find her?"

She nodded. "I'll call her back, see where she is."

"Probably at home," Haley said, "worrying about you."

"You didn't bring her here?" Dakota straightened from tying Sal's boot laces.

Haley shook her head. "She needed to rest, and I told her we'd let her know when Sal was ready for visitors."

He stood, grabbing his jacket from the chair as he headed toward the door. "I'll go to her house."

Talia glanced at Victoria.

Sal said, "We've already had this conversation. Allyson is where I'm going. She's what the future looks like for me, and you all can either get on board or this isn't going to be fun for any of us."

Talia shifted, her gold purse held tight against her side. "That's it? Just put up or shut up?"

Sal figured he would get a call from Mason later, one where the Secret Service agent explained to him that he needed to speak to Talia with more respect. "I'm not putting up with any of you picking on her, or blaming her for anything. Not anymore."

Talia pressed her lips together. "Fine. We'll try and be nice."

Because she spoke for all of them? He'd always figured if anyone was the ring leader, it was Dakota. But here it was. Talia, the heart and soul. The one they gathered around and protected. He'd been part of that group, but now his focus was shifting. And he hoped Allyson's focus was going in the same direction. That they were moving toward a future where they were happy and settled.

Victoria cleared her throat. "It's time for me to go down to the FBI office and talk to them. See if I can't straighten this whole thing out." She paused. "Find out why we're being targeted now and maybe even get the heat off us."

Haley gasped. Dakota said, "Wait just one second—"

"My mind is made up."

Talia said, "It can't be. They'll arrest you."

"We all know you have pull," Sal said. "But no one has that much pull. You'll be walking into handcuffs and we know it."

Would she really take the heat for them? She would allow herself to be arrested and likely charged with something?

He could hardly believe Victoria was really okay going to jail for the task force so that the rest of them could go free.

"It's a shame Welvern isn't there to vouch for us." Josh scratched at the scruff on his jaw. "But that might be exactly why Kennowich is going ahead with this play right now."

And Victoria was going to turn herself in.

Why did that seem so out of character? If he was honest, he half expected her to have split already. Saved herself. Why did he keep thinking the worst about her?

"I know what you think of me." Her gaze remained on him. "And I know it's not much."

"That's not what this is." He knew what she was capable of, and he had huge professional respect for her. Why she'd met with Kennowich was her business. And he figured there was at least an adequate explanation. She didn't do anything without a reason.

"But I have—"

"They're on their way," Talia said, looking at her phone. "We have less than fifteen minutes."

Victoria turned to Talia. "I need you to get me proof that we're being targeted, because we're going to take Kennowich down."

Getting that, specifically, wasn't going to be easy.

"And I want to know who was behind the drone attack."

Talia nodded at the boss. "I'll go to Mason's office. He'll be able to hold off the FBI long enough for me to at least try to do that."

"I'll go with her." Dakota strode to Talia. "We'll keep each other safe and make sure she gets where she needs to go."

"Thank you." Sal figured if he couldn't protect Talia, he would feel better knowing Josh and Dakota were going to do it.

Even Victoria looked relieved.

Haley pushed off the wall where she'd been leaning. "I'll go to the office and purge everything sensitive. Hopefully before the FBI show up with their warrant."

"I'll make sure you get there." Josh shared a look with Dakota. She nodded and he walked to stand beside Haley. Niall was still in California, looking into Kennowich.

"My emergency protocol is already running," Talia said. "You'll just have to do physical documents. The program will get rid of anything Kennowich might have planted when he tried to hack the system with that drone—or since then."

They nodded to each other, and all headed out.

Sal needed to find Allyson. But he also didn't want the team getting arrested. Once suspicion was directed at them, the hit to their reputation would never heal. In the federal community they would always be looked at with doubt. Case numbers would go down. Assistance from other agencies, and local law enforcement, would dwindle.

Was this really going to be the end? Or could they fight to get the black mark removed before it even settled on them?

But how was he supposed to stop it? Previously he would just have gone rogue and got close to the bad guy. Kennowich would see that coming a mile away, and he couldn't help but think there were multiple aspects to this that he wasn't aware of.

Still, what Sal needed was to get them all out from under FBI suspicion. And he had to do that before Kennowich's plan could drag them down.

Alternatively, if he could just get all the suspicion on *him,* then he could take the fall. But they'd have to help him do that, and no one on their team would agree to do so.

Besides, it almost seemed like Victoria might already be planning that move.

After he got to Allyson and made sure she was okay, he could figure this out. If Haley had just brought her here, instead of excluding her, then he wouldn't have to now find her. He sighed.

"You'll find her." Victoria moved to the door. "Not that I even want to talk about Allyson. This all started because of *that woman.* Kennowich would never have targeted us without her connection to that friend of hers."

"You have to know that's not true." He faced her. "He had us in his sights before that. Just as we did on him."

"She was the weak point. His way in."

So this was all Allyson's fault, at least in Victoria's mind? "Don't you show up at the FBI and tell them that this is all on Allyson." That wasn't her play, was it? "You do that, and I'll *bury* you."

Victoria flashed teeth at him, not in the least a smile. "Now the truth comes out. We see how shallow your loyalty has been. One woman, and you falter."

"And that little meeting you had with Kennowich last night?" He folded his arms across his chest. "You wanna talk about loyalty, you're gonna have to answer some uncomfortable questions."

"Let's walk."

She moved to the elevator. After the doors slid shut and they began their descent, she turned to him. "The choices I make don't require explanations. This is bigger than you realize."

"That doesn't fly with me." He'd have said a week ago that he knew who she was. The woman had secrets, yes. But she worked on doing the right thing, and he often saw the war in her when she failed to hide it. "I know you want what's best for the team, but it's not going to be throwing Allyson in the line of fire."

"Seems to me like she put herself in the middle of this."

"You can't pick and choose. You'll ruin someone's life."

"Lives get ruined every day." Victoria shrugged one shoulder. "It's just a question of adequately managing the fallout."

The doors slid open. "Was that what the meeting was last night? Managing fallout?"

"An attempt at a solution." Victoria led the way. "It didn't work, but I have more options now than I had to work with before."

Across the parking lot he saw three black SUVs pull into the lot. The FBI was here.

Victoria twisted and pulled a weapon from the back of her waistband. "Go. I'll hold them off."

The vehicles screeched to a halt. Multiple doors slammed and agents took cover behind open doors.

"Put your weapons down and surrender!"

Victoria stood there, as though waiting for something.

A split second later, someone opened fire.

22

———

The gun poked Allyson in the back. "Take a seat."

She moved down the slim hallway to the main body of the aircraft and scanned the interior. It was fancy. Not like any airplane she'd ever ridden in before. It really was too bad the reason she was in this one today.

A single man sat in a lush chair halfway down the left side. *Kennowich.* There were seats for five more, but she figured she might wind up being the only other passenger.

She turned back to the FBI agents. The female. Miller. The younger one had stayed in the car— he seemed antsy to get out of there after getting paid for his role as driver.

"Thank you." The man stood up from his chair. Kennowich had removed his suit jacket but still had his tie tight to the top. "That'll be all."

As though the two FBI agents were the hired help.

The man owned the space like any good CEO did. A man with power who knew exactly how far he could flex it. What did he have on these agents to induce them to hand her over to him?

This was the guy who had convinced Vanessa that the only thing to do was to disappear from everyone in her life, make everyone believe she was in danger, and work for him. For years.

Vanessa had pledged her loyalty to him and never once walked away. She'd allowed the people who cared about her to think she was dead.

Now he had these FBI agents backed into a corner. Doing favors for him.

Had they also convinced the rest of their agency that the Northwest Counter-Terrorism Task Force were the real bad guys? She'd thought they wouldn't be swayed. Unless Kennowich had hacked the task force office and planted convincing evidence, which these agents had then revealed to the rest of the FBI.

Now he had her.

But why?

Kennowich held out a securely closed manila envelope, stuffed to bursting. He tossed it at Miller who caught it with his left hand and the gun he held in his right. He stowed his weapon and looked inside, then nodded to the female agent.

To her credit, she had the decency to look guilty enough to be nauseous.

But Allyson wasn't going to give her more than that. After all, she'd just handed Allyson over—tied up—to a man who had already kept one woman in captivity. For years. Then there was all the other corruption Kennowich had carried out—deplorable acts the task force had told her about.

"That's it?"

The female agent didn't glance back at her. She just walked out with her colleague and left Allyson here.

"Have a seat."

Was she supposed to be satisfied with the one consolation the FBI agent had given her? A tiny chance at a way out.

Maybe it would save her life, and maybe it wouldn't. Allyson wanted to trust that it would help. To believe that God would move…and get her out of here. But when the airplane door was shut by a uniformed male pilot, hope waned.

"Sit down."

Along with her hope, energy also fled as the plane began to

move. Allyson landed in the nearest seat, then straightened to face Kennowich. He knew he had her at a disadvantage, but that didn't mean she needed to add to it. She had to focus.

He wasn't going to break her. No matter what this was.

As she studied him, she also tried to figure out what this was.

What kind of prominent businessman undertook something this complicated? There had to have been a reason it was necessary to send Vanessa to her. She didn't doubt that when he spoke he would be charismatic. Some people gravitated to that type of personality, allowing themselves to be swept up in it, malleable and codependent. Like Vanessa had been?

She couldn't speak for anyone else—definitely not Vanessa—when she didn't know exactly what had been in her head. Whether he'd worn her down slowly, or she'd jumped in freely, thinking it was an amazing chance at a great life. She would never know.

Her former friend had ended up in love with Kennowich's head of security. But what had the path to that entailed? Allyson hardly wanted to know.

And she definitely wasn't going to ask.

"And so you are here."

Allyson said, "In a plane?"

"Surely you're more intelligent than that. I have read your file." He spoke with a lilt that indicated an upper-class background. A mid-century highbrow education. Now he was probably pushing eighty. White hair. Manicured hands that couldn't hide the age spots.

"Why am I here? I didn't need to be dragged into this, and yet you sent Vanessa to me. For what?" It almost seemed like a sick joke. And maybe she shouldn't put that past a woman who had betrayed her. Who had never been her friend in the first place.

"Your role has been played," Kennowich said. "Except that I have incurred substantial losses, and you're in the position to enable me to recoup those losses. In full."

She had no idea what that meant, but several scenarios ran through her mind. The last was the worst.

He had to have seen it on her face, because he said, "As fun as that might be, it's not what I'm referring to."

"I'm not going to be a mule for you."

"I run a pharmaceutical company. Do you think I also am a drug dealer?"

"I figure you have people for that." She paused. "You probably even have someone to tie your shoes for you."

"Expendable people do jobs such as those. Don't you think you're worth more than that, Agent Sanchez?"

"You said my role has been played. Obviously you're now going to sell me, like you did Talia." Not a one-time transaction, but a way to make money every day. Maybe for years.

Allyson fought down a swell of nausea.

He flashed bright white teeth and chuckled. "Vanessa was scheduled to provide an associate of mine with a kidney."

Her stomach dropped again. Bile hit the back of her throat.

"Thankfully you're the same blood type. I'll be able to recoup my losses, and then some."

Allyson swallowed down the rest, or it would have ended up on the carpet. Was he going to take more than just one kidney? "I'm not going to allow you to do surgery on me. You have to know that I have a team and they're looking for me."

"They won't find you in time."

"It doesn't matter how far this plane flies." She tried to sound less scared than she really was. "Deputy Alvarez isn't going to stop looking for me."

"He's a little…preoccupied right now."

But he wasn't dead. *He wasn't dead.*

If he had been, Kennowich wouldn't have wasted the opportunity to rub that in her face.

He said, "The task force is no longer. It's only a matter of time before they are stripped of badges and freedom. That's what happens when you get in the middle of my business. Now all I need is to get the financial recompense out of you, and then I can make a clean break. Wipe the slate in North America and start over somewhere the authorities aren't quite so…tiresome."

The cockpit door opened then and a flight attendant approached. Slim hips, pressed clothes, and gelled hair.

She waited until he was close enough, then jumped up. She swung her bound hands over his head. She pulled back, pressing her arms against his windpipe before he could react.

Kennowich just stared at her.

"I'll kill him if you don't land this plane and let me go. I'm not going to let you do *surgery* on me."

The pilot guy didn't even struggle. A loyal subject?

Allyson kept squeezing until he was about to go limp. What was she going to do when he was on the floor? She couldn't kill an unconscious man—not even to save her own life.

Kennowich smiled at her and shrugged. "Kill him."

The man's body flinched, pressed against hers. So he didn't want to die? She might be able to work with that. It was enough to let her know he didn't entirely agree with the boss.

The man shifted then, and reached back. She realized he was laughing.

She heard the crackles and realized what was about to happen. She tried to move out of reach, but the prongs touched her side and she fell into unconsciousness.

———

THE SECOND he realized Victoria was in danger, Sal dived on her. They rolled across the ground and came to a stop by the elevator. He lifted up enough to see a man several cars down, ducked behind a vehicle. He had a rifle in his hands, braced on the hood of a car.

The shooter.

Between them and the FBI, Sal figured they thought it was the team shooting at them. More fuel to the fire against the task force.

Sal said, "Get to cover."

He left Victoria and ran for the guy who immediately saw Sal coming towards him. He swung the rifle around to point it at him. It was the man he'd followed in the pickup truck, to the house where Allyson had been held. And he now wore an FBI badge.

A man the FBI had been tracking.

Sal ducked behind the wheel of a truck and pulled his weapon. What on earth was going on? He waited for a break between shots and then lifted up. He fired twice.

One skimmed the side of the guy's head, above his ear. Sal thought he saw a flash of blood as the guy turned. He stumbled and dropped the gun, then took off running. Not working with the agents here, trying to round up the task force. This guy had been acting on his own.

Sal raced to the gun, but didn't touch it. He wasn't about to get his prints on it if there was a chance they were being set up for something more than those gun store robberies.

More shots were fired. Sal ducked, and then realized it was the FBI agents who'd driven up. A team sent to arrest them.

Car tires squealed around a corner and he saw more vehicles approach.

Victoria was huddled behind the nearest car to where they'd rolled. She was on her phone, talking animatedly as she stayed in a crouch. Calling in for reinforcements? Maybe she was on with Josh. Or Niall, though he was still in California.

Car doors slammed and Sal spotted Daulton, Carl, and a couple of other ATF agents. Daulton strode over to the FBI agents and said something Sal was too far away to hear.

"Victoria Bramlyn." The lead agent called out across the parking lot. "You will lay your weapons down and come out with your hands up."

Victoria said one thing, then hung up the phone.

"Salvador Alvarez. You will lay your weapons down and come out with your hands up."

If he was going to do what the agent ordered him to do, the guy could at least mix it up. Add in some variety.

Before Sal could respond, Victoria stood up with both palms raised. "It's just me. Sal is gone."

What was she doing?

"He needs to come out as well. We saw both of you."

"He ran off and left me."

Daulton, at least, didn't look convinced.

The FBI agent said, "Walk toward me slowly." He moved to the edge of his door, still behind cover, even though all the ATF agents were standing in what would be the line of fire if anyone was actually shooting.

"Alvarez shot at us," the FBI agent said. "We're going to find him."

"Let me and my team do it." Daulton pulled Victoria toward him, and then moved her in the direction of the FBI agents. A smooth move that effectively put his team between them and Sal. "You guys have your hands full with this one."

They headed out as a group. They'd see him if they came far enough. Was Daulton intending on arresting him, or did he just want to talk to Sal?

"We're going to perform a thorough search of the area," the FBI agent called out. Still, he wasn't going with them. He was putting cuffs on Victoria.

She looked kind of pleased. But Sal was far enough away, he could be reading her expression wrong.

Sal stayed where he was, though he slid the weapon out of reach. It didn't need to look like he was about to pick it up. Then he laid down his weapon and lifted both hands. Just in case he was misreading Daulton's intentions.

He could grab either one fast enough to defend himself.

As soon as Daulton was within view, Sal waved. He stayed ducked down. As he'd figured would be the case, Daulton didn't even react. Neither did his men who spotted Sal also. He waved at the rows of cars. "Spread out. Let's find this guy."

Then he made his way between the wall of the building and the car hoods where Sal was crouched. He stopped two feet away and scanned the area. Then he lifted his phone to his ear and said, "What's with the guns?"

"Shooter dropped the rifle," Sal told him in a low voice.

"Where's Agent Sanchez?"

"What do you mean?" Sal didn't like the sound of this.

"Where is she?" he continued to speak into his phone. "I figured you knew."

"Haley took her home."

"She's not there. Front door was open and there was a phone on the counter."

"Did someone take her? Maybe the FBI."

Daulton shrugged. "I figured you had her with you."

How was it possible that neither of them knew where to find her?

The FBI agent called out across the parking lot. "We're taking her in!"

Daulton nodded, moving the phone away from his ear and stowing it on his belt. "We'll let you know if we locate Alvarez!"

Sal heard the cars retreat. He was trusting the ATF. More than he trusted the FBI, and maybe even more than he trusted his own team right now. It seemed that Victoria wanted to get brought in for questioning. Maybe even arrested.

He just had no idea why.

Sal couldn't let that happen to him. If someone had Allyson—again—then being free was the only way he could figure out where she was. If she had been taken, that is.

Daulton gathered up the rifle, and Sal grabbed his gun. He slid it back into its holster and straightened. The rest of the ATF agents wandered back to them.

Daulton shook his head. "The FBI considers your team rogue. They're putting a strong case together, and it doesn't look good."

"Kennowich is pinning this all on us. We're not rogue, but I don't care about the case. Not if Allyson is in danger." He lifted his chin. "We need to find her."

"Far as I can see," Carl said, "you're the one who put Allyson in danger in the first place." The guy was scared for her.

"I'll make some calls. Check in with the agents talking to Sanchez's neighbors." Daulton motioned to their vehicles. "Let's get out of here."

They were on the road, Sal in the middle row of three, when Daulton hung up the phone. "A neighbor saw her get walked out of her apartment by a female FBI agent and two males. We've identified her, but we don't know where she is."

"It's a start," Sal said. "Can you get a photo of the agent?"

When he got it, they all took a look. Even the agent driving. No one had worked with her, and the ATF agent who'd seen her before didn't remember her name. If Welvern was up to it, Sal could have talked to him.

"I can find out where she is if you have her phone number."

Daulton twisted around from the front seat.

Sal said, "Call the Secret Service office and ask for Assistant director Armstrong."

Daulton shot him a quizzical look but did as he'd asked. He had the call on speaker when Mason picked up the phone.

"It's Sal. Is she there?"

There was a shuffle on the line, then Talia said, "Kind of in the middle of something here."

Sal explained what he needed, giving her the female agent's name and number. "We think Allyson might be in danger. This woman might know where she is."

Talia was quiet for a second, then she said, "I'll track the number."

"Thank you."

She hung up.

Two minutes later, they got the address where the female agent's phone was currently being used to scroll Facebook.

The place was a rundown, tiny, neighborhood-dive bar. The

ATF agents led, with Sal in the mix. He didn't need to be the one singled out as having accosted an FBI agent.

The agent sat on a stool at the end of the bar, an untouched open bottle in front of her. Before any of them spoke, she looked up from her phone. "Make it fast. My partner will be back soon, and I don't want him to know I spoke with you."

Daulton said, "Where is Allyson Sanchez?"

"Kennowich had us bring her to him. We put her on a plane."

Sal held back the urge to rage at her. "Headed where?"

"I don't know."

"Is that supposed to be an answer?"

The agent sipped her drink. Sal wanted to swipe it out of her hand and watch it shatter against the wall behind the bar. She set the bottle down. "I figured it would come to this." She glanced at Daulton. "I want a deal."

———————

23

The motion of the vehicle stopped. Allyson blinked and saw only trees. For a second, she thought they'd returned to the house in the mountains where she and Vanessa had escaped.

Everything that had happened that day, and since, rushed through her brain as she came awake.

The car door was opened from the outside.

Allyson slid toward the opening and was caught before she hit the ground. Huge hands hauled her out, and half-walked, half-dragged her a couple of steps before the door slammed behind her.

She flinched. The air she sucked in smelled like pine trees and was cool enough it raised bumps on her skin. She looked through the curtain of her hair as they hauled her along, not bothering to put in any effort. They didn't need to know she was coming around. The lingering effects of being stunned made her extremities tingle.

The place looked like a manicured country estate.

Not the mountain location home she'd been in last time. This place was styled like a rustic log cabin, but it was the size of a mansion.

Her hands were still bound in front of her, the way the FBI

agent had done. Wrists facing each other with enough space between them, a healthy inch so that she could get free if she got half a chance to so. The agent had to have known she'd given Allyson this way out.

Several people walked with them, but only one carried her. Kennowich led the group. *He's going to take my kidney.* The words rushed back to her. Would he take *much more* or was it *everything*? That part she couldn't remember. But did it matter? She would be dead, and he'd have gotten his money back.

Not the worst way she could cross into the beyond, but was today really the day she would meet Jesus? She'd kind of thought she'd be able to get married. Have kids. Not everyone got that chance, but she'd wanted to have it.

The front door swung wide.

"Good to see you, sir." The voice had a British accent.

Seriously? The man had a butler, like some TV billionaire superhero. Didn't matter which universe, there seemed to be one either way.

This was Kennowich's element. The place where money bought people's loyalty. A middle-of-nowhere estate where he could do whatever he wanted and get away with it.

"Take her to the surgery suite."

He turned and walked away, leaving her alone with the butler. She wanted to throw up on the fancy tile right there in the foyer.

Instead, the second the front door shut, she planted her feet and flipped up her head as she stood up. She got the lay of the land as she twisted into the man who'd been holding her. She slammed her interlaced fingers into his stomach.

He doubled over, coughing.

Allyson slammed her hands into his back, between his shoulder blades.

He fell, reaching for her legs as he landed on the ground. She scrabbled back and slammed into the front door, then launched off it.

One kick to his head, and he was out.

Allyson dropped to one knee. Over the bent one, she brought her hands down and snapped the plastic ties.

Then she searched the man for a gun.

She found a pistol but no phone. It was loaded. Allyson held it out in front of her. The lingering tingle wasn't going to give her an accuracy that would win awards, but all she wanted or needed to do was as much damage as possible.

No. She needed stealth until she found a phone and called for help. Then she would have to hide somewhere long enough for rescue to come. And who knew how long that would take?

Allyson snuck down the hall so she could find a back exit.

Or should she set a fire and burn the place down while waiting for help? She shook her head as she peered around a corner, saw no one, and started running. She probably looked like a bedraggled crazy person, but adrenaline pushed the tingle out in favor of a surge of energy she'd badly needed.

Think. Think.

Phone.

Back exit.

Help.

What would Sal do? Okay, so that was cliché, but if anyone could survive something like this, he could.

She raced down one hall, then another, trying to figure out where a landline would be while also looking for a discarded cell phone. And who didn't just carry one around with them every second? She didn't like hers, but she still tucked it in her back pocket. Usually.

The next open door was a small study. On the desk was a landline phone. She got a few angry tones while fat fingering the buttons to try to get a call out. Finally she heard it ring, thanking God—and pledging Him whatever he wanted from her—that she'd actually memorized Sal's number by dialing it a hundred times from the courthouse phone during their case. Not that she was a total stalker weirdo, she just remembered it.

"Alvarez." He sounded out of breath.

She made a "huh" sound, the only thing she could say before she realized she wasn't alone. Someone was in the hallway outside the room.

Allyson dropped the handset and ducked through a door in the corner, out of sight of the hallway door.

As soon as she crossed the threshold, she spotted a yellow couch. Two women sat there. Both turned to her as she stood in the doorway, heaving for breath.

The TV was on, playing some daytime awful soap opera with weirdly good-looking guys, and underhanded women who stabbed each other in the back.

Her mind wanted to drift to what Kennowich had them there for, but she shut it off.

One looked down at the gun, held loosely in her hands in front of her.

Both were young. College age, like Vanessa had been when she'd been abducted. Glassy eyes, but she couldn't see any additional evidence they were high from this distance. They stared at her. Passive, which spurred all kinds of horrible ideas she'd been trying not to think of.

Allyson said, "You ladies wanna get out of here?"

They looked at each other. The brunette said, "This episode isn't finished."

Allyson heard someone behind her, in the office where she'd made the call. "I have to go. Come with me, if you want." They would slow her down. Two people were harder to hide than one. She could come back for them, right? Or this could be their only chance, and she would never get another.

"She thinks we wanna leave." The blonde smirked. "Better run along little lab rat."

Allyson ran to the window.

"They're always locked," the brunette said. "You need a key."

Allyson looked around for another way out. There was only one door, unlike the last room. She couldn't go back to it, because it led to the gunmen who were in the study where she'd been just minutes ago.

"Ugh, fine." The blonde muttered to herself. "There's a door behind the curtain, okay? Take it and go down the hallway. Keep going left, every turn. You'll get to the patio. Eventually."

Allyson was going to have to believe her. Same way she had to believe Sal was now coming for her. That he'd realized what that call was, and now he and her team were going to show up, guns blazing to rescue her.

There was a door behind the curtain. So she went through it.

She had to have faith. Right now that was in short supply, but she needed to fall back on God. He had always been there for her, especially right after Vanessa's disappearance. And before that, when her father had died.

Right now she needed Him more than she ever had.

Allyson made her way down one hall after another. They all looked the same, which made her wonder if she'd taken a wrong turn. Or if this was nothing but a labyrinth and she was going in circles.

Finally she spotted a glass door and ran outside.

The second her feet hit the concrete of the patio, a body launched at her from behind. The guy landed on her, expelling breath from her lungs even as his weight ground her hips into the hard surface.

Allyson cried out.

He hauled her up and back inside, where he threw her to the floor. She looked up to find Kennowich standing in front of her as she reached for her gun…

It was still outside on the patio.

"As amusing as that was, the doctor is ready for you."

———

"You're sure it's her?" Sal gripped the phone and stood to the side as the ATF agents swung their giant duffel bags of gear into the rented SUV. It took longer than anyone had liked to check all their gear—and guns—through security to get there. But this was the final leg of the journey.

"I'm sure."

He hung up on Talia. "She says we're good to go."

As soon as they drove out of town up, they were planning to head into the hills where custom mansions had been built on huge lots, one belonging to a subsidiary of one of Kennowich's companies.

Carl slammed the back door. "Let's go."

"One second." Sal had spotted a familiar face pull up behind their vehicle. He lifted a hand to Niall, who raised his chin in a nod.

They all climbed into the SUV, Sal in the front passenger seat. He hissed as he tugged his seatbelt on.

"Okay?"

He nodded.

Daulton pulled out into airport traffic with Niall in the car behind them, being accompanied by a handful of local ATF agents based in California. It wasn't like they could call the FBI, considering they'd probably all get arrested.

"Update me," Daulton ordered.

"Victoria is with the FBI, being questioned. Talia found out through Mason, who is a known associate, but they're keeping him informed at least. Just not the fine details. Probably because the FBI wants him to turn over Talia." Sal paused. "Haley surrendered herself to the FBI along with a flash drive of evidence compiled against Kennowich, including what he planted in our system. Dakota and Josh are in a meeting with the FBI in the DEA office, downtown Seattle. My guess is a negotiation of their intent to cooperate."

Daulton blew out a breath. "I appreciate you doing this for Allyson while your team is being dismantled."

Sal didn't know how to respond. He did want to be there and helping them. But the threat to Allyson was real.

Kennowich wasn't going to destroy her if he had anything to say about it.

The last thing he wanted was for her to show up years from now, after no word. Meeting a completely different woman. One who had been destroyed and remade by this man.

No matter what happened to the team back in Seattle, they would now always be painted with the stain of suspicion. Whether the FBI got charges to stick, or not.

The ATF had sent an email outlining exactly what their agents had done to Allyson, along with the location of the female agent and her partner they'd handcuffed to the bar—everyone in there making sure the crooked cops didn't get away.

Maybe that would help.

Right now Sal just wanted to get to Allyson so he could help her. The team had each other, and they had help from multiple agencies. She had no one except the people there right now to go after her.

"You guys have a thing?"

Sal knew what he was asking. "I've been half in love with her for a long time. We haven't been able to see a way to make it work, and it hasn't been easy to figure out, but I think we are on our way."

He hadn't been able to figure a way to have the future he wanted with her. After this, would she want to retire with him to his mountain? It was a dream he wasn't sure would come to fruition, but he was certainly going to try.

Why come this far, only to be denied the shot?

God, help me get her back. Keep her safe until we reach the house and can get her out.

Carl directed Daulton from the backseat to a predetermined spot where they would park the car out of sight. The approach would be made using as much cover as possible, considering the sun was still high in the sky.

Yes, they could have gotten a warrant and shown up loud. But with the FBI breathing down their necks, it would have taken too long. Sal figured the second they showed up, Allyson would've been either dead or Kennowich would have moved her.

Something in him wouldn't let go of the idea that time was seriously running out for her.

He needed her back. Whether that got him arrested or not didn't matter. What mattered was getting to her before she was killed—or hurt in some other horrible way.

Sal's teammates had suffered trauma because of Kennowich, and they'd survived. He held onto that same hope for Allyson. She was made of equally strong stuff. Determination. Strength. A solid faith.

He knew she could survive a lot, though he was really struggling with the ideas swirling around of what she was having to endure. The question had to do with Kennowich, and the lengths he would go. What he wanted from her.

They loaded up and approached the house through the woods, spread out in formation according to the plan they'd formulated. It wouldn't be good if Kennowich escaped. All of them got in position and radioed in. The satellite images Talia had managed to find and send over clued them in to a few entrances they could actually breach.

At the signal, they entered the house. Sal turned the first corner and encountered a gunman. Thick neck, thick everything else, dressed in a suit with a shaved head. His brain registered, "goon" right as the man drew a weapon.

Sal shot him before he could get a round off.

At next corner, Daulton approached from the other side. "Watch out!"

Sal turned as the assailant fired. He killed the guy, then turned back to find Daulton on the ground breathing hard.

"That's gonna leave a mark."

Sal held out one hand, and they clasped wrists. He pulled the ATF agent to his feet, and they continued on through the house.

"West side is clear."

"Copy that," Daulton replied into his radio. "Keep working through the rest of the house."

Sal kept going. They couldn't end up empty handed. They had to find her. She *was* here.

She had to be.

Then, when he knew she was all right, he could head home and fix what was happening with his team.

"Got eyes on Kennowich," the voice came low over comms. "Looks like he's in a home office. He's got papers shredding, and he's getting on the computer."

Daulton keyed his radio. "Lock him down."

"Copy that."

Sal heard their shots, even from this distance. Then a gun went off. If Kennowich was dead, he wasn't going to shed a tear.

"He's on the run."

"Copy that," Daulton replied. Then to Sal he said, "I'm gonna—"

Sal tipped his head. "Go. I'm good."

He was going to find Allyson, and he wasn't going to abandon that search until he knew for a fact she was safe.

Sal stopped at the next corner, remaining behind the wall for cover while looking around. A man wearing green scrubs emerged from a break in the wainscoting. A hidden door. After looking both ways, the man scurried down the hall.

He ran to the door and pressed against it to get it open.

On the other side was a glass wall. Beyond that was what appeared to be a surgical suite. Allyson was laid out on the table, face down. She had her head turned to him, and her eyes were open. Glassy, full of pain and fear.

A surgeon stood over her with a scalpel poised. The wound in Sal's abdomen pulsed with pain.

He lifted his gun and fired two shots through the glass.

Blood spread across the man's chest and he fell to the floor.

24

Allyson cried out before she even realized where she was, or what was happening. "Whoa." The man leaning over her wore a uniform. "You're safe. It's all over."

She shoved him out the way, then sat up. And cried out again.

"You need stitches. Probably inside and out. It's pretty deep." He was an EMT.

She was in an ambulance.

Where was Sal? Wasn't he here?

The EMT touched something to the skin above her hip. It was gooey and cold. She sucked in a breath and forced herself not to look at it. "Do I still have a kidney?"

The EMT blinked. "Do…what?"

"Can you tell?" She tried to twist then, so she could see the wound. Her head swam, and she wanted to throw up. Had he given her something for the pain? Probably, otherwise it would likely hurt a whole lot more than this. "Is it gone?"

Kennowich had threatened to take even more than that. But he hadn't, because Sal had stopped him. Hadn't he? Or was the sight of the man she loved nothing more than an apparition?

She shut her eyes, not wanting to believe it had been nothing but a figment of her imagination.

"They tell me you've been through an ordeal."

Allyson kept her mouth closed and concentrated on not freaking out. Wasn't Kennowich here somewhere? Maybe this was a trick. Or a dream.

Maybe this EMT was part of Kennowich's operation. Get her to relax, so they could harvest a bunch of organs from her.

"You're awake." Daulton stood in the open doors of the ambulance.

She nodded.

"You okay?"

I think so. More like she *hoped* so.

"…need to talk to her." Someone she couldn't see. Her head swam with pain, and she couldn't figure out who it was.

"Chill, *muchacho.* Give them a second." Another voice, the person out of sight.

Daulton glanced off to the side, then nodded to someone. "You're good?"

What on earth was going on? Who was he even talking to? "Where is Sal?"

"He's about to go help get Kennowich to surrender. But he wants to talk to you first." Daulton assessed her with his gaze.

"Trust me." Carl spoke, but she couldn't see him. That was who was off to the side? "That isn't a good idea."

"Just get out of my way." She knew that voice.

"Your funeral, dude." She saw Daulton take a step back, then heard Carl say, "You should have seen her when she broke her toe. Bit everyone's head off all day every day for a week."

"I don't have a broken toe," Allyson called out. "That was just because you guys annoy me."

Sal stepped between the open doors.

"You still have to get Kennowich?"

He nodded. "We think he barricaded himself in the barn."

"I'll wait." She shot a look at the EMT. "We're not leaving until he's in custody."

"We've got this," Sal said.

Allyson shook her head. "I'm not leaving." The quaver in her voice betrayed her.

Sal studied her for a second, then said, "You're safe now. Nothing's going to happen to you."

"I'm not sure I'll believe that until I know he's in custody." Or dead. "He was going to sell my organs to 'recoup his losses'."

Sal looked like he was going to be sick. "Seriously?"

She nodded. "You saved my life."

He climbed in the ambulance then, moving toward her with purpose. The EMT was out of the way, tapping the screen of a tablet, when Sal sat beside her and gathered her in his arms.

"Easy," the EMT warned.

Sal's hold on her loosened until she squeezed him with her arms. Allyson ignored the pain in her side, on her back, and just held on until her breathing calmed. Until her heart eased its mad thump, threatening to pound right out of her chest.

"I'm going to go bring him in now." He spoke low, his mouth close to her ear.

Allyson nodded against his chest.

He pulled back, asking the EMT, "You're taking her to the hospital?"

She grabbed his hand.

The EMT said, "She needs a whole lot of stitches. And that's the best case scenario."

"Fine." He wanted her to go while he brought in Kennowich? She didn't need to stay here if the guy who'd done this was here as well. She wanted to run as far away from him as fast as she could. "Let's get this show on the road then." The words came out louder than she intended.

Allyson was more scared than she wanted to admit at the idea that Kennowich might still be out there. That he could escape.

Sal had to have noticed her fear, even though she said nothing about it. He touched her cheek. "Everything is going to be just fine."

She couldn't accept sympathy or empathy though. She would

dissolve into inconsolable emotion if she did. Sal leaned in and touched his lips to hers.

Allyson gave him a small smile. "Please go catch him."

If he had to kill Kennowich, she wouldn't exactly object. But having the man in custody to answer for her kidnapping—among other things—both times, was the best scenario.

Allyson looked down at her hands, and the red lines where she'd been tied up. She extremely disliked being a captive, and though she had enjoyed breaking her captor's noses, the gun had been better.

No matter what they'd done to her, she found a whole lot of satisfaction in recompense. Probably more than she ever should as a woman who had to operate within the boundaries of procedure and who needed to trust God to keep her in His hands.

"I'm angry, as well as scared."

"That's understandable." His gaze was soft. "You'll get past this, and your emotions won't be so strong."

"I trusted that God would save me."

"He did." Sal nodded, so sure of what he believed.

"Because He sent you?"

"No." He squeezed her fingers. "Because He hears us, and His delight is to be our rescuer."

Allyson needed time, and the headspace, to think about that. Everything was all over the place right now. "Go, get him."

Yes, she was shutting down this conversation, but that was because she needed to ponder it. And right now she was keeping him from doing his job. She should probably get a journal or something. Write all her thoughts down so she could process the whole thing. Right after her middle quit hurting.

Allyson swayed on her seat. He caught her and helped her lay down.

"Time to go," the EMT said.

Sal touched her face, moving in close to her. He spoke softly when he said, "Be safe. And I'll be there soon." It seemed like he wanted to leave about as much as she wanted him to leave.

She nodded. He kissed her again, softer than she wanted. But she couldn't deny the sweetness. Then he was gone, closing the doors of the ambulance behind him.

"Let's get you to the hospital so we can get you patched up."

———

THE AMBULANCE DROVE OFF. Sal turned away and headed back to where Daulton and Carl stood in a huddle with the others.

Sal's fingers curled into fists by his side.

Carl saw him approach and wisely took a step back. "I was just warning you."

Daulton said, "Figure this out later."

"Nothing to figure out." Sal shot Carl a pointed look. Though, later they were going to have a conversation. Carl had a thing for Allyson, and now that it was looking like Sal and Allyson might actually have something…he was getting snippy.

Not Sal's problem.

It was entirely up to Allyson who she fell for. Sal had tossed his hat in that ring, and he was goal oriented.

"She's good?"

He nodded in answer to Daulton's question. "For now."

Sal was about to ask a question when they all took a step back. They each made a gesture of serious relief. Faces washed over, letting go of tension. Carl ran his hands down his cheeks. One of the agents scrubbed at his bald head. Daulton shut his eyes for a second and blew out a long breath that probably had nothing to do with the fact he'd caught a bullet to the vest.

The ATF group supervisor opened his eyes then. "He was really going to take her organs?"

Sal nodded. They'd all been listening in on his conversation with Allyson, wanting to know that she was all right now. That she was safe.

They'd found her, rescued her.

Carl muttered a few choice words Sal agreed with if he was

honest. They just weren't the kind of words he'd have said aloud. What he said was, "I know."

She'd been seconds away from getting carved up by Kennowich's surgeon.

"What kind of freak keeps a medical suite in his house?" Carl looked like he wanted to punch someone.

Sal got the conversation moving. They all felt the relief now that Allyson was safe, and it was helpful to air their thoughts and feelings. But reality had to be faced.

This job wasn't done. "What's the update on Kennowich?"

"Still holed up in the barn, as far as we can tell. The men on the perimeter report no movement." They started walking toward the outbuilding, set back from the house and surrounded by trees. Like an eyesore no one wanted to acknowledge.

The homeowner had a staff, so he didn't need to worry about things like yard work.

"Let's roust him out."

"Problem." Daulton shifted an iPad so Sal could see it as they strode around the house. "Cellar on the original plans. He could be barricaded in there, and we'd never breach it. He could have a stock of weapons and traps set."

"Call your breecher, then."

"That would be me," Carl said from behind them. "You want the door opened in two seconds so you can serve a warrant? I'm your man. But we used up what I brought on the doors, so we're lacking in plastic explosives. Plus I'd have to get in there to see the layout. Then I'd know what we need to get in. And how much."

If Kennowich was even down in the cellar. Maybe he was just hiding and didn't know there was another level under the floor because he didn't spend that much time in the barn.

Or it had been converted into a panic room at some point, and Kennowich could survive down there for months.

Sal ground his molars as he stared at the barn. "Let's get eyes inside."

No one moved. He glanced over at Daulton and saw the man's raised eyebrows.

"Or, you know, whatever your orders are." Sal wasn't the ranking agent here. And he wasn't the one who cared the most about Allyson. He just had different feelings for her than the rest of them…except maybe Carl.

But she was safe now and headed to the hospital.

It was time to take down Kennowich.

"The FBI is on their way. We've got an agent already going through all the computer files and papers he didn't manage to destroy," Daulton said. "We have men and women in custody, and the agents with them could use backup."

Sal nodded. Niall had been out front, standing over a huddle of handcuffed men sitting on the driveway.

Two agents, along with Carl, headed off to do just that, leaving Daulton with Sal. Beyond them, Sal could see an agent on the barn's front door. Two more were stationed around the outside. All of them were getting antsy.

The ATF group supervisor lifted his chin. "Which brings me to your team."

"You have an update?" Sal turned to face him.

"It's tied to the FBI agents on their way. They want in on the search for Kennowich on account of what Haley turned over to them, and what they were sent by Talia." He gave Sal a pointed look, as though he might not be sure he'd gotten their names right, so Sal nodded.

Daulton continued, "Especially when they got my report I sent from the plane about the agents who handed *my* agent off to a suspected criminal. I'll be forwarding additional information shortly about what that suspected criminal intended to do with her."

He looked sick, and Sal didn't blame him. It would take a while for Allyson's team to let go of this. Before then, there would be nightmares along with an irrational need to protect her.

It was only because Kennowich still hadn't been taken into

custody that all of them hadn't gone with her in the ambulance. Carl had wanted to until Sal had told him if one of them went, then it was going to be him.

Once the FBI got there to do cleanup, Sal was pretty sure the ATF would just hand over the whole case in favor of being with Allyson.

Sal would be first to head to the car.

"The FBI also wants to talk to you."

"They can read my report," Sal said.

"Kennowich is a person of interest in what should be an ongoing investigation. They want him in custody for questioning. They'll want to speak with Allyson as well, particularly concerning the agents who delivered her to Kennowich."

"So long as they're not going to try and bury it." Sal moved to study the window that gave him a view into the barn. It was clouded, but he watched. What had grabbed his attention? Maybe it hadn't been movement. Could be there was a bird in there, or the wind had blown something.

Kennowich was likely holed up in that cellar, biding his time until he could call for his lawyer like any good, rich criminal did.

"I doubt Victoria Bramlyn will allow them to do that," Daulton said, following Sal closer to the barn. "Not with the way I heard she's tearing into the FBI office in Seattle about what's happening with your team."

The barn door swung open. Before he could figure out what was happening, a horse tore out of the dark interior. Kennowich sat astride the animal, feet in stirrups, one hand using a length of leather to smack the animal's flank where he sat.

"Yah!"

The man they needed to take into custody tore across the clearing and into the trees.

25

———

"All done." The doctor smoothed down the edges of a bandage he'd secured over her brand new set of stitches.

Allyson stayed quiet while he gave the rest of his spiel about showering and keeping it clean. Taking it easy.

She could still feel each pull of the needle, the tug of the thread as it ran through her skin. Maybe when she could push that away, she could worry what was next as far as cleaning up.

"I'll go get your discharge paperwork."

"Great."

As he disappeared through a curtain, she pushed herself up to sitting. The room spun. The curtain shifted and a figure appeared. Allyson blinked while her brain put the pieces together of who it was.

"Niall." The lips on his young face curled up. He was cute, in a "younger brother" kind of way. Probably older than he looked, but definitely younger than she felt, even on a good day.

Dirt smudged the shirt he wore under his jacket. The ball cap read NCIS, and his badge was on display. Gun tucked out of sight. Enough credentials visible to get him in here without too many questions.

"Right." She'd have gotten there. Her brain would have caught up to when she'd first been introduced to him at the office.

"We all figured a familiar face would be better."

But not Sal's face, or one of her team? Allyson blew out a breath, waiting for the odd feeling to subside.

"You have that look, like right after you give plasma or something." Niall frowned. "Do you want me to get you juice, or a cookie?"

"Both would be great." So long as she didn't immediately throw them both up. "But—"

He was gone.

She wanted an update first. There had to be news about what was happening. But she figured Kennowich wasn't in custody yet, or Niall wouldn't have been sent to babysit her.

Though he wasn't doing much good here, fetching her—

The curtain parted and he appeared with a can of orange soda and one of those 100-calorie snack packs of cookies. He grinned. "Vending machine special." He handed them over. "I figured that would be fastest."

"You're here to keep me safe?"

He nodded and perched on the end of the bed. Outside the curtain the sounds of a big city emergency room were like a low murmur. Like a hive of bees, busy at work.

"While Sal does…what?"

He glanced at his phone. "Brings Kennowich in, right?"

Allyson studied him. They weren't willing for her to get upset, so they were going to stick with the story. "I'm a big girl. You can just tell me."

What had happened at the house since the ambulance left? She figured it had been a couple of hours, even though she'd been a high priority because she was a cop and because of the type of injury she'd been brought in with.

Now her middle was numb from warmth, and she was being released. All patched up. Stitched up.

"Niall."

He glanced over at her, eyes narrowed.

"I'm fine." Okay, so that was a lie. "Whatever it is, I can handle it."

The thought that Sal was seriously hurt—or worse—because of Kennowich, rolled through her. Allyson's hands shook. She bit her lips together and waited.

"Sure you can." He shook his head.

"Niall. Just *tell me*." Or she would just get his phone, and call Daulton herself. Get updated on what had happened at the house since she left.

She shifted her foot, and kicked at his hip. "Now."

He tucked his phone away and stood. "It's being taken care of."

"Good." She shifted to get out of bed. "Let's go help."

He flinched toward the curtain, as though ready to go with her.

"So he does need help."

"He's tracking Kennowich. That's not a group effort." Niall folded his arms. As though he needed to do that in order to hold himself here. To keep from joining the fight, and possibly getting in the way.

Sal had always been so solitary, Niall was probably accustomed to holding where he was instead of jumping in. He was a capable man. That was the biggest reason he fit so well with that team. Why he was such a good marshal.

They had to be self-sufficient. They were trained to be capable, to solve problems.

To get the guy.

"We can help."

Niall shook his head. He was about to say something when his phone chimed. He looked at the screen. "He's talking to Talia." Niall glanced up and held her gaze. "They're dealing with it."

"So what can we do?"

"There's nothing to do but wait. You're safe now, and we're here."

"Nope. Wrong answer." She looked around for her shoes. Where had they put them? She couldn't go help Sal without shoes on her feet.

Allyson couldn't even remember if she'd worn any in the ambulance. What she remembered was Sal sitting there, holding her. Telling her everything was all right now.

She closed her eyes, wanting to hold on to that memory, to never let go. What if he was hurt? Allyson wasn't so sure that after coming this close to what she wanted, she would be able to live without ever having it. God wouldn't be that cruel, would he?

No. That wasn't how He worked. He didn't give and then take things away for spiteful reasons. There was no one taking pleasure in suffering that also had the power to provide relief. Not unless they were a human, like Kennowich.

"Look, I'd like to go help him." Niall lifted both hands, palms facing her. "Probably as much as you want to, but we can't."

"I just need a pair of shoes."

"If there is something we can do, someone will tell us what it is. Right now we're just going to stick to our part."

She understood that. Everyone was a piece in a bigger puzzle, and the team only worked effectively if everyone undertook their role. Going too far out of bounds caused confusion.

Still, she said, "So your team is in custody, under suspicion, and Sal is "who knows where" in the line of fire, and you're just going to sit here?"

"I'm standing." He didn't move. Determined to follow orders, something she admired as much as she disliked, especially when it didn't help. He said, "And the team isn't under suspicion, not as much now."

"Seriously?" What all had happened while she'd been Kennowich's captive?

He shrugged. One shoulder, and a shift of the skin over his nose. "Talia's good. And Haley." The note of pride was clear in his voice. "And whatever Victoria told Homeland about the FBI when she got to their office. It's being cleared up, which is why the

FBI from San Francisco is on their way *here* to talk to you. Which means when they get here, you need to be *here*."

Allyson shot him a look. "Find me some shoes."

"Sanchez—"

"You can call me Ally." She moved to the edge of the bed right as the doctor showed back up, holding a pink sheet of paper.

She took it from the doctor before he could say anything. "I need a change of clothes, shoes, and a gun. But not necessarily in that order."

There was absolutely no way Allyson would stay here and wait for the FBI when Sal could use their help. Objectively she understood that there were plenty of good FBI agents. Probably most of them. Still, those agents were the ones who'd turned her over to Kennowich. She wasn't going to trust a single one of them for the rest of her life.

Not now.

"We're—"

"—going to go help Sal. Got it?"

SAL TUGGED ON THE REINS. The horse slowed its steady gait to a stop. Well trained, no matter that it was Kennowich's animal. Someone—probably a hired hand—had worked with it.

Sal patted the horse's neck and spoke a few nonsense words while he scanned the trail ahead.

He'd been in pursuit of Kennowich for hours now, high in this mountainous area of northern California. He'd never visited this part of the country before. It might be nice, but it wasn't home.

And if it took much longer to catch up to Kennowich, he was going to lose his mind.

The only thing that kept him from losing it so far was Talia's assurance that the man was ahead of her. Still on his horse. Headed uphill.

Where he was going, Sal had no idea.

He'd thought Kennowich had a plan. Somewhere he was going, like a backroad where he left a car just in case. Sal half expected to come across a secret airport, constructed out here in the middle of nowhere.

But there was nothing.

No houses. No routes of escape. Just mountains and what was turning into an endless pursuit.

The horse's skin was covered with sweat.

Sal dismounted and grabbed the reins. He led the horse to a stream to the west and made a call as he walked.

Talia didn't even let it ring twice before she answered, "Matrice."

"Still got him on your radar?"

"I had to patch the FBI office in San Francisco in on what's going on. They're on the line also."

"I've been behind him for nearly two hours now," Sal said. "His horse has to be tired because his pace has slowed. He's still pushing it though."

"Copy that," a male voice he'd never heard before said. "Keep herding him north. Our agents are approaching from northwest and northeast."

"Copy that." Sal figured he'd give like for like, and it was efficient. "I'm ready to get this guy in cuffs." Where he thought he was going was a major source of irritation. "There's nothing out here to the north?"

He wasn't herding Kennowich as such, but Sal had angled to the right half an hour or so ago and sped up in order to try and get the man to change direction. It mostly worked. Though Sal had to wonder if Kennowich was just running away, or headed somewhere prearranged, or if he was purposely leading Sal on a mountain chase.

Talia said, "Miles of mountains. Won't be long before you're in Nevada at this rate."

Sal actually liked the Nevada mountains. "Nowhere you think he might be headed?"

"The Reno airport?"

Sal would have to look at a map, but figured it unlikely Kennowich that would ride his horse all the way there. "We need to take him down now."

He wasn't all fired up to have the FBI as the ones helping. The agents in Seattle had gone from ally to enemy pretty fast. They'd tried to round up his team for questioning. Their agents had handed Allyson over to Kennowich.

He knew these agents from the San Francisco office weren't in question. Most federal agents—like most cops—wanted to do their jobs right. They followed procedure, and they looked for ways to help people. To see justice done.

He just couldn't let go of the unease that had stuck with him after the adrenaline dissolved. He'd rather be out here with his team, the ones he trusted more than anyone else, if he had to have backup.

Talia must have heard something in his voice, because she said, "Dakota's been calling me every five minutes, asking what's the latest and whether she should get on a plane."

"Special Agent Pierce is being questioned by agents in Seattle, as far as I'm aware," the FBI representative said.

"She's never liked sitting still." Sal felt the smile across his mouth, glad for the distraction of all that Dakota represented. "Tell her I'm okay."

"Will do." Talia was quiet for a second, then said, "Kennowich turned east. He's rounding a mountainside that looks like a cliff."

Sal heard a wolf howl. The horse shifted, and he led it away from the stream. "Time to move."

Talia gave him directions.

The FBI agent was quiet for a while, then came back on the line. "All positions report. Six minutes to takedown."

"Copy that."

Talia echoed his response.

Sal hauled himself back on the horse and followed the map on his phone that showed where he was in relation to Kennowich. He moved to the rear, between the two groups of FBI agents he could now see, and secured the horse so he could retrieve it later.

Alone, he trudged between the trees. Each step sank into the soft earth, coating his boots with mud. He liked this work. The lengthy pursuit, followed by the takedown of a high-value target.

So why did he want to be at the hospital with Allyson instead?

As soon as Kennowich had fled the barn on the horse, he'd rushed in to saddle another one and then taken off after him. Twenty minutes had passed before he spotted the man up ahead. That was when he realized he'd blown off the ATF team's involvement and gone off by himself.

Same old, same old.

Only now everything was different. Not the part where Talia helped, and the FBI assisted in the capture. *He* felt different.

He wanted to call Niall, who was retasked by Talia to stay with Allyson because Sal had asked her to. He hadn't liked the fact she would be alone, not knowing what was happening.

Sal's phone buzzed with the command to move in.

He started the approach, seeing that Kennowich had dismounted his horse. The man then smacked the horse's flank to send it off running. Sal couldn't figure if he actually knew what he was doing around the animal or not. Probably because he didn't know what Kennowich was up to at this moment, and it irritated him that he had no idea.

He glanced once more at his phone and saw the other agents converging.

Their target stood alone in a tiny clearing, the cliff face of the mountain in front of him. His back to Sal.

Standing still. Doing…what? Did he know he was done, that they had him cornered? It seemed too easy. Like he'd walked himself to this very spot. And for what?

Sal cleared the last tree and came into view. "Malcom Kennowich!" He called out in a loud commanding tone, "Federal agents. You will lay all weapons down and put your hands up!"

Kennowich spun, already firing.

Sal squeezed his own trigger. Two of Kennowich's bullets missed Sal, but the third caught him in the chest.

He staggered back a step and went down to one knee.

FBI agents shouted, racing over.

Toward Sal.

Kennowich's teeth flashed white. The world swam in and out of view as Sal tried to figure out what had happened.

More shots echoed across the mountainside. Birds fluttered into the sky.

Sal blinked, looking up at the blue.

26

———

Niall raced the car down the mountain highway while dread swished around in Allyson's stomach to the motion of the turns. *Sal.* He'd helped her so many times, now it was their turn to help him.

Sure, he was tracking down Kennowich. He did that kind of work all the time. Why would this be any different? Still, there was a part of her—call it discernment, or something else—that wasn't going to relax until she saw him for herself.

The second the phone rang, he handed it to Allyson. Talia. She swiped the screen and the call came through the rental car speakers. "Niall's here, and so am I."

"Good." Her voice was breathy. Whether that was from stress or exertion, Allyson didn't know. And there wasn't time to ask. Talia said, "I've got you on GPS. Keep heading along that highway. It'll be another ten minutes."

She'd already texted Niall general directions before they'd left the hospital.

"Copy that," the NCIS agent said.

"Are we worried?" She knew she was but wanted to hear their take.

Talia was the one who answered. "I've lost contact. They were about to take down Kennowich, but everything went dead. As though someone covered the entire area with a blanket. No GPS. No cell contact. Even the radios went offline."

Niall gripped the steering wheel with renewed intensity. "So we have no idea of the outcome of the operation?"

"Right," Talia said. "I tried a backdoor I have into Sal's phone, but it won't connect. So either they knew about it, or it's a fluke."

"Who?" Allyson asked. "Kennowich?"

Talia paused. "Or the FBI agents who went with him to do the take down."

Silence filled the car. She stared out the windshield remembering how she'd opened her front door to those agents. She'd gone with them, trusted them. In the end, it turned out Kennowich had paid them off for handing her over to them.

Was the corruption in the FBI more widespread than those few agents? That would mean not only did Kennowich have agents on his payroll in Seattle, but also here in California.

His business was based here, so that made sense.

It was also a completely terrifying idea, considering he also had holdings all over the US and abroad. What if Kennowich had men and women in law enforcement, and even in government, all over the place?

There would be nowhere safe to hide from him.

Nowhere he couldn't go to find a safe place to lay low and escape the justice that sorely needed to be brought against him.

For the first time, Allyson felt the fires of vengeance stoke in her. This case was the first time things had gotten personal for her, aside from the day Sal had been hurt—a one-time occurrence, thankfully. This was huge. Widespread, like an infection in the body.

They would need serious medicine to root it out.

A rustle came over the phone line. In the background she heard a man say, "I vouched for those agents, personally. I work with those men."

Talia sighed. "Special Agent Billings from the Seattle office of the FBI, who has formerly worked at the San Francisco office, disagrees with our theory that the agents sent to help Sal aren't, in fact, friendly."

Neither of them missed the tone in her voice. Allyson glanced at Niall, who met her gaze for a second before looking back at the road.

Allyson said, "Any evidence that there's corruption in the FBI, more than just the couple of agents who handed me to Kennowich?"

The FBI agent on the line was quiet.

"That appears to be a simple case of blackmail, though we're still unraveling the threads. The rest of the team is here." She paused. "Haley says hi."

Niall smiled. "Hi, Sweetness."

Talia chuckled and relayed the message. Then she said, "The state of the FBI in San Francisco is out of my purview, I'm afraid. But I've put in a call to Daulton to be aware, as a team showed up at the house to help. He's keeping watch on all the evidence that's being collected on Kennowich from his hou—take the next right. It's a fire road."

Niall took the turn.

"I'd like to see him explain why he had an entire surgical suite in his vacation house." Allyson realized what she'd said only after it came out of her mouth.

Talia said, "Ally," her tone soft.

She didn't correct her that only friends called her that. "So we don't know who to trust."

Niall asked, "What about Victoria, what does she say?"

"She isn't here," Talia said. "She's at the office of Homeland Security, not at the Secret Service office or the FBI, though that's where I thought she was. I haven't heard anything in a while. She's gone radio silent."

"Let's find Sal and Kennowich," Ally suggested. "Then we can get back to Seattle and figure out the rest."

"Agreed."

Talia said, "Follow that road north. It winds around the mountain, and you'll come up on where two FBI vehicles should be parked."

They followed her directions and found no cars.

"This is ominous."

She glanced at Niall, wondering why he'd think that. Then she looked at the empty space where tires had left ruts in the dirt and had to agree with his assessment. "Let's go."

She shoved the car door open and got out.

Sharp pain rippled through her side, but she ignored it. There was no way she would sit here and let Niall go alone. The man was wearing dress shoes. Hers weren't much better, nothing but borrowed running shoes from one of the nurses, but they would do fine.

"You good?"

She glanced at Niall. "I won't last hours, but I'm okay for now." Mostly she was ignoring the pain, but that didn't really work. There wasn't any way to completely put the sensation aside, she just needed to try to focus on other things. She was going to be snippy until they found Sal and she could rest.

He walked with his phone held out in one hand, gun in the other. She had his extra weapon.

Talia said, "Half a mile uphill to the northwest. Follow the dots."

It didn't take long to come upon the clearing.

The first dead man lay awkwardly against a tree. Blood covered his chest. "He's an FBI agent." She didn't crouch, that would hurt. And if these guys had betrayed Sal, she didn't even want to know. Today had been…just too much.

"Over here!"

She spun too fast to see what Niall had and cried out in pain. Then she saw him. Sprawled on the ground, hog tied. Gagged. A knot was raised on one side of his temple, but his eyes were open and clear. The side of his shirt, where he had stitches from being stabbed, was damp with blood again.

"Sal." She sank to her knees while Niall cut him loose, relaying to Talia what they'd found about the dead man and the state Sal was in.

"You guys need Life Flight?"

Sal said, "No," but it was muffled.

Niall finished cutting him free. "He looks all right."

She pulled the gag from his mouth so that it hung down his neck. Sal sat up. "I'm good. You guys?"

Of course he sounded more worried about them. He sat up, stretching out his limbs as he moved.

She nodded. "We're good."

Sal squeezed the back of her neck, then leaned in and touched his lips to hers. "Good."

Talia's voice came through the phone speaker. "Where's Kennowich?"

———

SAL STOOD, holding Allyson's elbow. Not quite sure if he was holding her up, or himself. Probably both. "You're okay?"

"I'm here, aren't I?"

"So am I," Talia called through the phone.

Niall lifted it in front of him. "Sorry. Little distracted." He glanced at both of them.

"Good to hear your voice, Talia." Sal closed the gap between him and his teammate. His friend. They slapped each other's backs.

"Got the drop on you?" Niall's eyebrows lifted.

Sal nodded to his question.

Allyson joined their huddle, standing close to him. "What happened?"

"Last I heard," Talia said. "Was that you were moving in to do the takedown."

Sal nodded for Niall and Allyson's benefit. He wanted to tug her under his shoulder, have her be close to him. He'd kissed her already, though. Staking his claim—finally—in front of one of his teammates.

He pushed aside those thoughts he'd like to sink into. Kind of like the way he'd love to sink into a close hold and more of that kiss they'd shared before.

But not yet.

"I got hit." He touched the vest covering his chest and rubbed at a spot that would probably be a gnarly bruise tomorrow. "By the time I figured out what happened, they had me surrounded. Disarmed me and tied me up."

Boy was he itching to pay them back for that.

And yet, they hadn't killed him. Probably should have considering he was never going to stop looking for them. Not until he had each one in custody and Kennowich behind bars where he belonged.

Niall shot him a grim look. "They left with Kennowich?"

Allyson seemed to feel the same. Or she still wasn't okay from the cut she'd sustained. The woman had some color in her cheeks, the red of exertion. Underneath it, she was still very pale. "He's gone? Again?"

Sal tugged her to him then and kissed her forehead. "We'll find him."

"The FBI here has dirty agents in it as well?" She shook her head, wide eyed.

As though he'd sensed Sal and Ally needed a moment, Niall wandered off. "I'll check the body for anything that might help." He asked Talia a question over the phone as he walked away.

Sal tugged her to face him, but she was already moving that way. Allyson slid her arms up his chest and locked her hands behind his neck. She couldn't hide the wince of pain, though. She lowered her hands and slid them around his back before she leaned her forehead on his shoulder.

Sal rubbed her back, keeping away from her injury, though his fingers felt the edges of it.

She sucked in a long breath. It broke a couple of times as she pushed it out. "I'm spent. I don't think I have the energy to go after Kennowich. But he'll get too far if we don't move now. The longer that goes on, the farther away he gets." She leaned back and looked up at him. "I don't want him to get away."

The implication of her words was more than face value. He nodded. "We're not going to let him." But he could see she was exhausted. He felt banged up. Then stiff on top of that, from being shot and tied up.

He tugged on her hand and pulled her over to where Niall was working on two phones, only one of them his.

"Maybe you could stay in the car." He wasn't about to suggest that she should stay here with the dead guy until the coroner got here.

She was already shaking her head before he even finished saying it. "I'm not leaving. And I'm *definitely* not going home to my apartment." She glanced up at him, a note of fear on her face. "It feels like every time I leave your side, I get kidnapped."

"That's not going to happen anymore." He stopped and turned to her without dropping her hand. "No one is leaving anyone else."

"Well, I assume I'll be able to use the restroom by myself. Because otherwise that would be very awkward."

Sal barked a laugh.

He saw Niall glance at them out the corner of his eye but didn't take his gaze off Allyson. He moved closer and touched her cheeks. "I'll allow it."

"Thank you, O gracious one." Whatever sarcasm she'd intended to be there was negated by her smile.

"You're welcome." After they were married, this would be easier. But for now, he would enjoy what he guessed was going to be a wonderful and totally frustrating season in his life.

Hopefully a short one.

Talia's voice came through the phone speaker. "Either of you care to know what I've found while you were smooching?"

Ally grinned at Sal. "Smooching? I don't recall any of that."

Niall was still bent over the phones. "Appreciated." As though they needed his input on kissing.

Sal turned to the phone. "And what is that, Talia?"

"Kennowich's location." She was about to say something else when there was a muffled crackle on the line. Then Talia spoke low, as though to someone else there with her. After she was done she said, "Special Agent Billings agrees with our assessment that the entire team of FBI agents are dirty rotten scoundrel liars."

"That isn't what I said." Billings bit the words off. "I want a picture of that dead agent, and then you all can get on the road."

"We have to walk back to the car first." Niall took the picture, and they headed out toward the fire road where they'd left the car.

The agent kept talking as they walked. "I'll need you to ID each one of them. Get it all squared away, who was there and who wasn't. If you're saying they were all present to help Kennowich get free..."

"They all were," Sal said toward the phone Niall still held out. His hand had to be getting tired by now. "The whole team from San Francisco, at least the ones who didn't go to the house to meet Daulton, were there for Kennowich."

Talia blew out a breath that crackled against the phone's microphone. "Okay, I've got a thread of a lead in the phone that connects to an app. The kind where you send a message and it's gone two seconds after it's read."

"And you can read it?" Sal was impressed.

"Well," Talia made an embarrassed noise. "Your dead guy back there was taking screen shots of conversation about coming there to get Kennowich. Maybe he wanted to protect himself, but now I've got all their usernames. I'm running a search in the app to see if any of them are connected to it."

"You can get their locations from that?" The FBI agent on the line was the one who asked.

"Uh…yeah."

Sal chuckled as they reached the car. Even he knew that stuff was child's play for someone like Talia. "So where to?"

He climbed in the back with Allyson and sat close to her while Niall drove. As he'd said, there was no way he was about to let her go. However, that didn't mean he wouldn't rule out leaving her in the car, safe.

Niall handed the phone back to Sal, who took it off speaker and held the warm device to his ear. He said, "I can't believe that the entire team was there, as part of Kennowich's operation. Could he really have turned that many FBI agents?"

The agent on the line was the one who answered, "I have the photo your colleague took of the deceased man. I'm running it through facial recognition, specifying employees of the Department of Justice."

"Thank you." Sal did feel bad. The guy seemed genuine, as though corruption within the ranks of the FBI would be a source of grief for him. A reason to lose faith in his agency.

"They're headed to the airport," Talia said, her voice softer than he'd heard in a long time.

Sal relayed the information to Niall. Allyson's head lolled on his shoulder. She was asleep? That was good. She needed to heal, and her body could do that while she slept, better than at any other time.

He held her, unwilling to contemplate the fact he'd nearly lost her. And she'd also nearly lost him and would have if those corrupt FBI agents had decided to give up all sense of right and wrong. They could have easily put a bullet in his head and simply walked away. But they hadn't.

Thank You, God.

He had kept her safe when Sal had been unable to do it. Something he would be eternally grateful to the Lord for. *Help me to never take You for granted.*

Niall drove them to the airport, and they took a side entrance for freight transport closest to the collection of cell phones registering on Talia's GPS search, all connected to the same app with their usernames. No way would a man like Kennowich board a plane on a day like today as though he were any other real person. He probably had a private plane chartered to take him to some non-extradition country where he would attempt to flee justice.

Sal said, "Drive faster."

Niall pulled away from the security booth where they'd shown two badges because Allyson didn't have hers. Sal needed to get her badge and gun for her so that she could have them—something important for a cop to have in order to feel like themselves again after a terrorizing ordeal like the one she'd been through today.

"Found them," Talia announced to him just as car brakes squealed behind them. "That's Daulton and his guys. I called them and they're here to back you up along with a bunch of local ATF special agents."

"And the house?"

"Locked down for now," Talia said. "So go get Kennowich, yeah?"

"Yeah."

"Good." She paused. "Because his plane is on the runway, and it's about to take off."

27

———————

Niall hit the gas. Allyson came awake, swaying in the backseat. She braced a hand on the seat, but it wasn't the seat. It was Sal's knee. She blushed and pulled away, noticing him smile at her. The action took years off his face, but didn't completely erase the worry lines or the stress.

Niall swung the wheel hard to the right and said, "Still got that gun on you, Ally?"

"Yep."

"Sal?"

"I'm unarmed."

She grasped for the one Niall had given her, so Sal could have it. "I'll just—"

"Duffel bag," Niall said.

It was by her feet, behind the driver's seat. She tugged it over, but Sal caught it. "Let me." He pulled it onto his lap, rummaged inside, and came out with a shotgun and a box of shells. He eyed her. "I have a vest, but you don't."

"Didn't matter last time."

He made a face and dragged one from the bottom of the duffel, which he shoved at her. She blew out a breath. "Fine, I'll put it on."

Sal said, "You'd better be joking."

"I don't want to die."

"Good."

Niall chuckled as he drove like a crazy man across the airport. "Pretty solid, as far as life goals go."

Allyson smiled. Sal leaned forward and touched his lips to hers while the car careened wildly. She laughed. "Try not to kill us before we get there, Niall."

"Yes, ma'am."

She would let that slide. For now.

Allyson glanced back and saw her team was right behind them. She could make out their faces in the front seat and sent them a jaunty wave. All she saw was Carl's head shake. Like she was the crazy one.

No one else she'd rather be racing through an airport with, backing her up on the biggest take down of her life. Especially on a day when she was nowhere near one hundred percent and neither was Sal.

"There it is."

She looked where Sal indicated, the phone quiet now. Talia was probably on the phone with air traffic control, or the airport's manager person—while she also planted a virus in their systems that would down all planes. Or some other "Talia-style" plan designed to save all their bacon from being overcooked in the nick of time.

The plane ahead was one of those tiny ones rich people flew around in so they didn't have to mingle with the normal folks who lined up for the bathroom and didn't want to pay for the in-flight sandwiches. The same one he'd flown her to California in? Maybe. She didn't want to think much about it.

The plane rolled slowly across the blacktop, headed for the runway where it would take off at full speed. Bound for somewhere exotic where Kennowich could disappear.

"Get in front of it." She patted Niall's shoulder, so he would know she was serious.

"What do you think I'm doing?"

Sal was loading the shotgun, deep in his own thoughts. Still, he said, "Watch it, bud."

A muscle in Niall's jaw clenched. He kept driving, racing alongside the airplane. The car engine roared as it picked up speed.

Allyson heard the whir of police sirens behind them. "I'm guessing airport police aren't super happy with us?"

Sal leaned over to look out the window, where the airplane nose was now right above them. "I guess it's not really copacetic to play chicken with an airplane." He motioned to the pilot with two fingers, swiping them down. "Like that was what we'd planned on doing today."

Allyson had to smile. There was so much tension. This was incredibly dangerous, and yet neither of these men showed their fear outwardly. Her team also used humor to blow off steam in situations like this. Sometimes it was grim, but it was a coping mechanism.

Niall pulled the car directly in front of the airplane. She carefully turned to look out the back window. Enough so she could see the nose and the two angry pilots waving their arms, but not so far it hurt too badly. Did the pilots recognize her from the last time she'd been taken on their aircraft? Did they even care?

The NCIS agent hit the brakes a few times, lighting up that red display at the top of the back window. The plane got dangerously close. Enough she couldn't hold back the fear. "Whoa."

Sal squeezed her shoulder. "It'll be okay. They just need to pull over."

She wanted to laugh, but didn't figure it would come out right. "Done this before?"

"My pit maneuvers are famous," Niall said. "Planes just make it more interesting."

"He's decided he's going to retire and be a race car driver."

Allyson wasn't exactly sure how that would work out, being a retiree who also screamed while going hundreds of miles an hour around a track—or whatever speed those cars went. It seemed kind of boring to her, going around and around the same track for hours. But if that was what he wanted to do, she supposed it was all down to him. "Uh…best of luck to you."

Sal barked a laugh. "That was nice. Very cordial."

She leaned over and hissed. "I couldn't think of anything else to say."

He seemed to think that was also very funny. Niall tapped the brakes again, and she nearly hit her head on Sal's chin.

She glanced out the back window to see the airplane now surrounded by vehicles. "It's slowing."

Five minutes later the airplane was at a full stop.

They surrounded the door as it flipped down and two men climbed out. Badges for the FBI were on display on their belts. "I'm sure we can figure this out." The one who'd spoken was huge. T-shirt tight on his shoulders and biceps, with tattoos poking out from under the hem on his arms.

Allyson's teammates gathered around them. She glanced at Daulton, considering at least six people had this FBI agent and his friend in their crosshairs.

He nodded. "Good to see you, Sanchez."

She nodded back, not sure what to say that wouldn't sound lame or make her start crying. She'd never live that down.

Sal said, "Send Kennowich out. That's who we're here for, and you don't want to be caught protecting him when it'll cost you more than you bargained for."

The FBI agent grinned. "Malcom Kennowich is a businessman, and he is under our protection."

"Send him out."

"So you and these ATF agents you've hoodwinked can continue to harass him?"

A police car pulled up, followed by another. Multiple uniformed cops climbed out. Officers. A sergeant, even a captain. The captain strode over. "One of you fellows care to explain what this is?"

Sal lifted his chin. "Wanted man on that plane. Can't let him leave."

"That remains to be seen," the FBI agent said. "You got a warrant? Evidence?"

"He kidnapped me," Allyson said. She glanced at the police captain. "Malcom Kennowich told me he was going to harvest my organs to recoup his losses." She twisted slightly and lifted the hem of her shirt so everyone could see the bandage. "And he nearly succeeded."

"Send him out," Sal ordered. "Unless you're determined to aid him since he is *under your protection*."

Was it more than he-said-she-said? It had to be. She was the evidence, the witness to many of Kennowich's crimes. If these FBI agents were trying to protect him, that meant they were dirty. Right?

"You can't let him get away." She sounded desperate, but what other choice was there? There was one truth she understood right now.

Allyson wasn't interested in Kennowich being taken to jail.

She wanted to be the one to kill him.

———

"Send him out," he asked again.

Sal kept his cool. He had to. Despite the cops' reactions to Allyson's obvious desperation to catch this guy, they had to get the result they needed instead of being forced into either waiting or backing down. They might not know what she'd been through, but it was clear this was personal.

Not necessarily a point in her favor right now.

He didn't take his gaze from the two armed FBI special agents in front of him, despite being aware the cops were moving closer.

This could go real bad real fast if he didn't play it right.

Movement in the doorway preceded a man stepping all the way into view. Kennowich stood in the doorway.

He moved all the way to the top step of the dozen or so that would get his feet on the tarmac. "I'm sure the airport staff would appreciate us wrapping this up quickly. I know I would."

It was the first time Sal had seen him up close, in person.

On the surface, Malcom Kennowich appeared every bit the high-powered businessman, if tired, at the end of a long day.

Or after a hike through mountains.

Still, there was something else about him. Darkness in his eyes, the gaze of someone who had seen much and done even more to others. This wasn't a man who tricked people into being convinced of his purity. This man had a core of evil inside him.

"I've done nothing wrong." He linked his hands in front of him as he descended to stand behind the FBI agents.

"You're really going to protect him?" Sal asked the one closest. "What does he have on you that makes you so eager to betray your oath?"

Sal figured he could guess. The top sellers were indiscretions he was blackmailing them over, or the need for cash for whatever reason. Didn't take a rocket scientist to figure it out.

The police captain stepped forward. "Right. Here's what we're gonna do. Everyone is going to head over to the police station. We're going to sit down and figure this out."

"I'll bring my lawyer." Kennowich's eyes glinted. Not a smile as such, but the effect was there.

"I have no doubt about that." The police captain took another step. "Because I happen to know exactly who you are."

The FBI agent shifted. The tiniest movement, but Sal caught it and spotted the shift toward his gun. This guy was prepared to shoot a police captain for Kennowich? That wasn't coercion against his will. The agent was sold out to the cause, or he'd been the recipient of the "benefits" of an arrangement with Kennowich for long enough that he wouldn't give it up. Like the supplier of a drug addict's favorite substance, whatever that might be.

Allyson closed in as well, closer to the second man guarding their suspect. "He's going to jail." She addressed all of them who close enough they could shoot each other at point blank range. That was the last thing Sal wanted, but he had to be prepared.

Sal said, "Malcom Kennowich, you're coming with me."

"Actually, he's coming with me." Victoria stood just beyond the police captain. "Malcom? We had an arrangement."

28

Allyson gaped. Victoria could not be serious. She'd made an arrangement with Kennowich, the man who'd hurt so many?

Kennowich said, "That we did."

"One you broke." She didn't even acknowledge Sal or Allyson standing there, but kept her attention on Kennowich. "When you had an ATF agent abducted."

"You wanted evidence the FBI is dirty? I got it for you." He grinned, which came out looking more like a sneer. "Widespread corruption."

The FBI agents started to spin around, reacting to what he'd said.

Sal apparently couldn't stay silent any longer. "Because you corrupted them."

Kennowich laughed.

Sal walked past the two FBI agents, tugged on one of Malcom's wrists and asked the police captain, "Do you have cuffs? I seem to have lost mine."

Allyson would like to have had hers. That would have been satisfying. She glanced at Victoria, trying to see some expression of emotion on the woman's face. There was nothing. Did she feel nothing?

Kennowich protested. "Director Bramlyn, we had an arrangement." He twisted to look at Sal. "You do not have the authority to—"

His bluster was lost in the confusion as the police captain moved for his gun. "No!" Allyson brought hers up.

One of his officers—the sergeant—reacted before Sal even realized the FBI agent had spun as well. Weapon first.

He fired.

Sal fired.

Allyson fired.

The man beside her fired.

Everyone hit the ground. Sal heard a number of thuds, and groans, but managed to get Kennowich rolled over onto his face. His knee smarted where he'd landed on it earlier.

The sergeant's gun still smoked, the FBI agent he shot lay on the ground. His gun had fallen from his hand.

The other agent also lay dead.

Victoria had hit the deck.

"Ally?"

She winced. "I'm good." Her voice was barely above a groan. "But that really hurt."

The sergeant moved to her and helped her up. "Thanks."

Sal said, "Cuffs?"

The police captain frowned at him. "Not sure you're going to need them."

She looked down at Kennowich and saw the blood pooling on the concrete underneath him.

"I guess not." Sal walked to the captain and stuck his hand out. "I really appreciated your assistance with this. We never would've been able to do this ourselves." He all but completely ignored Victoria, who was now standing. He didn't even acknowledge her existence.

"You'll have to thank your guardian angel for that. I was just following orders."

"I'm sorry?" Sal cocked his head.

The police captain motioned to Victoria. "She explained everything and made sure we knew you guys were good." He shot Allyson a wry smile and continued, "I also got a call from the Seattle office of the Secret Service. What followed was an interesting conversation I wasn't sure I believed." He shot Sal a smile next. "But she convinced me. I'm just glad we got here in time."

Allyson said, "Talia." She glanced at Victoria, but the director never took her gaze from Kennowich's dead body.

"She said that was her name." The captain glanced at Kennowich as well. The man had bled out on the tarmac. "I'll call CSU." He took a step back. "And for the record, I knew all about this guy. You don't have a law enforcement career in this town and not know who he is. I've been wanting to nail him for *years* but couldn't get anything to stick. The FBI refused to get on board. Guess now I know why." He paused. "I'm kind of glad I got the chance to be the one who took him down."

Kennowich had been taken out. So had the FBI agents, determined to evade custody. Determined enough to force a gunfight.

Later, Allyson and Sal would have to answer for every part of this. There would likely be a lengthy investigation, given the apparent corruption in the FBI. She had no idea how widespread that was, but even one bad cop was unacceptable to her.

Allyson's team approached from all angles, along with Niall. Daulton said, "You guys good?"

She nodded. Sal tugged her to his side and said, "We're good."

And yet, he still didn't acknowledge Victoria's presence.

The plane was searched, and duffel bags of money in several currencies were discovered, along with clothing and toiletries.

"He was going to run."

Sal nodded against her temple. "We stopped him and uncovered more of his poison." He leaned back and looked down at her. "It's over now."

Niall wandered over, hanging up his phone call. "Haley is good. Everything with the FBI has been handed over to Homeland Security Investigations. Dakota and Josh are good, and Talia is still with Mason. They've basically been at his office this whole time, getting evidence while my fiancé turned it over to the FBI."

"That might not have gone too well," Allyson said.

He nodded. "Good thing she kept copies because Dakota told me we don't know who to trust over there. Haley said agents from Homeland that Dakota knows showed up and escorted her to their office." He made a face and blew out a breath. "They'll want to speak with each of us as they unpack what happened, but we're out from being under any kind of suspicion given where the FBI is at right now."

Allyson exhaled. "Sounds like a serious level of corruption has been uncovered in the Seattle and San Francisco offices of the FBI. Who would have known how far Kennowich's reach had spread."

Niall smiled down at her. "Sure you're okay? That was some spill you took."

Sal caught her wince. She said, "I'm good." Then she turned to him, imploring him to believe her.

"That's not going to convince me."

"Fine," she said. "I could sit down." But he needed to talk to Victoria. How could she convince him to hear the woman out?

Daulton strode over. "You're on vacation for the next two weeks. If I need anything I'll call you."

Sal had to cough to cover the chuckle. She shot him a side glance that made him laugh louder.

Over by the police vehicle, Victoria had started to walk away.

"You should go talk to her."

A sober look crossed his face. "I know."

He moved in for a quick kiss. Just a gentle touch of the lips, then, before he moved away, Sal whispered two words low enough no one could hear him except for her.

"Love you."

———

"ARE you just going to walk away?" Victoria turned, eyebrows raised. Sal caught up to her. "No explanation?"

She said, "You really want to hear all that right now?"

He wanted to hear something, for sure. Especially since he'd be leaving for the airport soon. His focus would need to be on Allyson. Making sure both of them get every injury seen to so there are no lasting problems.

What he didn't need was split focus when he'd finally started to make headway with the woman he loved. The case was done— or so it seemed—so he wanted answers to the questions he had so he could get on with the next part of his life.

Finally, she sighed. "The FBI were the ones who robbed those gun stores. They're the ones who were behind most of this. When I realized that, I put the pieces together and contacted Kennowich."

She'd contacted a known criminal? "Kennowich is the one who set up the team to go down for the gun store robberies."

She shook her head. "That was all backlash from the FBI. They're the thieves."

"And Kennowich taking Ally?"

"Which time?" She didn't smile. "Vanessa and Peter were working with the FBI. At first, she showed up here on assignment from Kennowich, who we *were* trying to bring down. But that quickly changed. When Allyson and Vanessa were taken from the park, that was in conjunction with the FBI so they could set up the team to take the fall for the gun sales. They were going to pay off Kennowich and start a new life somewhere else." She paused. "The FBI are the ones who sent that drone to open fire on the task force office."

"Because of you." Because of backlash from the FBI. "You've been investigating their agents?"

She nodded.

It occurred to him that she had saved their lives during the drone incident. She'd had bulletproof glass installed.

He was angry she hadn't told the team what was going on, but she had protected them.

"You've been working on a completely different case?" He folded his arms across his chest even though it pulled the edges of the stab wound open. "Does anyone else know?"

She shook her head. "Welvern has been helping me. He came to me when it became clear there was corruption in his office. We realized it spread further afield. There's a disease in the FBI."

"Because of Kennowich." He was the one getting FBI agents to do his dirty work. Sal had confronted one of them himself, when Victoria had orchestrated Allyson's kidnapping.

"Kennowich was just a symptom of a larger problem."

"So you've been running an investigation into FBI corruption," he said. "For how long?"

"Months."

"This was all about them, not Kennowich? He was going to testify against FBI agents in exchange for immunity?"

"Just a deal. Not a free pass." She shifted her weight from one heel to the other. "The…surgery he was having done on Allyson Sanchez violated that deal." She shook her head. "He was just supposed to hold her until I got there with Homeland Security. It was about setting them up."

"But I got there with the ATF first."

"I'm glad you did."

He nodded. She would have been too late. Kennowich would have "recouped his losses" and gotten away with it. "You can't play people like this. And you don't make deals with them."

"Maybe in your world."

He wasn't going to be able to convince her. Why did she think they lived in different worlds? Because she was a spy? "You've been playing a dangerous game."

Investigating FBI agents. People who had operated under the cover of their badges, playing both sides and getting away with it.

"I'm sorry for the hurt that's my fault." She glanced to the side. "But we needed a way to uncover what the FBI was doing and get the proof to make it stick."

"We've been tracking Kennowich for months."

"He's dead now." She shrugged one shoulder. "You got your man."

She wasn't going to comment on the destruction he'd caused? She'd just been planning on making a deal with him? Sal didn't want to know what it would be like to have to live with those decisions. Maybe she was right, maybe he didn't live in the same world.

Sal blew out a breath. "You've really been working to uncover corruption in the FBI all this time?"

"I think we've finally gotten it all. Homeland Security is sending agents to do a sweep right now, picking up everyone we can prove was part of it."

"I can't believe you've been working this all by yourself," he said. "You never told anyone?"

"I had Welvern." There was a tone in her voice when she said, "had."

Sal studied her. She looked…alone. "Go to him."

"Don't worry about me." She tried to smile, but he didn't believe it. "I always land on my feet."

She took a step back. "I'll expect your resignation in my inbox by Monday morning."

"Are you kicking me off the team?"

"Do you want me to?"

"Would you do it anyway, if you thought it was for my own good?"

She chuckled, a delicate sound he hadn't heard much. "Goodbye, Sal. Have a nice weekend."

EPILOGUE

Three weeks later

CONGRATULATIONS.

Sal smiled at the text, the last in a chain from the task force group chat. It included everyone except Victoria.

No one had seen her since she walked away from the airport.

Sal set the phone down by the coffee pot and prayed—again —for Victoria. For her to find peace, and be safe. There wasn't much else he could do. Not when Talia had every resource looking for her.

Victoria knew how to hide.

And she had good reason to be living under the radar right now, considering the chaos going on at FBI offices all down the west coast. The arrests had been in the double digits, with more corrupt agents being discovered since that first round. More were probably hiding, trying to get away with what they'd done.

Some might even be looking for payback.

The Northwest Counter-Terrorism Task Force had been folded into the Seattle office of Homeland Security, part of Victoria's arrangement with them. Each was still part of the task force, just with a new boss and a new office.

Except Sal, who had quit.

Allyson had done the same a couple of days later.

They'd worked their last days as federal agents and then made an appointment with his pastor in Wyoming. The wedding had been a small ceremony yesterday in the church where Sal had been baptized as a child.

Sal poured two cups of coffee and stepped outside the door of his Airstream.

"Shhh." Allyson put her finger to her lips.

He stopped and looked. A deer and its fawn had wandered between the trees. He walked to her and handed over her mug. She was curled up on a camping chair, wrapped in a blanket. The fire pit had a roaring blaze going, wafting smoke into the air.

He sat in the chair beside her and sipped. He turned the mug in his hand and heard his wedding ring clink against the side.

Sal stared at the mountains.

Allyson glanced over, a smile on her face. "Good morning, Mr. Alvarez."

He leaned close enough to kiss her. "Good morning, Mrs. Alvarez."

"What are we going to do today?"

He grinned. "Bored already."

"No." Yes.

"Liar."

She shoved at him, but it had no strength. "I want to go for a walk. Read the newspaper. Maybe get lunch in town."

"And a job?"

"One each, or one for both of us?"

He could go either way on that. "Like a private investigator business?" They could work together, side by side.

She shrugged.

"We can do whatever you want." He sipped some more coffee and stared at the mountains. Soon they would have snow, which meant he and Allyson needed a permanent roof.

"Maybe I want to work the checkout at the grocery store. Or

be a librarian." She twisted toward him, and he didn't see one hint of pain at the movement. "I could learn how to make cappuccinos, or open a bookstore."

Sal grinned. He caught her chin gently in one hand. "Honey, you can do *whatever you want.*"

"I love you."

"That's good, because I love you, too."

"That's good," she said. "Because I finished my coffee already. I need a refill."

Sal's laughter echoed across the Wyoming Mountains.

———

Hope you enjoyed this story, please be leave a review at your favorite retailer!

Sign up for my newsletter and stay informed on new releases, participate in events, and get free stuff!
https://authorlisaphillips.com/subscribe

The story concludes in *Final Stand,* turn the page for a sneak peek now!

Find *Final Stand* at select retailers
https://books2read.com/u/boaonZ

———

A vendetta.
The biggest case of her life.

Victoria Bramlyn has been a spy, a State Department Director, team leader and friend. But there's one role she's never realized. The woman in Mark Welvern's life.

When the capture of a corrupt FBI agent and one of the FBI's Ten Most Wanted is finally within her grasp, Victoria has to make one last choice between the people she loves and the score she needs to settle.

Mark has loved Victoria for years. But there just might be too much history between Victoria and Mark for them to make a relationship work. When the truth about everything she's done comes to light, his loyalty to her is tested and he is forced to decide between duty and having what he's always wanted. Will he give it all up for her?

Love meets obligation head on in this explosive conclusion to what readers are calling, "a five-star series!"

The Northwest Counter-Terrorism Task Force is on the case.
https://books2read.com/u/boaonZ

ALSO BY LISA PHILLIPS

Northwest Counter Terrorism Taskforce series:

First Wave - Book 1

Second Chance - Book 2

Third Hour - Book 3

Fourth Day - Book 4

Final Stand - Book 5

Find out more

https://authorlisaphillips.com/northwest-taskforce

Or, buy the complete series at a discounted rate!

Northwest Counter Terrorism Box Set

ABOUT THE AUTHOR

Follow Lisa on social media to find out about new releases and other exciting events!

Visit Lisa's Website to sign up for her mailing list to and stay up-to-date, get free books, and be included in special promotions!

https://www.authorlisaphillips.com

Find out about Lisa's books based in LAST CHANCE COUNTY at
https://lastchancecounty.com

www.ingramcontent.com/pod-product-compliance
Lightning Source LLC
Chambersburg PA
CBHW020104310726

48970CB00002B/470